D1160974

Dragonfire ~ Dragon Claimed ~ Ignite
Fever ~ Dragon Lost ~ Flame ~ Inferno
A Dragon's Tale (Whisky and Wishes: *A Holiday Novella*,
Heart of Gold: *A Valentine's Novella*, & Of Fire and Flame)
My Fiery Valentine ~ The Dragon King Coloring Book
Dragon King Special Edition Character Coloring Book: Rhi

DARK WARRIORS SERIES
Midnight's Master ~ Midnight's Lover ~ Midnight's Seduction
Midnight's Warrior ~ Midnight's Kiss ~ Midnight's Captive
Midnight's Temptation ~ Midnight's Promise
Midnight's Surrender

CHIASSON SERIES
Wild Fever ~ Wild Dream ~ Wild Need
Wild Flame ~ Wild Rapture

LARUE SERIES
Moon Kissed ~ Moon Thrall ~ Moon Struck ~ Moon Bound

WICKED TREASURES
Seized by Passion ~ Enticed by Ecstasy ~ Captured by Desire
Books 1-3: Wicked Treasures Box Set

HISTORICAL PARANORMAL

THE KINDRED SERIES

Everkin ~ Eversong ~ Everwylde ~ Everbound
Evernight ~ Everspell

KINDRED: THE FATED SERIES

Rage

DARK SWORD SERIES

Dangerous Highlander ~ Forbidden Highlander
Wicked Highlander ~ Untamed Highlander
Shadow Highlander ~ Darkest Highlander

ROGUES OF SCOTLAND SERIES

The Craving ~ The Hunger ~ The Tempted ~ The Seduced
Books 1-4: Rogues of Scotland Box Set

THE SHIELDS SERIES

A Dark Guardian ~ A Kind of Magic ~ A Dark Seduction
A Forbidden Temptation ~ A Warrior's Heart
Mystic Trinity (a series connecting novel)

DRUIDS GLEN SERIES

Highland Mist ~ Highland Nights ~ Highland Dawn
Highland Fires ~ Highland Magic
Mystic Trinity (a series connecting novel)

DRAGON ETERNAL
© 2022 by DL Grant, LLC
Cover Design © 2022 by Charity Hendry Designs
Formatting © 2022 by Charity Hendry Designs
ISBN: 978-1-942017-91-2
Available in ebook, audio, and print editions.
All rights reserved.

Excerpt from: **DARK ALPHA'S COMMAND**
© 2022 by DL Grant, LLC
Cover Design © 2022 by Charity Hendry Designs

Sneak Peek from: **DRAGON LOVER**
© 2022 by 1001 Dark Nights
© 2022 by DL Grant, LLC

www.DonnaGrant.com
www.MotherofDragonsBooks.com

DRAGON ETERNAL

A DRAGON KINGS® NOVEL

Dear Reader —

I don't remember when I first fell in love with dragons. I might not be able to pinpoint the exact time, but my love is profound and endless. From an early age, I was drawn to all things mythological. For most of my younger years, my room (and everything else!) was unicorns.

While I had access to my parents' extensive library, where I was encouraged to read whatever was there (and there was everything from all genres), I don't recall reading too many stories with mythical or paranormal elements. When my father was still alive, he used to ask me often why I wrote PNR. From my very first book I ever wrote, it always skewed to the paranormal. I couldn't tell you why I started writing PNR/fantasy, only that I loved it. I meshed it with my love of all things Medieval. Trust me when I say that they weren't an easy sell to agents or editors. But I never gave up.

I still remember the day I got the call for my PNR historical series the *Dark Sword*. It was with a publisher (and editor) I'd longed wanted to work with. That contract started a working relationship that has given me so many opportunities. It was that editor who came to me and asked me to spin off the *Dark Sword/Dark Warriors* series. I had pitched dragons to her before, and she passed. But, like I said, I never gave up. So, I pitched them again. This time, she said yes.

She gave me the freedom to do whatever I wanted with the series. Those first three novellas sold amazingly. It was my first time hitting the *NY Times* and the *USA Today* bestsellers lists. From those first stories, readers were as eager to read about my Dragon Kings as I was to write them.

The *Dark Kings* series spanned 18 books, 7 novellas, and 2 short stories. So far.

When I spun off that series to the *Dragon Kings*, you once again proved that you weren't finished reading about the Kings. I'm delighted to present the fourth book in this series. There are characters from the *Dark Kings* series that pop in from time to time, but this spinoff opens up a new world, one that is waiting to be explored—and beings anxiously waiting to be introduced to you. With new characters, new paranormal beings, and of course, Dragon Kings, there is so much coming!

Writing DRAGON ETERNAL was a true delight. I have a soft place in my heart for Shaw that will forever be his. I know you're going to love him as much as I do.

Xoxox,
  DG

PROLOGUE

Before

She had never been so scared. Or hungry.

The clamor of the city was deafening. Nia wanted to cover her ears with her hands and hide in the small room. But hunger forced her from the safety of her home.

A shiver rocked her as the chill of the winter morning slammed into her the instant she stepped outside. Her bare feet were cold on the stone streets. Her old garments were so threadbare it was like having nothing covering her skin to guard against the frigid wind. She missed the warmth of her younger sister and baby brother, but they were counting on her. Their mother hadn't been back in days. She had never been gone so long, and Nia knew that something bad had happened.

They'd finished off the last of what meager food they had the day before. Baby Chanler had been screaming for milk. Nia had given up her share of food to her younger sister, Myria, and she had attempted to give Chanler some as well, but he refused it. He had finally stopped crying a few hours ago. That's when Nia had decided to venture from their home and try to find something for them to eat.

She had no coin. Nor did she have anything to barter. Her only option was to steal. If she were caught… She tried not to think of what would happen. Whatever she did, she needed to do it fast. Her vision swam, and her stomach knotted painfully before making her nauseous. She swallowed and focused on her surroundings. She couldn't get sick. Her siblings were counting on her. She wouldn't fail them. Nia had promised that she would look after them until their mother returned.

Nia's mouth watered when she smelled fresh-baked bread. Her gaze locked on the vendor's stall to her right. The bread was so close, as if beckoning her to take a loaf. She looked at the baker. He was speaking to others. If she kept low, she could sneak up, take one, and be gone in a blink. Yet, she hesitated.

Stealing was against the law. If she were caught, they could force her to go in front of the priests. Their punishments were harsh and severe. They would take her away from her sister and brother, and then who would look after them?

Nia licked her lips, her stomach cramping at the thought of that soft, warm bread on her tongue. Her mouth watered as she imagined sinking her teeth into it. Just one loaf. That's all she needed to get her, Myria, and Chanler by until their mother returned. She was resourceful. Her mother had always said that.

And Nia *never* let her mom down.

Fear mixed with her hunger. She didn't want to do this, but she didn't have a choice. She took a deep breath and steeled herself. She stayed low, keeping out of sight of any adults as she crept forward, hiding behind barrels and people until she was right next to the baker's stall. She could no longer see him.

Nia looked around. Not a single adult met her gaze. Some never saw her. Others pretended she wasn't there because if they looked too closely at her, they would see that she was starving. Then, they would have to make a decision whether to help her or not. Her mother always said that was too heavy of a choice for someone to make.

The only ones who saw her were the other kids in the same situation as she was in. Some shook their heads, silently telling her not to chance it. Others watched her with wide eyes, waiting to see what would happen.

Her stomach cramped again. Today was the one day she *wanted* to be ignored by everyone. She desperately wished to be nothing more than a shadow until she could get the bread and return to her siblings.

Nia closed her eyes and whispered a quick prayer as she pressed her back against the stall. The ends of the loaves hung over the side of the table above her head. Within reach yet so far away. The vendor hovered. He was used to thieves trying to steal his wares. He was quick to grab them. She would have to be quicker.

Her eyes opened as she tilted her head back to look up. Her gaze locked on the loaf directly above her. The smell was so heady, she grew dizzy. Her hand shook as she lifted it slowly. She was poised to snatch the end of a loaf and retrace her steps when the crowd began to part. Conversations halted as everyone craned their necks to see who it was.

Nia froze. She waited, wondering if anyone had noticed her, but everyone was focused on whatever was happening. Her prayer had been answered. She smiled as she looked up at the row of loaves hanging off the edge of the table once more. Her fingers nimbly wrapped around one as she yanked it against her. She remained frozen, listening for anyone shouting: "*Thief!*"

But there were no such words.

She tore off a piece of bread and stuffed it into her mouth as she began her route back to her siblings. All the fear that had churned so vigorously within her was gone. She swallowed the bite and took another, weaving through the crowd. She was so happy, tears gathered in her eyes. She had gotten food for them.

Her smile grew as she spotted the alley that would take her to the back stairs leading to their rooms. She broke free of the crowd and started to run when someone suddenly yanked her off her feet.

"Let me go!" she screamed.

But the strong arm around her remained unmoving. She flailed her arms and legs in an attempt to get free. Suddenly, someone else yanked the bread from her grasp.

"No! No, please," she cried as she reached for it.

That's when her gaze fell on the armor of the man who had her food. She stilled and glanced at the arm holding her. More armor. Not just any armor, though. These soldiers wore the dark blue colors of the Divine. Nia felt as if she had been dunked in ice water.

She looked into the eyes of the one who held her meal. His face was expressionless. The two soldiers didn't speak as they began walking her back to the crowd, which she realized was now staring at her.

"Please. I need to take that bread to my siblings," she pleaded.

The man holding her made a sound. "She reeks."

"The poor always do," the other muttered.

Nia was embarrassed by their words. She didn't smell anything, but she did feel hunger, and so did her brother and sister. She tried to elbow the man holding her. "Let me go."

He sighed loudly, her hit glancing off his armor and hurting her more than it did him. But she wasn't going to give up. She kept struggling, all the while watching the other soldier walking to where eight men with bulging muscles stood holding a covered litter. The curtains didn't part, but she saw the soldier's mouth move and then his head nod. He turned to her and the brute holding her and motioned them toward the litter.

"No!" Nia screamed. "I need to get to my sister and brother! They need me!"

The man unceremoniously dumped her to the ground, then pointed a gloved finger at her and stated, "Stay."

Nia shivered on the cold stone, her heart hammering in her chest. She wrapped her arms around herself and tried to find a way to escape. The two soldiers walked down the alley where she had been, then went up the stairs. She waited breathlessly for them to return. What were they doing with her siblings? She wouldn't let the men hurt them.

Before she could even dare to grab one of the soldier's weapons, the men returned, carrying her siblings. Nia got to her feet. She was ready to rush to them when she heard the soldiers' whispered words.

"The wee one has been dead a few hours."

"More kids left to starve to death."

Nia shook her head. *No.* They had to be wrong. Chanler had been sleeping when she left. Myria had been hungry, yes, but she had been alive. Tears welled in Nia's eyes. She hadn't been gone that long. The men were wrong. They had to be.

"No," she whispered when they handed her siblings off to someone else. "Myria! Chanler!" she shouted, but neither of them woke, neither of them cried for her.

Nia had seen a lot of death in her young years. She knew what it looked like. And she knew her sister and brother were gone.

All the fight left her. She wondered what she was going to say to her mother. How would she explain that she had let her down? Nia wrapped her arms around herself once more, but nothing could make her warm again. She didn't want to tell her mom about her siblings. That meant she had failed in the one directive her mother had given.

Nia barely realized she had been lifted off her feet. Only when they dropped her into a cart full of other children who looked as hungry, dirty, and scared as she did, did she begin to comprehend that life—at least as she knew it—was over.

She whipped her head around and put the area to memory. She would return one day and let her mother know that she was alive.

CHAPTER ONE

Cairnkeep

Shaw stood with his eyes closed on the cliff near Cairnkeep and
listened to the dragons. The flaps of their wings, their roars as
they called to one another, and the whoosh as they flew. He had
missed the sounds the most.

He drew in a deep breath and slowly released it, enjoying the
feel of the sun upon his face. The dragons' peaceful noises calmed
the rage inside him. Most of his Dragon King brethren
pretended that fury didn't exist. But it was there.

Always.

Until now. For the first time in ages, he felt as if things were
back to normal.

Except, they weren't.

They were far from it, actually. Yet, for this moment, he
could pretend as if they were on Earth, that the dragons had
never been sent away, and that they had never heard of humans.

Sadly, all of that was simply wishing. Because the mortals had come, there had been a war, and the dragons *had* been sent away. For so long, Shaw, like many Dragon Kings, had feared they would never find their dragons again.

He opened his eyes and looked at the mountains around him. Zora. A realm the Dragon Kings only recently discovered that had been the dragons' home since that fateful day on Earth. Zora was a spectacular realm. Majestic mountains, breathtaking plains, stunning forests, and everything in between. Every vista was dazzling in its splendor. The sky was brighter, the oceans bluer, the grass greener.

Shaw felt whole once more. And it was all because he was with the dragons.

Yet he knew his time on Zora was limited. He and the other Dragon Kings were there simply to seek out something that had been able to attack and killed dragons—something that had never happened before.

The crunch of grass alerted him that someone approached. He glanced over to find Merrill. Shaw had never been much of a talker. Merrill made up for that since he never seemed to shut up. He wondered if Merrill would give one of his pep talks. The thought nearly made Shaw smile, but he swallowed it before Merrill could see.

"I'll never get tired of this view. Or *any* view with dragons," Merrill said. "I saw all of you every day. I suppose that should be enough, but it wasna."

Shaw grunted. The Kings had hidden their identities from the humans on Earth, only taking flight at night or during storms.

"I missed seeing my Oranges. I missed gazing at my clan,"

Merrill continued, his dark blue eyes on the dragons in the distance.

Shaw glanced at him. The pain etched on Merrill's face was the same every Dragon King endured from the instant they'd sent their dragons away to save them. But this was the first time in ages that he had seen it on Merrill's face. Shaw frowned, a small niggle of worry taking root. Then he realized who he was thinking about.

If anyone had gotten past the anger, heartbreak, and misery, it was Merrill. He had been born blessed with a sunny outlook. There were times that Shaw had been jealous of Merrill's ability, but Shaw had accepted who he was long ago.

Merrill pulled his gaze from the dragons and shuttered his agony. "I wonder if they're changing up our patrol area. The desert area I had was pretty, but I'd love to see some water. Maybe look for some caves."

Shaw shrugged. He had no idea why he and Merrill had been called back to Cairnkeep. For weeks, each of the Kings had had a designated area along the dragon border in hopes of finding the new threat. It was bad enough that this new invisible foe had killed dragons, but the twin rulers of Zora—Brandr and Eurwen—had also been attacked.

"I think this has something to do with Cullen."

Shaw frowned at Merrill.

Merrill ran a hand through his dirty blond hair and jerked his thumb over his shoulder. "Cullen arrived a few minutes ago. I was hoping he'd bring his mate, Tamlyn, with him. I can no' wait to meet a Banshee."

Shaw turned to face Cairnkeep. The twins hadn't built a large castle or any such structure. They had kept things simple with separate cottages to call their own. Shaw didn't blame them. He wouldn't have built anything if it were him. Then again, the twins were half-dragon, half-Fae.

And were incredibly powerful as children of the King of Dragon Kings—Constantine—and a royal Light Fae—Rhi. The twins had seen the mistakes the Kings had made on Earth, and they had been determined to do better when humans began arriving on Zora.

Shaw had to admit that Brandr and Eurwen had done things well. They had sectioned off a good-sized area for the mortals and told them to do with it what they wanted, but that they wouldn't get more land. So far, the humans hadn't tried. They would. Eventually. Shaw was curious to see what the twins would do when that time came. Hopefully, he and the other Kings would still have access to Zora to find out.

"I wonder how long we'll be allowed to stay after we find this new enemy," Merrill said.

Shaw shook his head and shrugged.

"It's easy for them to look at our decisions and point out where we went wrong, but we did the best we could," Merrill continued. "It also seems like the twins' relationship with Con and Rhi is improving. I think that's a move in the right direction."

Shaw shot him a dry look. Merrill was crazy if he thought millennia of contention between parents and children could be healed in a few months. Granted, Con and Rhi hadn't even realized they *had* children. That was because Erith, also known as Death, had intervened to save Rhi after she was attacked. By taking the embryos so Rhi could heal, Erith had created a ripple through time that had affected everyone. Rhi hadn't known that she was pregnant, and once she was healed, Erith hadn't been able to put the babies back.

So, the twins had a healthy dose of anger toward their parents. Like Merrill had said, it was easy for someone, especially a child, to look back and point out the mistakes of a person's past. Con was far from perfect, but he had set aside his wants and needs—and his love for Rhi—for the Dragon Kings.

Fortunately, Rhi and Con had found their way back to each other—as all of them had known they would. Now, the couple was getting to know their children.

"Here they come," Merrill said.

Shaw spotted the dragons flying toward them. He caught sight of Con's gold scales as well as Cullen's garnet ones. It wasn't long before he spotted Vaughn's teal scales, and beside him, Eurwen's peach body and gold wings. The last one to arrive was Brandr. His gold scales faded to beige on his stomach.

Shaw walked alongside Merrill toward the others as Cullen joined them. Dragons had always been solid colors on Earth because they'd kept to their clans. They hadn't stayed in those clans after finding Zora. They intermingled, which Shaw liked. That meant that Brandr and Eurwen weren't the only dual-toned dragons now, though their coloring came from the fact that they were half-Fae.

"Thank you for coming so quickly," Eurwen said as she smiled first at Merrill and then at Shaw. She had Rhi's silver eyes and Con's blond hair. Her fair coloring set her apart from her twin with his black eyes and black hair.

Brandr crossed his arms over his chest and widened his stance. "We realize that you two were asked to come to Zora to help us search for our new enemy, but there has been a development."

Shaw's gaze moved to Cullen.

"What might that be?" Merrill asked.

Cullen blew out a breath before his pale brown eyes looked between the two of them. "In my region, I saved a woman and a young lad. That woman, Tamlyn, is my mate."

"We heard," Merrill replied.

Shaw nodded when Cullen looked at him.

"What you might no' have heard yet is that Tamlyn's Banshee ability allows her to save children with magic from being killed." Cullen glanced behind him, his gaze focused in the distance as if he couldn't wait to get back to his mate. "The city, Stonemore, has a law that states that anyone with magic is to be killed. When they discover children with magic, they take them to the priests and then execute them."

Merrill looked aghast. "Bloody hell. Bairns? Who would do that?"

Fury ripped through Shaw. Just one more reason to loathe mortals.

And another reason for why he and the other Kings should have wiped them out when they had the chance.

"They do that so they doona have to fight adults later, those who have the audacity to stand against them," Con replied.

Shaw realized what the group wanted of him and Merrill. "You want us to go into the city and find these bastards."

"Yes, and no," Vaughn said.

Rhi suddenly appeared. All Fae could teleport. Even the twins were able to do it for short distances. Rhi pulled her long,

black hair away from her face and put it in a ponytail.
"Everything is fine with Tamlyn and the others."

Relief filled Cullen's face. Shaw watched him curiously. There
was no doubt in his mind that love existed. Too many of his
brethren had found their mates to say otherwise. Yet some were
meant to love. And some weren't.

He was in the latter camp. Shaw became a Dragon King to
keep his clan safe and rule justly. Once the dragons left, his
purpose had shifted to ensuring that the Kings survived and
remained together. And he couldn't do that if he was weak—and
falling in love would make him vulnerable.

A muscle worked in Brandr's jaw. "Cullen is known in
Stonemore now. In order to save Tamlyn and a group of kids, he
shifted and gained the attention of everyone in the city. No' a
smart move."

"What kind of Dragon King would I be if I'd allowed them
to die, simply to stay hidden?" Cullen demanded, his anger
palpable.

"Suffice it to say that everyone is on high alert," Rhi added.

Merrill ran a hand over his jaw. "What is it you want us
to do?"

"Infiltrate the city," Eurwen continued. "Separately. Have no
contact with each other that anyone can see. They'll be searching
for magic, which means you'll have to make sure not to use any
that anyone might see."

Cullen nodded in agreement. "You should be able to
communicate using our telepathic link. The only time I wasna
able to do so was when our new foe was close by."

"They were there?" Shaw asked, suddenly anxious to get to
Stonemore.

Cullen's nostrils flared. "You can no' see them. No' straight on. Out of the corner of your eye, it's almost like seeing a wave in the air. A shimmer. That's it, or them, or whatever or whoever the bloody hell it is. It took me down in dragon form. Be warned, when struck with its magic, I couldna move."

"Whatever magic they use freezes you," Eurwen added. She stepped closer to her mate, Vaughn.

Brandr dropped his arms to his sides. "I've never encountered anything like it before. I didna see it coming."

"None of us did," Cullen said.

Shaw filed that information away.

"What's our objective?" Merrill asked.

Cullen snorted, a muscle jumping in his jaw. "If it were up to me, I'd tell you to kill any priests you come across. Then find the Divine, whoever the bastard is that's ruling Stonemore, and put an end to them. Immediately."

"But it isna up to you," Brandr snapped. He glared at Cullen.

Eurwen lifted her chin. "We need more information on the city. Its inhabitants, who the Divine is, the priests, who might help free the children. Anything and everything. The more you can get, the better."

In other words, they were spies. Shaw could think of a million different ways to use a Dragon King—including what Cullen wanted—but that would have to wait for another day. For now, he would get all the intel they wanted.

"The sooner we get there, the sooner we find what's needed," Merrill said.

Con stepped forward. "Make sure we doona start a war."

"Seems like that has already happened, starting with the killing of children," Merrill added, a spark of anger in his eyes.

Con shrugged. "Be that as it may, this isna our realm. We're guests. Eurwen and Brandr are in charge."

Shaw had only ever taken orders from Con. He almost asked what Con would do if he were in charge, but that probably wasn't the best question to pose at the moment.

"Watch yourselves. Doona underestimate the mortals at Stonemore," Cullen cautioned.

CHAPTER TWO

Stonemore

Shaw stepped out of Ferdon Woods and gazed at the red sandstone city before him. Stonemore was impressive, built into the middle mount of the Tunris Mountains. There were eight levels in all. He lifted his eyes to the very top where a grand structure sat, seeming to stare down at the rest of the city. The place the Divine ruled. Shaw couldn't wait to come face-to-face with this so-called ruler. No doubt he would give Shaw a number of reasons for why he thought it a good idea to kill children.

He pushed that from his mind for the moment. Shaw's gaze moved from level to level until he looked at the tall, wooden gate that appeared new. The guards watched him from the gatehouse. Merrill was already inside. Shaw had walked among humans before. Nothing about the mortals on Zora worried him. From

everything he had learned so far, they acted just as those on
Earth did.

Shaw adjusted the pack draped over his shoulder and headed
for the closed gate. He halted before it and lifted his head to the
guards. Cullen had schooled both he and Merrill in the clothing
and accents used, which was a combination of those spoken in
Asia and India.

"What brings you to Stonemore?" one of the guards shouted.

Shaw stared at the man and his armor for a long moment.
Then, he replied, "I'm visiting the city."

"Do you have magic?"

Were the occupants really relying on people to give their
word? Shaw nearly snorted at the thought. He hated to lie, so he
tried another tack. "Why would anyone with magic come to this
city, which is known for its strict rules?"

"Be sure you hold to them," the guard warned before calling
down to someone.

The gates creaked and swung open enough for Shaw to pass
through a moment later. He looked at the four soldiers on either
side of the inside gate. They held their hands on the hilts of their
swords as if they expected to be thrust into war at any moment.
He took in every detail before walking on.

The city was crowded. And loud. He already missed the easy
sounds of Cairnkeep. Shaw steeled himself as his gaze moved
around him. The abject poverty startled him. There had been
those who had more than others in his clan, but he'd never let
any of his clan starve. It always outraged him how easily humans
could ignore those in need, especially when they stood right
beside them. A little kindness went a long way.

But it wasn't just a few who were starving here, it seemed.

The majority of those on the bottom level seemed to be. Surely, the wealthy saw them when they left the city. Shaw fought the urge not to use his magic to produce food for those in need. It wouldn't do him any good to be found out within seconds of his arrival. Yet, it was difficult for him to turn a blind eye to those slowly starving to death.

He put his hand in his pocket and drew out a coin. Cullen had shown him and Merrill the coin earlier, and they had each created some with magic. Shaw walked to a small boy whose eyes were vacant and haunted, the look of someone long past famished. He squatted before the lad and picked up the boy's hand before placing the coin in it.

The lad blinked and focused on Shaw's face. His dark eyes lowered, and he saw the coin. He stared at it for a long minute before slowly looking at Shaw.

"Get yourself something to eat," Shaw urged him.

It took him two tries before the lad said, "Thank you."

Shaw gave him a nod and watched as he walked away, a group of children quickly following. Shaw remained long enough to see the lad buying bread for himself and the others. Then, he turned and started up the street that wound through each level. The architecture was simple and basic once he moved past the gatehouse. He spotted some stairs that would quickly get him to the next level, but he decided to use the street and get a better feel for the city and people.

So far, he didn't like what he saw. Sure, the red sandstone gave the city a pinkish look, which was majestic against the dark mountain, but he was not impressed by anything yet—and he didn't imagine he would be.

The second level showed poverty mixed with the middle

class. The inhabitants wore better clothing but still ignored those in need. The buildings appeared as if more thought had gone into their design and structure. Some would still call them simple, but there was beauty in simplicity at times.

By the third level, he realized that each layer of the city denoted the hierarchy of the citizens. The poorest were on the bottom, with the wealthiest on the top four and those in the middle stuck in between. Even greater care had been taken with the third level's design. There were beautiful patterns cut into the sandstone, giving each building its own look. The clothing was still basic, but the material was better, and the women had added jewelry.

On the fourth level, Shaw was struck by how different the women's hair looked from the first three levels, those who usually wore it long and plaited or pinned up. The women here went to great lengths to try various hairstyles. Men also flashed jewelry on their wrists and fingers. Apparently, this was the upper-middle-class section of the city. And everyone here knew it.

Not only were the residents of Stonemore subjected to class segregation by the coloring of their clothes—the wealthy favored dark blue, while the rest chose greens, browns, reds, and oranges—they were forced into it by the levels. No one on the first four wore blue.

Shaw kept walking until he came to another gate that led up to the fifth tier. Armed guards stopped anyone who appeared as if they didn't belong on the upper levels. If Shaw were to see any of those, he would have to find another way in—or sneak in. He grinned to himself. Sneaking it would be. He'd rather rely on himself than trying to gain someone's trust in the city.

He made his way back through the streets. Shaw spotted

Merrill talking to a rug vendor on the third level. Neither of them looked at the other. Shaw kept going until he stopped at one of the pubs. He stepped inside the dimly lit room, and the smell of stale ale, smoke from pipes, and food struck him.

A well-endowed woman with pinned-up, sandy blond hair shot him a smile as she passed, carrying tankards of ale. She set them down at a table and then returned to him. "Welcome to The Full Fiddler. You lookin' for a room?"

Shaw nodded once.

Her hazel eyes looked him over once before she turned and walked to the bar. "I expect payment upfront."

Shaw's black trousers and beige shirt signaled that he was a traveler. He followed her and drew out a few coins. He laid them on the bar and raised a brow.

"That's a week's worth," she whispered, then swiped the coins into her hand and smiled. "For that, you get my best room."

He followed her down a short hall before taking a set of steep stairs. She proceeded along the narrow corridor to a room at the end. She unlocked the door and pushed it open before walking inside.

"This one has a view," she told him.

Shaw glanced out the small window to see the tops of the trees from the forest and the two lower levels. "Thank you."

"Oh, so you *can* talk?" She laughed at her joke, her big breasts bouncing as she did. "You won't find a better meal anywhere else, that I can promise."

"And the ale?" he asked.

She smiled, shrugging. "After a few pints, it won't matter anyway." She tossed him the key and sauntered out, closing the door behind her.

Shaw opened the mental link the dragons shared and said Merrill's name. "*I'm at The Full Fiddler.*"

"*My rooms are on the second level, opposite end. The Fancy Pea. This certainly is an…interesting place. Watch yourself. There are soldiers and priests everywhere.*"

Shaw severed the link and dropped his pack onto the bed as he walked to the window. He braced his hands on either side of the glass and looked down onto the street. He hadn't spotted any of the priests Cullen had spoken about on his way in, but he saw them now. They wore long, red robes. The Priest of Innus, they were called. Shaw's hatred was strong but that had nothing to do with the religion and everything to do with them murdering children with magic.

The sight of a red-robed priest who also wore armor caught his attention. So, these were the ones chosen by the Divine to protect the temple and the priests above all else. From what Cullen had shared, none of the soldiers had chosen this path. The Divine tapped them for service, and they had no choice in the matter. They had to give up their lives, families, and friends.

Shaw wouldn't learn much by watching. He had to get out and mingle with the people. Not once had he ever questioned Con's directive, but he had to wonder why the King of Kings had sent *him* when Shaw detested interacting with others. He would do it, but that didn't mean he liked it. He better served in the shadows, by watching.

He moved away from the window and walked out of his rented room, locking the door behind him. Shaw made his way downstairs. The owner smiled when he took a table at the back. She walked to him, swaying her hips seductively.

"What can I get you?" she asked while leaning forward so he got a better view of her impressive breasts.

She was attractive. And clean. He could glean some information from her. "You spoke of your food, and I find I'm peckish."

"You won't be disappointed. That, I can guarantee," she said with a wink.

He found himself grinning. Shaw studied the room after she walked away. There were tables of various sizes, and for midday, there was a good crowd. Some ate, but most just drank and talked. Men catching up with their friends or complaining about their wives.

Apparently, the conversation in a pub was generally the same no matter what realm in the universe you visited.

A plate of meat and what Shaw thought was some kind of vegetable—possibly a potato cousin—was set in front of him, along with a pint of ale. "You're going to love this. I'm Jane, if you need anything. And I really hope you need something."

Her invitation was clear. Shaw met her gaze and smiled. He waited until she'd walked away before tasting his meal. She was right. The food was excellent.

CHAPTER THREE

Nothing had turned out like she'd expected. Then again, Nia had learned to adjust to the changes and use them to her advantage. She had come a long way from the young girl starving in the streets. Few could have turned things around as she had, but that happened when you grasped any change as good.

She sat in her opulent rooms on the sixth level of Stonemore and stared at the rolled missive in her hand. It was a new directive from the Divine. Usually, Nia opened them immediately, but something about this one sent a chill of foreboding down her spine when it had been placed in her hand. Not only did she not want to open it, but she also didn't want it anywhere near her.

Unfortunately, she didn't have a choice.

Many told her she'd never had a choice. Not from the instant the Divine picked her out of the crowd that fateful day. The truth was, she hadn't. She had done what she had to do to survive. That didn't mean she didn't have dreams. It simply meant that she understood where she was in the pecking order.

Nia set the message on the table and rose. She poured herself her favorite tea—jasmine rose—and added honey before stirring. She intentionally kept her gaze from the table...and the note. After stirring the tea, she moved to one of the second-floor office's large windows. They were her favorite part of the estate with their magnificent views.

During her downtime, she was never far from them. Whether just sitting beside the windows in a large, comfortable chair while reading, opening them to let in the breeze, or simply gazing out—as she did now—she soaked up every opportunity.

Because she had spent years without any windows.

The door to the room opened as Sadie entered, carrying a vase with freshly cut roses from the garden. The heady scent filled the room. Nia loved all flowers, but she had a fondness for roses. When the Divine had granted her access to the estate, the first thing she had done was add a garden.

"Ma'am? Are you feeling well? You look pale," Sadie said.

Nia shook her head. She never spoke about her thoughts with anyone, much less one of the servants. "I'm fine." When Sadie turned to leave, Nia called out her name. "Are you happy here?"

"You treat us very well, ma'am," the slave replied with a smile. "Much better than my last master."

Nia swallowed her anger. "The man who raped you."

"He used all of us. It was his right."

His right. That was horse shite, but Nia didn't voice her thoughts.

"You give us all hope, ma'am," Sadie continued. "You were once just like us. Now look at you. You have your own estate."

Nia forced a smile. Neither mentioned that she was just as much a slave as Sadie. The only difference was that Nia didn't work for anyone but the Divine. Still, the Divine had complete control.

Sadie smiled again and departed, the door closing softly behind her. Nia returned her attention to the window. A soft breeze rustled through the trees below her. Her gaze moved to the forest beyond, but it was too far away. She couldn't tell if the limbs moved. Her thoughts bounced around from one inconsequential thing to another until she'd finished her tea.

Her heart thudded against her ribs. She debated getting another cup, but she could only hold off the inevitable for so long. Slowly, she turned and retraced her steps to the table. She gently set the delicate teacup on the tray and straightened, her gaze locked on the missive. She let out a sigh as she reached for it.

It had been years since her fingers had fumbled so to unroll the paper. And all the while, she kept thinking that she might be worried for nothing. It was probably a visiting merchant from another city, and the Divine wanted to make sure they had a proper evening. Sometimes, she didn't even have to use her body. Occasionally, the men and women simply wanted someone to talk with or to hold.

Nia knew all about loneliness. She had suffered from it greatly in her early years when she'd yearned for her siblings and her mother. She'd eventually grown out of it. Much later, she learned the significance of having time alone. If she had a choice, she would suffer the loneliness to be self-sufficient and make her own decisions. The ability to not have to answer to anyone ever again. *That* was her ultimate goal.

Somehow, someway she would make it happen.

She focused on the bold script and began to read.

My dearest Nia,

I know I said that you had a month off, but something has come up. Something, I daresay, that will interest you. Two Dragon Kings are in Stonemore. Merrill and Shaw. There is no mistaking them. They aren't dressed as one of us. Search them out. Pick one—your choice. Use all your skills to seduce him until he is in love with you.

Then, bring him to me.

If you succeed, I'll grant your greatest desire: your freedom.

D

Nia's knees went weak, forcing her to drop the missive and grab hold of the table. The paper re-rolled and rocked gently back and forth before going still. She stared at it while her mind stayed stuck on: *Dragon Kings*. Two were in the city. Only a short week ago, a dragon had terrified everyone by flying over Stonemore. Now, two *Kings* were here? Why?

Her legs steadied enough that she could stand, but she remained bent over. Partly because her dream was nearly in her grasp. Yet, a tiny voice in the back of her mind reminded her what hadn't been in the note from the Divine—what would happen if she failed. Nia knew what that was. She'd be killed.

She had seen the Divine take many others' lives, those who failed in whatever mission they had been sent on. To Nia, there was no other option. She would succeed. She had to. Her freedom was right there, so close she could almost taste it. Despite the rampant fear she felt for anyone with magic, much less a Dragon King, she would find a way to achieve what the Divine asked.

The taste of freedom was so strong it overshadowed her terror. She would be able to choose what she wore and whether she wanted to take anyone to her bed again. She could also leave Stonemore. She was dizzy from all the thoughts rushing through her mind, visions of the future she had dreamed of being so close she could almost touch it.

Nia straightened and whirled around to hurry to her chamber across the hall. She went to the wardrobe and looked through the dozens of items until she found the one she wanted. After ringing for Sadie, she kicked off her shoes and sank onto the stool before her vanity.

"I'm going out," she told Sadie when the servant arrived. "I have to look my best."

Sadie didn't ask questions as the two of them got to work. In less than an hour, Nia stood in front of the mirror, examining herself. She ran her hands down the dark blue tunic that showcased her small waist while the plunging neckline showed her full breasts. The cuffs of the long sleeves were embroidered with silver roses. The dark blue skirt brushed the tops of her sandaled feet and molded to her hips. The long length of her brunette waves was gathered artfully away from her face to fall down her back.

"You're stunning, ma'am," Sadie said as she gazed wistfully at Nia's reflection.

Nia touched her hair. "You're amazing with what you do with my hair. Thank you."

"I love hair. It's my favorite thing."

Nia wished she had something she loved to do. She shoved aside that thought. There would be time to figure that out once she had her freedom. For now, she needed to focus on the task at hand. She wasn't worried about seducing the Dragon King. No man or woman yet could say no to her. The tough part would be hiding her fear. But she would manage.

The worst part would be getting the King to the Divine. It might be one of the hardest tasks she had been given, but Nia didn't know how to quit. There wasn't a time limit, so she would keep at the King until she had him eating out of her hand. Then she would deliver him to the Divine. After that, she didn't care what happened. She would have succeeded. Which meant she would be free.

The instant that happened, she was getting as far from Stonemore as possible. She didn't care where. If she never saw the city again, it would be too soon.

The sun hung over the horizon by the time Nia left the house. She used her carriage to take her to the gate that separated the upper levels from the lower. From there, she disembarked and waved her driver away. If things went as planned, she wouldn't need her carriage tonight.

Nia nodded to the soldiers guarding the upper levels as she left behind the luxurious homes and shops and mingled with what the wealthy described as trash. It was laughable since Nia knew that some of those so-called wealthy had once lived in the lower parts of the city. She had come from such beginnings. But no one ever mentioned that. It was as if they wanted to ignore where they had come from.

She refused to forget. Her mother had done the best she could, and she had been good to them. She'd taught her children to be good, and to do good. One day, Nia would be able to be all the things her mother had wanted for her. For now, she was still surviving.

The unease from earlier returned, and she tried to shove it aside. She was good at that. Usually. But she kept thinking about there being Dragon Kings in the city. It would take every ounce of skill she had to complete the task ahead. There was a time and a place to give in to emotions, but now wasn't one of them. She had to be at the top of her game. Once she found the Kings, anyway. The Divine's missive hadn't said where they were or what they looked like. Only that there was no mistaking them. That meant they must be easy to find. At least, that's what Nia hoped.

She hadn't gotten into her finest dress to waste a night. She would track down the Kings. The first one she saw would be her target.

She meandered through the lower levels for over an hour without finding them. Had the Divine set her up? Was this some trick? The Divine had connections that astounded Nia, but that didn't mean the Divine could determine when a Dragon King entered Stonemore. What would a King be doing there anyway?

Nia found herself near the temple. The priests watched her as they came in and out of the building. The way they stared at her with lust in their eyes turned her stomach. She was used to men gazing at her with licentious thoughts, but there had always been something about the priests that put her on edge from an early age.

She paused and remained in the courtyard, moving as far away from the temple—and the priests—as she could. Finally, the group of them began to disperse. Just as she was releasing a breath of relief, two soldier priests looked her way. Nia kicked herself for staying in hopes they would lose interest. The priests and soldier priests ran the city. Even the Divine was hesitant to step in where they were concerned.

Nia usually made sure to keep far away from the priests and soldiers. The worst thing would be to let them know they'd made her uncomfortable. These men liked their power. All men did, but these even more so. She wondered if they would feel so powerful if they were castrated.

The closer the soldier priests came to her, the more she wanted to flee. Images of a horrible night flashed in her mind. She had been frozen, unable to move. Because if she did, she would start screaming. She knew better than to get close to the temple. But it was too late now. They had her in their sights.

She was so lost in thought that it took her a moment to realize that a large form had moved closer. He said nothing, just stood near her, staring at the soldier priests. She kept her gaze on the soldiers and her attention on the man. Eventually, the two soldiers paused and turned to walk away. Shock went through her. She didn't know why such good fortune had come her way, but she wasn't going to concern herself with it. The soldiers never did anything like that. If they wanted something—or someone—they got what they wanted. Always.

Nia breathed easier when the soldier priests no longer watched her. She finally turned to face the man. He casually leaned his tall form against the wall, but nothing about him was laidback. She gazed at his profile and strong jaw and then moved down to his beige shirt and black pants. He still stared intently at the soldier priests with his arms crossed over his chest—as if daring them to walk closer. If that unwavering gaze had captured her like that, she would've stopped in her tracks, too. There was something about him. Some essence that let others know not to mess with him.

He turned his head to her. She found herself gazing into the most amazing green eyes when he did. They were a vibrant green ringed with a deep green. The only other time she had seen that color was on a fern. Thick, black lashes framed his eyes and drew her gaze up to black brows. His face had a rugged look, one that might almost be considered harsh but somehow worked perfectly with his wide lips and stubborn chin.

His hair was as black as night and just brushed the tops of his shoulders. She wondered if the thick strands were as silky as they looked. That thought fell away when he turned to her more fully, and she got a glimpse of his broad shoulders. Tall *and* strapping. Nothing about him was polished. His raw masculinity made her blood heat. She couldn't catch her breath.

Or stop looking at him.

This man wasn't just handsome, he was appealing in ways she couldn't begin to name. Her targets had been attractive a few times, but she had never met anyone like him. One side of his lips curved into a smile, and she realized that she had been staring. Nia inwardly shook herself. She didn't have time for this. She had to find herself a Dragon King.

"You look calmer now."

She reached for the wall beside her at the sound of his amazing accent. It was deep and oddly lilting, and his vowels were pronounced in a way she had never heard before. She needed to hear more of it. "Excuse me?"

He jerked his chin to the soldiers. "You looked anxious. I'm new to the city. I hope I didna overstep."

Did he just mesh the *did* and *not* into one word? It almost sounded like didna instead of didn't. She stared at him, trying to think of something to say so he would keep talking.

His smile faltered. "I must have."

"No," she hastily said. "You didn't overstep. I apologize. I'm flustered. I'm usually here with my maid, but she wasn't feeling well. I thought I could come alone."

"You should be able to move about in your own city."

She smiled when he said about as *aboot*. Where was he from? "We should, yes."

His eyes crinkled at the corners.

She glanced at her feet. The strange sensation in her belly made her want to giggle, something she had never done in her life. She smiled warmly. "Thank you for your assistance. I'm Nia."

"My name is Shaw," he replied with a bow of his head.

Her knees nearly buckled when she heard the name. *This* was Shaw? A Dragon King. She was actually standing in front of a magical being—the most powerful on the realm. He looked normal. He spoke normally, but she knew that he was anything but.

Get control of yourself before he notices, she chided herself. After everything she had endured, Fate owed her one. Nothing had ever fallen so easily into her lap.

That voice. That face. Will it really be that much of a hardship to seduce him?

The answer was a resounding no.

If she could get past the deep-rooted fear.

"Lass?" he asked with a frown. "You've gone pale."

Nia swallowed and turned to her years of training to school her features. "I'm still a little shaken. Would you mind walking me past the temple? I think if I had a drink of something it might settle my nerves."

He pushed away from the wall and towered over her. "Of course. I'll take you anywhere you wish to go."

If only she didn't know who he was. If she didn't, she could almost believe he would protect her against anyone. He had that kind of quality about him. But she *did* know. And that was the problem. She swallowed, not having to fake being upset. "I like to walk. It probably wasn't wise to come alone."

"I take it you doona live on this level."

She shook her head, lulled by his voice. "I live on the sixth."

"I'll make sure you safely get wherever you wish."

A stranger to the city. One that compelled the soldier priests to turn away. A man who had an air about him that was different than anyone she'd ever encountered. Even if she hadn't known his name, she would've guessed him to be a Dragon King.

She had found him by accident, but now that she had, she couldn't let him go—even if she wished she could. "A drink first, if you don't mind."

"Right this way."

He walked her to a café. It was farther down the street as if he were conscious about getting her away from the temple. She was thankful for that, at least. It made her curious about him. Was he being nice to get something? Or was this just who he was?

Once they were seated and she had ordered for them, she turned to him. He was so close, she could reach out and touch him. His nearness both calmed and flustered her. Just as her excitement to have found the King warred with her panic at being near him. The two emotions swirled within her, neither gaining ground.

His fern green eyes held hers. No longer did he look as if he were about to murder someone. His expression wasn't exactly soft, but it had soft*ened.* The way he drank her in wasn't something new to her, but the sensations it caused certainly were. She had never experienced desire before.

But she suspected that was exactly what she felt.

"Why do you no' like them?" Shaw asked.

She folded her hands in her lap and didn't pretend not to know who he referred to. "I never said I didn't."

He quirked a brow, not buying her words. "It was written on your face."

"They make me uncomfortable. They always have."

He studied her for a moment, his fern green eyes steady on her face. "It's because you innately know there are things about them that are no' what they seem."

"I never thought about it like that." Was she really hanging on his every word? What was wrong with her?

Why was she even questioning it? Shouldn't she be happy that she liked conversing with him?

Shaw was still and comfortable, while she felt as if she were about to jump out of her skin. He unsettled her. She needed to change the topic and put it back on him. "Where are you from?"

"Far from here."

He glanced away, and in that moment, she saw how he sized up the room and the occupants with one look. Anyone who had been staring at him hastily looked away. No one even dared to look *her* way.

She fought to hide her smile. Did everyone realize who he was? Or was it just the look he gave them? Probably a little of both.

"You've traveled far, then. Why come to Stonemore?" she pressed.

"I suppose you could say that Fate led me here."

Nia grinned. "Fate has a way of doing things we don't plan."

CHAPTER FOUR

It hadn't been Shaw's intention to interfere. Nia had caught his eye earlier as she walked alone, seemingly so at ease. Then she saw the priests. Her visceral reaction had propelled him to act, even as he knew he shouldn't.

Her once-relaxed frame had gone rigid, her apprehension and agitation evident. Shaw had been observing the priests and soldiers for some time. It was obvious that they not only liked their power but also used it. The people of Stonemore had healthy respect for the priests and their soldiers, but none had shown outright alarm as Nia had.

Now, he sat with her at a small table. He was fully aware of her. How could he not be? She was a woman that everyone noticed. Beautiful didn't begin to describe her. Ethereal, striking.

Breathtaking.

She was all of that and more. Even if she hadn't worn the dark blue dress of the upper class, he would have known by the way she held herself. Only someone who lived in wealth behaved with such elegance and decorum.

Shaw had noted her beauty from a distance, but the full impact of it hadn't hit him until he got close to her. A wealth of long, brunette waves floated down her back to her waist. She had the thick strands pulled away to frame her face. Large, honey-colored eyes stared at him in an oval face of perfect symmetry. Her lips were full and utterly kissable. She had a long, graceful neck.

The deep V of her gown pulled his gaze lower, giving him a view of her décolletage. Then lower to her small waist and the flare of her hips. Nia's hourglass figure was as perfect as her face. His blood heated as lust surged through him.

"Do you not agree?"

He blinked. Shite. She'd been talking. What had she said? Oh, aye. Something about Fate. He needed to stay on top of things. "I do. Fate takes us where we need to go."

"It seems to have brought us together." She smiled softly while holding his gaze as a server delivered two glasses filled with some amber liquid.

Shaw put a hand on his thigh and left the other on the table. "I'm rather glad it did."

"Me, too."

They stared at each other for several heartbeats.

Nia was the first to look away. She lifted the drink to her lips and took a dainty sip. "How long are you staying?"

"I have no set time."

"Perhaps we can spend more time together," she said as her gaze swung back to him.

Shaw drew in a breath and released it. Bloody hell. The

woman was enchanting. He was ready to give her anything she wanted just so he could spend more time with her. "I'm no' part of your world."

"Maybe I don't want you to be."

There was a chance she liked to mingle with those of lesser standing in the city, but Shaw had a suspicion that Nia had whoever she wanted, whenever she wanted. Who was he to deny himself what would surely be an excellent time? Not to mention, he might gain some intel from her. "I'd be a fool to pass up the opportunity to spend time with you."

One dark brow quirked. "You keep talking like that, and I may never let you leave."

Shaw grinned, sinking into her honey-colored eyes. He reached for his glass and brought it to his lips before asking what it was. The liquid was warm and smooth as it slid down his throat. He smiled as memories of the past assaulted him.

"Do you like it?" Nia asked.

He replaced the glass and nodded. "Aye. We call it mead. I've no' had it in quite a while."

"I like that name. We call it honey wine."

Shaw's gaze dropped to her mouth as she took another drink. When she set the glass down, she licked her lips. Lust burned through him, scorching his veins. He fought the urge not to lean over and kiss her. The attraction he'd first felt had doubled in the short time he'd sat with her. Everything about her turned him on and made him yearn to know her taste and her body. If he wasn't careful, she would leave him in ashes.

"Should I ask what you're thinking?" She tilted her head, giving him a flirty side-eye.

"That I need to be careful around you."

Both brows shot up on her forehead. "Why is that?"

"You know why."

Her gaze dropped to the table as the corner of her lips curved into a seductive grin. "Tell me."

"You have power. Some might call it a gift. I'm sure other women have cursed you behind your back for the ease in which you can take a man to his knees."

Nia's eyes lifted to meet his. "You aren't on your knees."

"No' yet."

"You think you will be?" she asked with a charming grin.

Oh, aye. Shaw would have to be very careful around her. Not only did she know her appeal, but she knew how to use it. It had been a very long time since he had played such a game— or felt lust riding him so hard. He knew himself well enough to know that he could have a little fun while also staying on mission. And who better to get the lay of the city from than one such as Nia?

Shaw took another drink of mead. "Aye."

"You're very certain."

"Just as I am that you want it, too."

Shock flared in her eyes for just an instant. It was gone so fast that he might have missed it had he not been looking. Nia regarded him for a moment before saying, "You might be reading things wrong."

He shook his head and jerked his chin toward her. "No' when I can see how erratic your pulse beats at your throat."

To his surprise, she laughed. The sound was soft and sultry, throaty. He wasn't the only one it affected since those around them looked her way. Shaw liked how her eyes crinkled at the corners. The laugh had been uninhibited and wholly pure. It showed him that Nia had more layers than he originally suspected.

And he wanted to know every one of them.

"Thank you for making me laugh." She sat there for a moment as if soaking it all in. "It's been a while since someone has taken me by surprise."

He shrugged and idly turned the glass on the table. It was either that or reach for her. Now wasn't the time to get his hands on her. Because if he did, he would have a hell of a time stopping. Since they were in the middle of a café, he needed to control himself. "You're verra composed. I'll give you that."

She visibly swallowed, a flush creeping over her face. Desire burned in her eyes. She looked away to compose herself. When she faced him again, she was serene once more. "I'm curious about your accent. Verra. I've never heard that before."

Shaw fisted his hand on his leg. Bloody hell. He needed to stop thinking with his cock. "You think I'm hiding something?"

"Isn't everyone?" She shook her head, the dark locks moving with her. "Everyone has secrets. I don't think it's good to share such things."

"What secrets could you possibly have?"

"You wouldn't believe me if I told you."

Shaw was intrigued. "Try me."

She smiled and looked down. "I just met you. For all I know, you're a spy for the Divine."

Something in her words troubled him. Maybe because they'd hit a little too close to home. He *was* a spy. Just not for the Divine. "Your leader has spies?"

"Of course," she replied with a laugh as if it were nothing. "Everyone who lives in Stonemore knows that."

"Why would he need such a thing?"

Nia waved the server over and placed three coins in her hand. "You promised to walk me to safety. Will you still?"

"I always keep to my word."

Shaw got to his feet and followed Nia out, noting how everyone seemed compelled to look her way. As if they were as infatuated with her as he. Her beauty played a big part, as did the way her clothes molded perfectly to her body. But it was also how she carried herself. Confidence and sophistication set her apart from everyone on the lower levels. And he imagined on the upper ones, as well. Shaw hoped he got to see that for himself before he left Stonemore.

Nia paused once they were outside and then looked back at him. Her honey eyes beckoned guilelessly. He wondered how many times she had looked at others as she did him. She didn't play the innocent, and he was thankful for that. Instead, she owned who she was, almost using it as a shield. He could understand that.

They walked in silence for a bit. He didn't push her to answer his question about the Divine. He had spoken more that evening than he had in weeks, so he was happy for the quiet. He didn't need to fill the emptiness with meaningless words. Though, he was beginning to wonder what she was thinking. That was something new for him. He didn't usually spare a second on someone's musings.

"What do you think of Stonemore?" she asked.

He glanced at her. "It's like any city. Noisy, busy, smelly, dirty."

"You asked why the Divine would have spies."

Shaw focused on her words since he wasn't looking at her face. "Aye."

"To ensure the city stays as it should."

"What does that mean?"

Nia sighed softly and glanced around before moving closer to him and lowering her voice. "Religion rules the city."

"I thought it was the Divine."

"The Divine does, too."

"It can no' be both."

She glanced at him, her face impassive. "Can't it?"

Shaw shook his head. "I've seen something similar before. It does no' work in the end."

"It has here, and it will continue. The Divine will make sure of it."

He glanced ahead to see that they were approaching the gate that led to the fifth level. "Do you follow the religion?"

"Everyone does."

"Do you no' have a choice?"

She remained quiet as they passed two soldiers. When they were out of earshot, she said, "What a curious question."

But he noted that she didn't answer him, which was answer enough. "Nia..." he began.

She stopped and faced him as they neared the gate. The night put her face in shadows, but with his dragon vision, he could see as well in the dark as in the light. There was a tightness about her lips that hadn't been there before. Her gaze darted to the soldiers ahead. "Thank you for this evening. You came to my rescue and made me laugh."

"When can I see you again?" Shaw had wanted to phrase the question better, but the words had come out in a rush.

Her lips softened into a smile. "Soon. Be careful, Shaw. Don't trust anyone in the city."

Before he could reply, she lightly touched his arm and walked away. He stared after her, watching until she reached the gate. The soldiers nodded to her and let her through without making her stop.

Shaw pivoted and began retracing his steps. He opened the mental link. "*Merrill? Any luck tonight?*"

"*Some,*" Merrill replied. "*The people here are fanatical about their religion. And they detest magic. They think it's evil. How about you?*"

"*I, too, learned that religion is all-consuming. Though I doona think everyone is devoted to it. At least no' so with the woman I spoke with.*"

Merrill chuckled. "*You are no' the only one who met a woman.*"

"*Aye, but mine is from the upper levels.*"

"*Shite. Of course, she is. But...that's probably good. We can get two different perspectives about the city, the religion, and the leader.*"

"*The soldier priests made her uneasy. That's how I came upon her.*"

Merrill made an indistinguishable sound. "*I'm curious to know her thoughts. Are you with her now?*"

"*No.*"

"*Tell me you're going to see her again.*"

"*Oh, aye.*"

Merrill paused. "*We're supposed to keep a low profile, Shaw.*"

"*I'm aware.*"

CHAPTER FIVE

Iron Hall ruins

Cullen ran a hand down his face. The *conversation*—and he used that term lightly since he considered it more of a disagreement— had been going for hours.

His mate, Tamlyn, had refused to budge an inch. She glared at Jenefer, her hazel eyes flashing. "You aren't thinking this through."

"How many times do I have to tell you that it's what I have to do. Your place is here," Jenefer retorted, her brown eyes flashing dangerously.

Tamlyn threw up her hands. The light coming through the tree roots above glinted over her dark skin. "Your place is here, too."

"You aren't listening!" Jenefer yelled, the sound echoing through the underground city.

Cullen looked across the pool of water—a collection of the

beads dripping from the tree roots above—to Sian. The petite Alchemist hadn't said a word since her lover had declared her intent to leave Iron Hall to search for other Amazons.

He understood Tamlyn's thinking, but he also understood Jenefer's. All he could hope for now was that Tamlyn didn't ask him why he wasn't arguing with Jenefer like she was.

"We've always done things together," Tamlyn told Jenefer. "Always. It's been me, you, and Sian. Now you want to leave?"

Jenefer sighed loudly, her frustration evident. She brushed her hand over her blond hair that she had plaited into one thick braid. "I'm not leaving forever, Tam. I'm going to search for the other Amazons. We're going to need them. I don't care what the Dragon Kings say or what they plan. There *will* be a war. Those of us with magic will have to stand up for ourselves. Amazons are the greatest of all human warriors. *We need them.*"

"We have you." The look in Sian's pale green eyes beseeched Jenefer to change her mind.

Jenefer turned to her and smiled sadly. "I'm good, babe, but I'm not good enough to stand on my own. The more we have on our side, the better."

"Then I'll go with you."

Tamlyn threw up her hands in dismay. "Are you kidding?"

Cullen opened his mouth to attempt to calm Tamlyn when Astrid came running from one of the corridors. She was one of the six children that he and Tamlyn had saved from execution in Stonemore. From the moment Astrid had called him "*my dragon,*" she'd had his heart.

Given the speed the child was running, he knew she wouldn't stop. Cullen waited until she launched herself at him, then he grabbed her and swung her high. Her joyous smile made him melt. She started to say something, but he glanced at the others, silently urging her to remain quiet. Astrid nodded, and he put her on his shoulders.

Sian finally let her fury show. "What, Tam? You don't think I can handle it out there?"

"That isn't it at all, and you know it." Tamlyn put her hands on her hips and glanced at the roots above her. "I don't want any of us to leave. If one does, then…"

"I'm returning," Jenefer said again.

Sian shook her head. "You can't know that."

"I can, and I do," Jenefer countered.

Tamlyn turned to him. "Cullen, say something."

He'd been afraid she would say that. He looked at each of them and then sighed. "Jenefer's right. The more those with magic stand together, the better. If she can find more Amazons, then she should. Otherwise, you'll be fighting the same battle over and over again each generation."

"Unbelievable," Tamlyn whispered. The hurt on her face was like a knife to his gut.

Jenefer shook her head. "Don't be mad at him, Tam. This is a strategic decision. We've been oppressed for too long. I'm tired of hiding. I'm tired of running for my life. This realm was made with magic. Why should we have to keep who we are a secret? I'm not saying I want to subjugate those who don't have magic, but I've had enough. Our kind is being killed as children. You've risked your life time and again to help them. What's different now? Just because I have to venture out? That isn't fair."

"I'm scared you won't return," Tamlyn said in a soft voice.

The Amazon walked to Tamlyn and wrapped her arms around her. They embraced for a long minute. When Jenefer stepped away and turned to Sian there were tears on both her and Tamlyn's faces.

Cullen caught his mate's attention and motioned for her to follow him. He kept Astrid on his shoulders as he walked Tamlyn outside. She refused to look at him. Tamlyn made her way to one of the rocks near the hidden entrance and sat.

"Jenefer and Sian needed to be alone," he said to fill the silence.

Tamlyn braced her hands on her knees and shook her head. "My gut is telling me that Jenefer shouldn't leave."

Cullen didn't have the heart to tell her that fear was causing that feeling. The three of them had been all one another had for years. They had leaned on each other, forming an unbreakable bond. Now, that was being tested by one of them leaving.

"Do you want me to go with her?" he offered.

Finally, Tamlyn looked at him, and her hazel eyes softened. "Thank you for offering, but not only would Jenefer balk at the idea, but we're fortunate that you're able to stay here with me. I don't want to test things with the other Kings."

"I'll do whatever I must. Just like I did to ensure that you and the children were safely out of Stonemore." He squeezed Astrid's ankles, causing her to laugh.

Tamlyn lifted her gaze to the little girl. "Jenefer's right. We *do* need to fight. I'm not against taking a stand, it's just…"

"Her leaving," he said.

"Yes. I'm terrified it'll be the last time I ever see her."

"It might be. Now you understand how Jenefer and Sian felt each time you went to Stonemore alone to rescue a child."

Tamlyn's face scrunched in a wince. "You could've pointed that out earlier. I hadn't thought of it that way."

"You had things you needed to say. So did Jenefer."

Astrid began hitting the top of his head. "Cullen, Cullen. *Loooooook.*"

He lifted his eyes to see where she pointed and followed her finger to the top of the verdant canyon. He grinned at the sight of the wildcat. Ever since the beast had helped him in his battle with the foe the Kings were tracking, the cat returned to the canyon again and again.

"She's so pretty," Astrid said in her child's voice.

"And dangerous," Tamlyn added.

Cullen glanced at his mate and grinned. "She's our friend."

"Who would like to eat me."

"She knows what I am."

Tamlyn grunted. "She'd still eat me and Astrid."

"Not me," Astrid stated matter-of-factly.

He and Tamlyn shared a laugh. Cullen returned his gaze to the wildcat, who was now lounging on her side, cleaning her face with a paw.

"She needs a name," Tamlyn said.

Cullen had been thinking the same thing. "How about Nari?"

"I like it," Astrid replied.

Tamlyn's lips twisted. "I like it, too. Good choice."

Their conversation was interrupted when Jenefer emerged from the hidden doorway with her armor in place and her sword strapped to her back. Sian followed a few paces behind with bloodshot eyes and a red nose.

"The sooner I go, the sooner I can return," Jenefer said.

She put on a brave face, but Cullen saw the tear tracks on her cheeks and heard the anxiety that wobbled her voice. "If you get into trouble, head to the dragon border. The Kings know you and Sian. They'll protect you and get word to me."

"I'm headed far from the border of your land but thank you." Jenefer drew in a shaky breath and turned to Tamlyn. "Don't do anything stupid."

Tamlyn laughed through the tears that fell onto her cheeks and got to her feet. "I can't promise that."

"It's okay. I know Cullen will make sure you stay out of mischief." Jenefer flashed him a smile before embracing Tamlyn once more. The hug was fierce and brief. The Amazon quickly stepped away and dropped her arms. Then she turned to Sian. "I meant what I said. You believe me, right?"

Sian nodded her dark head. "I do."

"I'm coming back for you. I love you, Sian."

Tears came faster as Sian tried to speak. "I love you, too," she finally got out.

Jenefer squared her shoulders and looked at Cullen. He gave her a nod that she returned. Jenefer then gave a watery smile to Astrid before turning on her heel and walking away. No one moved as they watched Jenefer make her way to the end of the canyon and begin the climb up. Nari paused in her bath to watch her, and the Amazon gave the wildcat a wide berth. Then…Jenefer reached the top and started walking, soon disappearing from view.

Sian let out a sob and raced back into the underground city. Astrid started to wiggle. Cullen lowered her to the ground and watched as she raced after Sian. He ensured the child was safely inside before going to Tamlyn and wrapping his arms around her.

Her shoulders shook as she cried. He gave her the comfort

she needed until the tears finally dried. Even then he didn't release her. Of all three of them, Jenefer was the most competent to go out on her own. Not just because she was a skilled fighter, but because she saw their world as it truly was. Sian and Tamlyn sometimes had a difficult time facing facts.

"How did you do it?" Tamlyn asked.

Cullen frowned. "Do what?"

"Watch your family and friends, your clan, leave when the dragons were sent from your world to ours? You lost everyone. Potentially forever. I'm losing one person who has a good chance of returning."

He ran his hands up and down her back. "We did it to keep the dragons safe. It was a difficult decision, and every King suffered tremendously. Some still suffer because of that decision. Jenefer is strong. If anyone can find the Amazons and get them to return, it's her. She's stubborn as hell."

Tamlyn chuckled and then sniffed. "What if she doesn't return?"

"Doona think about that now. Stay positive. If no' for yourself, then for Sian."

"Oh, Sian. This has to be killing her."

Cullen glanced at the entrance to the city. "She's strong. She'll find a way to keep going."

"We need to watch her for a while. Sian is strong, but she's also fragile. Does that make sense?"

"Love often does that to people. Her heart will hurt until Jenefer returns. Until then, all we can do is be there for her."

Tamlyn sniffed and leaned back to look at him. "Have I told you how wise you are?"

"No' nearly enough," he replied with a grin.

She leaned forward and kissed him. "Thank you."

He pulled her against him once more and kissed the top of her head. "Everything is going to work out."

One way or another, he would make sure of it.

All the Kings would.

CHAPTER SIX

She had spoken to a Dragon King. It was all Nia could think about after she left Shaw the night before. He had even filled her dreams—and there hadn't been any sign of fear in them. When she opened her eyes that morning, her first thoughts had been about Shaw.

Now that she'd had some time away from him, her trepidation and panic had faded away. Leaving her with thoughts of desire. Possibly because of her erotic dreams. She couldn't stop wondering what it would be like to have someone like him in her bed. His fern green gaze was penetrating, his voice deep and captivating. A thrill raced through her when she thought of his large hands. She could imagine them holding her, caressing her. Stroking her. Nia had studied every kind of sex there was. She could be shy and vulnerable or assertive and domineering. Normally, she could tell what her partner needed within moments of meeting them. Not so with Shaw.

She had been the closest thing to herself last evening. It

alarmed and frightened her on a level she hadn't experienced in years. She had learned to be whoever was needed in any given situation. How had Shaw stripped away all her defenses? Despite the fear that'd almost had her running away, he had charmed her. Not to mention, he had made her laugh. Whenever she looked into his eyes, she almost forgot who she was and what she was supposed to do.

If only he weren't a Dragon King. She would…

What would you do?

Nia turned her mind away from that question. It wouldn't do her any good to go down that trail. Her thoughts returned to her meeting Shaw. She cringed when she thought of the soldier priests. Shaw had protected her. Not because he knew who she was or why, but because he had seen how affected she was. Even now, it shocked her. No one intervened with the priests, but he had. She would be forever grateful to him for that.

It would be too easy to fall for his charm. That in and of itself surprised her. She knew all the tricks. She used them.

What if it isn't a trick?

"Stop," Nia told herself. To think like that would only make things worse for her. She needed to keep her eye on her goal, one that was within reach for the first time in her life.

No matter how Shaw made her laugh or want to smile, she couldn't forget that he was the Divine's enemy—and she answered to the Divine. Nia knew that better than anyone. There was no escape, no freedom. Unless the Divine granted it.

Nia shoved aside the covers and rose from the bed. She walked barefoot to the window and opened it. The morning breeze ruffled the thin material of her floor-length blue nightdress. She wrapped her arms around her middle and stared out at the gray morning being broken by the yellow-gold light of the sun.

Shaw had said he wanted to see her again. She needed to interact with him to cement her mission. Her skills in flirtation were top-notch, but she hadn't even had to dig into any of her bag of tricks. Things had come easily between them. That should make things simple and effortless.

When she thought of the times she'd had to seduce men and women who were so foul they literally turned her stomach, she wondered how she'd done it. Shaw was the opposite of foul. The attraction between them would make her assignment painless. After everything she had endured during her life as the Divine's slave, it was time she got to experience some pleasure.

Shaw's half-smile flashed in her mind's eye. Had he used magic to put her at ease, to make her forget all her training? That was the only explanation for Nia being herself. Or had she been? Did she even remember who she was anymore?

Survival had trumped everything else. She had said, done, and been whatever was demanded of her. It kept food in her belly, a roof over her head, and clothes on her back. Sure, she was a slave, but she hadn't worked any less than if she had been left in that dingy place that she had called home.

Nia had expected to spend her life as a servant. She liked to remain in the shadows and observe the comings and goings in the citadel. Those first years were eye-opening. While Nia rarely saw the Divine, her location in the lower part of the palace ensured that she witnessed many comings and goings.

During one such encounter, a soldier priest had taken notice of her. Nia closed her eyes against the memory, but there was no getting away from it. That day had changed everything. She'd gone from a servant in the shadows to being pampered as a courtesan. Her schooling had begun immediately. They taught her to read and write, but those studies were secondary to the chief education of seduction and sex.

Inwardly, Nia had screamed and cried at the direction her life had taken, but it didn't take her long to realize how she could use it to her advantage. When she did, she'd put everything she had into it.

And look at her now.

She was the only courtesan to live on an estate and not at the citadel. She had servants of her own. She even had a modicum of freedom. Mostly, it was an illusion. She might have her own place, but it wasn't really hers, and the Divine's people followed her everywhere she went, watching her every move. Still, she would take this over other options.

Nia drew in a deep breath and then slowly released it. No matter how handsome Shaw was, no matter how he made her smile and forget who she was, she would complete the task given to her. She dropped her arms and rang for Sadie. The servant arrived within a moment.

"Good morning, ma'am," Sadie said in a cheery voice.

Nia turned to face her. "I'll be going out for the day and probably into the night."

"So, something practical and comfortable but also eye-catching?"

"Exactly." Nia was reminded once more how good Sadie was at her job.

Another servant brought in breakfast while Sadie chose Nia's attire. As she ate, Nia thought of where she could take Shaw and what they could do. He'd made it clear that he was interested in her, which meant she should make sure they were alone together. A thrill shot through her at the prospect, but she hastily shoved it aside. Shaw was a means to an end. She shouldn't forget that.

With her meal finished, Nia dressed. This time, she had Sadie pin her hair up in a low bun. Sadie made the style soft and alluring by keeping Nia's locks loose. She turned her head one way and then the other to look at herself in the mirror before smiling at Sadie. "This looks amazing."

Sadie beamed. "I'm glad you like it."

Nia stood and moved to the full-length mirror. She had decided on a skirt, this one simple and light. The expensive dark blue material of the matching shirt was without adornment, but it was one of her favorites. She adjusted her breasts in the plunging neckline. Nia liked the asymmetrical cut of the shirt with one side longer than the other.

"Whoever your target is, they don't stand a chance."

Nia lifted her gaze to meet Sadie's and smiled. "No, he doesn't. I'm going to make sure of that."

"Should I get the house ready?"

"Please, do. Don't do anything too lavish, though. I want things to seem natural."

Sadie folded her hands before her. "He's not your normal, then?"

"Not even close."

A slow smile spread across Sadie's face. "I'll make sure everything is just as you like it."

Nia faced the servant and put her hand on Sadie's arm. "Thank you for everything that you've done for me."

"It's truly been my pleasure."

She gave Sadie a squeeze before walking out of her room. The staff ran efficiently. As soon as they'd learned that she was leaving for the day, they'd readied the carriage. Nia climbed in and wondered at the odd sensation in her stomach. It took her a second to realize that she was nervous. She couldn't recall the last time she'd felt such an emotion.

That wasn't the only one assaulting her, however. There was also excitement—at seeing Shaw. And a small thread of fear that she tried to ignore. It wouldn't do any good to give in to it when she had a job to do. Her thoughts returned to Shaw. Would he look the same in the light of day? Would he be as charismatic? Would his smile make her stomach flutter? Would she still want to grab his face and kiss him?

She was about to find out.

Just as it had the evening before, the carriage dropped her off at the gate to the lower levels. The soldiers from the estate didn't follow her because others were watching her. It was a reminder that she belonged to the Divine.

Nia welcomed the sun on her face. She lifted her hand to shield her eyes from the bright light as she thought about where to find Shaw. He hadn't told her where he was staying. She could have found out, but she didn't want to do that yet. She wanted to see if he would search her out. It was a gamble, but she suspected that he would, given his talk the evening before.

She moved away from the soldiers. After only two steps, her gaze landed on none other than Shaw. He stood unmoving in the bustling crowd, his eyes locked on her. Delight, apprehension, and nervousness whirled in her belly.

He was taller than most. She didn't know how she hadn't spotted him immediately. The sun glinted off his dark hair. His crooked smile caused her heart to race. And his eyes...the way they watched her told her that he had been locked on her from the instant she'd disembarked from the carriage.

Shaw made his way over to her. "Good morning."

Her lips parted at the smooth timbre of his voice. She had to swallow twice before she found her voice. "Good morning."

"I hope you doona have plans for the day."

Oh, if he only knew. "What did you have in mind?"

"Spend the day with me."

She searched his fern green eyes. Damn him for being even more handsome in the sunlight. To her surprise, the fear that had plagued her loosened its hold somewhat. "How can I refuse such an offer?"

"I was hoping you'd say that."

"Do you have a destination in mind?"

"Away from the city, perhaps."

Nia tried to look away from his eyes, but they ensnared her. The intensity of his gaze and his words made her heady. People surrounded them. The only place in the city they would be left alone was at her estate, but she didn't want to take him there yet —there were too many watchful eyes. And she was still finding her footing with him.

"How do you feel about a walk in the forest?" she offered.

A ghost of a grin played upon his lips. "Perfect."

CHAPTER SEVEN

The instant Shaw left the city he breathed easier.

"If you don't like Stonemore, why do you stay?"

He swiveled his head to look down at Nia. She kept her gaze on the well-worn path that led from the city to the Ferdon Woods. She wore dark blue once more. The clothing wasn't as dressy as it had been the night before, but the material spoke of wealth. He glanced at a long wave that had come loose from her bun. He wanted to touch it, but he stopped himself. "I never said I did no' like it."

"Your sigh says otherwise." She shot him a knowing look.

"Sometimes, I can no' stand the crush of people."

She chuckled as they reached the edge of the woods. "The lower portion of the city is more crowded than the upper."

Shaw reminded himself that he needed information. "How long have you called Stonemore home?"

"All my life." Nia hesitantly entered the forest.

"You never wanted to leave?"

"I didn't say that."

He frowned at her choice of words. "Is that an aye?"

"Aye?" she asked as she jerked her head to him.

Shaw shrugged and forced a smile. "It means yes."

"I like it. I might start using it," she replied with a smile. "I wonder if it would catch on in the city."

He highly doubted that, but he didn't say it. "What's your answer?"

"I'll leave eventually."

"What's holding you back?"

She stopped and nervously looked through the tall trees and thick undergrowth. "The forest stretches far on either side. Many dangerous animals call it home."

"There are dangerous animals everywhere."

Her honey-colored eyes met his. "Not the kind I speak of."

"It doesna matter if they're animal or human, there is danger. Sometimes, humans can be more deadly than animals."

"You speak as if from experience."

If only she knew. Shaw lifted one shoulder in a shrug. "Tell me of the animals here."

"There's the brineling. Huge beasts with two horns protruding from their foreheads and thick green skin. They breathe heavily but move quickly despite their size. If they see you, they'll run you down."

"How do you get away from them?"

She flashed him a smile. "By not meeting one."

"I'll keep that in mind," he said as his gaze scanned the forest. Sounds of birds and other animals filled it. The forest ecosystem was as simple as it was complex. His enhanced senses picked up a sound in the distance: heavy breathing. It was moving away from them, so Shaw didn't mention it to Nia since she was obviously ill at ease in the forest.

"The giant owls are a sight to behold at night," Nia said as she started strolling along the path.

Shaw was immediately intrigued. "How big are you talking?"

"The wingspan would be longer than you."

"Impressive."

"And deadly," she added. "Then there are the wildcats. They might be magnificent creatures, but they're incredibly lethal. You won't be able to miss them. They have black-spotted fur and green eyes."

Shaw thought about the wildcat that had fought with Cullen. "Have any been domesticated?"

"Never," she said with a laugh. "We keep our distance. One got into the city once. It wreaked havoc on the occupants until some soldiers cornered and killed it. Its hide hangs in the citadel."

He'd hoped that she would bring up the Divine. "Have you been there?"

"On a few occasions," she said, though she wouldn't meet his gaze.

Shaw noted that it was the second time she had refused to answer his question. Nia was forthcoming with information, but nothing useful. He wondered if she was intentionally holding things back from him. "Do you still think I'm a spy for your leader?"

"It wouldn't matter if you were. I have nothing to hide." She briefly met his gaze, a smile on her lips.

But it was different. Strained, tense. That set him on edge. Something had changed, but he didn't know when or how.

Maybe he had been too quick to think that Nia was just some beautiful woman. What he did know was that she definitely had something to hide.

"You said last night that everyone has secrets," he reminded her.

She paused to pick a wildflower, tucking the steam of the purple bloom behind her ear. "Because everyone does."

"That means you have something to hide."

Nia faced him then. "Nothing the Divine needs to be concerned with."

"Do you fear him?"

"Every leader is feared somewhat."

"That is no' what I asked."

"Things are as they are," she replied.

Movement in the trees off to the side caught his attention. He watched an animal that resembled a squirrel—though twice its size and brown in color—jump from limb to limb.

They started walking again. The deeper they went into the forest, the calmer he felt. He glanced up through the thick tree limbs to the blue sky above and the fluffy, white clouds drifting past.

"You are much more at ease here," Nia commented.

"I doona have to watch my back for thieves." Shaw glanced at her and shrugged. "You also seem more at ease."

She smiled as she watched a bright orange bird fly overhead. "There's less noise."

"Do you come often?"

Nia shook her head. "I might like the peace, but the animals scare me."

"People walk through the woods every day. I walked through them to come here."

"That's true."

He glanced ahead. "Have you followed the path through the forest?"

"No," she answered, her tone soft.

Shaw wanted to know what had happened, but he could tell that she wouldn't answer. It was time to turn the topic back to things that could benefit the Kings. "I've been to many cities in my travels, but Stonemore has to be one of the strictest when it comes to magic. Are the rumors I heard yesterday true?"

"What might those be?"

"That children with magic are killed."

She moved slightly away from him as if the distance would prevent her from answering. "There is a hard line about magic in the city."

"You didna answer my question."

Nia turned her head away from him. "Yes. Okay? Yes, they murder kids."

"Why does no one stand up for them? They're children."

"That's the way things are."

"Did you ever think there might be another way?"

Nia drew in a sharp breath and then released it. Her jaw clenched, and her nostrils flared. "It's the way things have always been."

Obviously, this was a sore subject for her. Shaw would approach it again later. Maybe when she got to know him better, she might open up more. At times, she seemed sincere and unguarded. And at others, like now, she was standoffish.

"My apologies," he said. "I shouldna push about your city."

She sighed and shook her head. "I shouldn't be so defensive."

When she looked his way, they shared a smile. It didn't quite reach her eyes as it had before. Shaw would have to work to rebuild what he had destroyed with one question. It might take more effort than he'd first thought getting anything from Nia. It was time to turn the topic once more. "Tell me about yourself."

She glanced at him, surprise in her eyes. "There's nothing to tell."

"I doubt that. You're a verra desirable woman. I've seen how others look at you. You could have everyone eating out of your hand if you wanted."

A laugh fell from her lips, the same beautiful sound as the night before. "Now you're just flattering me."

"You know it's the truth," he pressed, smiling.

Her eyes glittered when she looked his way. "If you're worried about a husband or a partner, don't be. I'm not with anyone."

"How is that even possible?"

"Life has a way of shoving you down a twisty road so you never know where you'll end up."

Shaw thought about his time before the humans had arrived when he was King of Sapphires. Life couldn't have been better. Then the mortals had arrived, followed by war, and then the dragons left, pitching him into a world of anger and uncertainty. "Aye. I know that road well."

"You survived it." Nia stopped again and faced him.

He turned to her and twisted his lips. Her gaze was direct, seeking. The air shifted around them. The walls she had erected lowered, and he saw the desire in her eyes. He fought to remember what they were speaking about. "So have you."

"In my own way. I'm a survivor."

"We have that in common." He stared into her eyes, wanting to feel her body against his, to know her warmth.

Her taste.

His gaze lowered to see her pulse beating rapidly at her throat. The hunger that had clawed through him during the long night roared its intent. They were alone.

She wanted him.

He wanted her.

No. *Want* was too weak of a word. He *craved* her.

"When are you going to kiss me, Shaw?"

Her words shredded the last of his control. He closed the distance between them, wrapping one arm around her as his other went to her neck. He gazed down at her heavy-lidded eyes. Her lips were parted, waiting for his.

"Oh, the things I'm going to do to your body," he whispered as he lowered his head.

CHAPTER EIGHT

Nia knew pleasure. She had studied it, learned it. Mastered it. She knew how to bring someone to the brink of orgasm with a single touch. She was an expert on how to take someone's desire and use it to her advantage. Her arsenal of tricks was wide and varied.

And not once in all her years as a courtesan had anyone ever made her feel budding excitement or the blossom of desire. Never.

Shaw had her on the precipice, teetering precariously as she anticipated his kiss. She couldn't drag enough breath into her lungs. His arm held her firmly against his hard body, his heat surrounding her, lulling her. His long fingers caressed her throat before wrapping around to her neck. Shivers of exhilaration moved through her.

She stared into his fern green eyes. He didn't hide his longing. Not now, and not when they first met. It transfixed her, electrified her. Her body shook with nervousness—and need. No matter what part she played in the sex game, she was always in control—because she hadn't known what it meant to *feel* desire.

Not until Shaw.

Her fingers tightened on his waist. She didn't remember lifting her hands, but now that she had a hold of him, she didn't want to let go. His stomach jumped when she caressed upward. Her heart skipped a beat at the knowledge that he might be just as affected as she.

You're a courtesan. You know how to make others crave you.

This was different. She didn't know how it had happened or when, but she couldn't deny it. It frightened her enough that she debated running back to the city. Then she remembered the Divine's promise of freedom if she delivered a Dragon King. After all the pleasure she had given others, wasn't it time for her to experience some of her own?

Her thoughts scattered when Shaw's fingers lightly brushed the back of her neck. Her knees became weak. She grasped his broad shoulders for support as his head lowered. Nia had only a heartbeat to prepare herself. Shaw's mouth was soft and tender as it brushed hers. That barely registered before he returned. This time, his lips covered hers. His kiss was, in turns, coaxing and demanding. He molded her against his body, besieging her mouth as if she were a war to be won.

He took his time learning her. The kiss deepened by degrees that she wasn't even aware of until they clung to each other, desperate to get closer.

Suddenly, he ended the kiss and stared down at her. She blinked in confusion. Her heart rate sped up, and her breathing turned ragged as if she had just run a race. No one had ever consumed her mind and body as he did. It was as frightening as it was exciting. Several ideas of seduction ran through her head to get him back to kissing her, but she found she didn't want to use them. Not on Shaw.

"We can no' stay here." His voice was deep and rough, raw from desire. "I want to focus all of my attention on you. No' the animals that could attack."

She tried to speak, but no words formed. Instead, she nodded in agreement.

Shaw said nothing as he took her hand and led her back through the forest. His strides were so long, she almost had to jog to keep up with him, but she didn't mind. She wanted to get somewhere private, someplace it was just the two of them.

They reached the city quickly. The soldiers saw them and opened the gates so they didn't have to pause. Those on the streets who saw Shaw's face hastily got out of his way. His grip on her hand was strong. She almost wished one of the priest soldiers would step into their path. She would love to see what Shaw would do. Then again, that would delay their alone time.

Shaw took the stairs between levels. Twice, he put his body between her and the crowd so she wouldn't get jostled. No one had ever treated her with such care before. She stared at his face, but he was too focused on their destination to look her way. The judgments and fear she had formed about Shaw because he was a Dragon King were called into question at every turn. She'd thought she knew him, but she realized—belatedly—that she didn't know anything.

Shaw paused to let two older women pass, yanking her out of her thoughts. Nia looked around and realized that they were on the third level. She had been so lost in her head that she hadn't paid any attention to their journey. Her lips parted to tell him that they could go to her villa when he pulled her into a pub.

Nia followed him through the building to the stairs and down the hall to what she assumed was his room. He tugged her inside before shutting and locking the door. Then he looked at her. Her stomach felt as if a dozen butterflies flapped their wings at once. So many others had looked at her with need, desire, and possessiveness. But no one had ever gazed at her with such raw hunger before.

"I spent the night thinking of all the ways I wanted to pleasure you," Shaw said as he slowly walked to her. "I could think of nothing else. You've no idea how difficult it was for me to let you go last night."

She swallowed. "I have an idea."

Was that her voice? She sounded…breathless, needy. Her blood ran hotly through her veins, converging between her thighs. Her sex clenched.

His face tightened as he fisted his hands at his sides. "I want to see all of you, but if I touch you now, I'll likely rip something."

Nia had no doubt he would do just that. She should fear the power he held, but she was too wrapped up in the promise of pleasure. She kicked off her sandals. Her hands shook when she unfastened her skirt and let it puddle around her feet. She had to pull the tunic over her head before she tossed it away. Then she stood in only the thin material of her short, wide-legged undergarment. Shaw's gaze locked on the pale blue item. Nia slipped her fingers into the waist and slowly pushed them over her hips and down her legs.

Shaw swallowed twice before he said, "Och, lass. You're prettier than anything I've ever seen."

So many had commented on her beauty, but something about how Shaw said it—or maybe it was the look in his eyes—let her know that he meant it. And *that* touched her deeply.

He reached for her then. His touch was tender as hunger flared in his eyes. She should be terrified. Here was a being with magic. And not just any magic—dragon magic. He was a Dragon King, an individual feared above all else.

Yet she wanted his touch as she had never wanted anything in her life.

Nia placed her hands on his stomach, feeling it clench beneath her palms. She glanced down at his abdomen. "Your turn. I want to see you."

His lips curved into a sexy smile that nearly made her swoon. By the gods, he was driving her wild. It had to be magic. That was the only explanation. She should be shocked. Outraged. But everything felt too good for her to care. Maybe she would be aghast at herself later when she was alone. Now, however, she was going to soak up every moment.

He flexed his fingers at her waist before dropping his hands to his sides. "Aye."

By the gods, his voice was amazing. It suited him. It was just as dark, sultry, and delicious as he was. It was a good thing his magic was causing her to think like this, otherwise she would be in big trouble. Everything she felt was too good to be real.

Shaw yanked off his tunic with such force that she heard the material rip. Her gaze fastened on his upper body, and her jaw went slack. She had felt his sturdiness in the forest, but now she got to see the ripped sinew that corded his neck, shoulders, and pecs. He breathed deeply, causing his chest to expand. Her eyes moved over the light dusting of hair and then dropped lower to his stomach where she could count every muscle.

All the moisture left her mouth when her eyes fastened on the delineated muscles at his waist that disappeared into his trousers. That's when she caught sight of the design. Her lips parted in surprise, but before she could ask, she blinked, and his pants and boots were gone.

A dragon, in a color that sometimes looked red and other times black, sat on his right hip. The dragon's wings were spread, the right wing fanning across his lower stomach. She walked to his side and saw the left wing curved against his lower back. The dragon's body ran from Shaw's hip and down his thigh, with the dragon's tail curling under his right butt cheek. Her gaze ran back up the design to see the dragon's head, which was turned to the right and looking up as if gazing at Shaw.

"What is that?" she asked, wanting to run her fingers over the beautiful design.

"A tattoo." He paused. "Touch it."

Her hand shook as she reached out and ran her fingers across the tattoo. It was smooth. She hadn't expected it to feel like his skin. Then she realized that she was touching *Shaw*. Her eyes moved lower to his thick arousal that jutted upward. She slowly let her gaze roam over his length before taking in his long legs.

His entire body was hard muscle honed to perfection. And he was all hers for the day. Suddenly, she was very happy the Divine had sent her to find the Dragon Kings.

Nia moved to stand before him and placed her palms on his waist, gradually moving her hands over his abs up to his chest.

The muscles flexed beneath her palms. She met Shaw's gaze and caressed over his shoulders until her fingers laced in the back.

"Woman, my control is nearing an end," he warned.

She grinned. "Then let it loose."

In an instant, he lifted her into his arms, carrying her as if she were the most precious thing to him. She slid her fingers into his midnight hair. It was just as thick and silky as she had known it would be.

Shaw placed a knee on the bed and laid her upon it. He braced his hands on either side of her, gazing down. He shifted to one side and set his hand on her lower leg. Without breaking eye contact, he leisurely stroked his hand up her calf and thigh. He paused at her hip, circling his finger over her hip bone before continuing the path over her side.

She watched how his eyes subtly changed with every part of her body he explored. Watching him learn her with his hands was extremely arousing. He lingered once more at her waist, moving his palm back and forth a couple of times in the indent. Then his hand caressed her ribs. Her breath hitched when his thumb brushed the underside of her breast.

Nia wanted him to take her breast in his hand so badly she nearly begged him. His gaze narrowed as if daring her to say the words. She swallowed them. Barely. She didn't know where Shaw would take her, but she desperately needed to find out.

Just when she thought that he would cup her, his hand shifted and moved to the center of her stomach. He slowly slid his hand up her abdomen and between her breasts to her neck. His fingers rested on her racing pulse as his eyes crinkled slightly at the corners. Yes, he knew exactly what he did to her. She almost told him that it didn't count since he used magic, but he couldn't know that she knew his identity.

"Stunning," he whispered as he lowered his head to hers.

She sighed into the kiss. He didn't ravage her as he had in the woods. He took his time, teasing her. She didn't care. It all felt so amazing.

He moved his weight on top of her. She moaned, loving the feel of him. His cock pressed into her, and her body clenched in anticipation. She couldn't wait to feel him inside her. It was too bad she couldn't do magic. Because if she had this kind of power over others, then she would never fail the Divine. Not that it mattered. She would bring Shaw to the Divine and win her freedom.

She pushed at his shoulder. He didn't budge for a moment, but then he gave in. That's when she knew that he allowed her to roll him onto his back. Shaw had magic, but she had power of her own. It might not be magic, but it had gotten her everything she had now.

Nia straddled him and ran her hands over his chest once more. She couldn't get enough of touching him. Everything about Shaw felt so wonderful. He watched her with those fern green eyes. She didn't need to know what he was thinking. She felt his desire lying hard at the junction of her thighs.

She reached back and shoved her fingers into her hair, scattering the pins. As her hair tumbled free, Shaw's eyes darkened. His cock jumped, and his hands clenched at her hips. But she wasn't finished yet.

Nia dropped her head back and ran her hands over her breasts.

CHAPTER NINE

Shaw was going to burn alive. The lust that surged through him was unlike anything he had ever experienced before. It seared him. Scorched him.

And he craved more.

More of the heat. More of Nia.

Her bewitching body was made to be loved. She embraced her sexuality, and she was more provocative for it. It wasn't just her stunning figure she used. Her hair was a seductive weapon of its own. The feel of it teasing his legs as she leaned her head back made his balls tighten.

Then there were her eyes. By the stars! Those honey-colored orbs were his undoing. He saw every flare of desire, every flicker of need that she felt.

Shaw groaned when she ran her hands tantalizingly over her breasts. He sat up and cupped one of her full globes. Her nipples had been hard since she'd disrobed for him, and he had been dying to wrap his lips around the tight bud. But it wasn't time for that yet. He wrapped the long length of her hair around his other fist, keeping her head back.

"Think to tease me, do you?" he said with a smile as he gently massaged her breast.

Her throat moved as she swallowed, her pulse racing. "Just as you're teasing me."

He smiled at her words. He loved how she wasn't afraid to match him word for word—or action for action. Shaw rolled the pert nipple between his thumb and forefinger. "How sensitive are your nipples?"

She didn't answer him immediately. He then gave the bud a little squeeze. A soft moan escaped her lips.

He grinned once more. "You like my fingers. How about my mouth?"

Shaw moved his hand and wrapped his lips around the nipple, giving a soft pull. A cry of pleasure filled the room. He felt her wetness as she sat on him, but he wanted more. He circled the nipple with his tongue before suckling once more.

She began rocking her hips. He almost lifted her to thrust inside her, but thoughts of her had tormented him all night. This might be their only time together, so he would make it memorable.

He moved his head to her other breast. His free hand returned to the nipple he had abandoned and teased it. Nia moaned as she moved her hips, seeking the pleasure he promised her. He could continue and let her reach fulfillment this way, but there were other ways that would satisfy them both.

Shaw untangled his hand from her hair and lifted his head. He had her turned around so that her back was to his chest before she even realized what had happened. It helped that he used magic to shift him so that he leaned against the headboard. With his knees bent, he placed her legs over each of his.

"Shaw," she began.

His left hand returned to her breast and her sensitive nipple while his other rested on her stomach just above her pelvic bones. Her hips undulated. She wanted him to touch her, and he would. Just not yet.

Her head fell back to rest on his shoulder, giving him a partial view of her face. Her lips were parted, her chest rising and falling rapidly. When he gently pinched her nipple, her nails dug into his thighs. He didn't mind the pain. It kept his control tightly leashed on his own raging need.

He kept her focused on her nipple, all the while slowly edging his way closer to her center. When he finally did touch her, she jerked in surprise. Her body softened as he gently circled her swollen clit. He teased the tiny bud until he felt her body stiffen once more. Then he slid a finger inside her.

Shaw squeezed his eyes closed at the feel of her wet heat. He wanted inside her right then, needed to sink deep within her and let himself go. The pleasure would be immense for both of them.

Somehow, he pulled himself back from the brink and began moving his finger in and out of her. He watched his hand as he heard her breathing hitch, and her soft moans filling the room. The way she responded to him made him want to see how far he could push her.

She was close. Oh, so close. Nia wanted to beg Shaw to let her climax, but she knew it would be pointless. Each time she began to crest, he shifted his attention somewhere else on her body and brought her to the brink again.

It was torture.

It was incredible.

Every nerve ending tingled with awareness. She felt how his body moved behind her, heard his harsh breaths, letting her know that he was just as affected as she. With every new part of her body he touched, he brought her more awareness and pleasure. She wasn't about to bring an end to that.

He shifted slightly. The steady rhythm of his fingers inched her closer to orgasm. Then she felt his hardness at her core. Nia forced her eyes open to see that he had moved his cock so that it lay against her. Each time she rocked her hips, the length of him moved over her clit.

If she had been close before, she was about to peak now.

Suddenly, his lips found her neck. His lips on her skin, one hand teasing her nipple while the other stroked inside her, combined with the feel of his arousal against her clit was all it took to make her orgasm.

The strength of it swept through her like a storm, bringing ripples of pleasure that rushed through her again and again.

The sight of Nia climaxing might be the most touching thing Shaw had ever witnessed. Her complete surrender was beautiful to behold. He waited until the last tremors left her body before laying her on the bed and covering her body once more. Her eyes opened to look at him. She reached up and gently touched his face. The moment was oddly touching.

She wrapped her legs around his waist and rocked against him. Shaw clenched his teeth when the head of his cock found her entrance. He pushed inside her slowly, giving her body time to adjust to him. Her sigh of contentment when he was deep inside was nearly his undoing.

"Don't hold back," she said just before pulling his head down for a kiss.

The taste of her was heady. Nia's kisses left his knees weak and his heart racing. With that kiss, the last of his control snapped. He began to pump his hips, his arousal sliding in and out of her tight body. Her legs tightened around him, and she matched his thrusts.

The hunger that had been clawing at him roared with the mounting pleasure. The world vanished. Time no longer existed. It was only him and Nia and the desire that consumed them both.

Nia raked her nails over his back as a cry tore from her throat. Something primal moved through Shaw when ecstasy filled her face, and her body clenched around his cock. He didn't stop moving. He couldn't now if he wanted. His orgasm was fast approaching. Even though he knew it was nearly upon him, he was shocked at the intensity with which it shot through him.

He didn't stop moving until the last of it had left him. When he opened his eyes, he saw Nia watching him. She placed a hand over his heart and smiled. Shaw gave her a soft kiss before moving his sweaty body from hers.

They both lay on their backs, staring at the ceiling. Shaw was in shock. He knew lust. He was well acquainted with the emotion. He assumed that was what he felt for Nia. After such a round of sex, he wasn't sure what it was.

He only knew one thing for sure—he hadn't had his fill of her yet.

He turned his head to find her eyes closed. He smiled and rolled onto his side to face her. Nia's eyes opened as she turned her head to him.

"Should I let you sleep?" he asked.

"I shouldn't tell you yes, that you wore me out. It might make that ego of yours inflate."

He chuckled. "You should see yourself when you climax. It's a beautiful sight. I'm going to see more of it."

"Oh, really?" she asked as she quirked a brow.

He nodded.

She rolled to face him. "You're awfully sure of yourself."

"Do you deny that we have a connection?"

"No."

"Do you deny that what we did felt good?"

Her smile faded. "Never."

"Unless you doona want me, we're going to have lots and lots of sex."

"Mmm. Who am I to refuse that?" she asked with a wink.

CHAPTER TEN

Merrill tossed back the last of his ale and let his gaze move around the crowded pub. The ale wasn't horrible, but it wasn't Dreagan whisky, either. By the stars, what he wouldn't give for a dram.

He forced a laugh when the soldier he was sitting with told a joke and looked his way. It hadn't taken long before he realized that the soldiers knew the most. Not just any soldiers, though. It had to be ones who patrolled the upper levels. Merrill had watched several as they went on shift and then were relieved. That's when he spotted Tomar.

The soldier was older and outranked many others. The lines on his face and the few gray strands at his temples mixed with his brown hair told Merrill that he had experienced a lot. Merrill followed him and learned where he lived. Then, it was just a matter of bumping into him, literally, and striking up a conversation. Tomar liked to talk.

That wasn't good for the Divine.

But it was great for Merrill.

He had already learned that Tomar believed that Stonemore was the greatest city on the realm—despite never visiting any others except in battle. Tomar had also lived in Stonemore for his entire life. He was the sixth generation of his family to become a soldier for the city.

Merrill watched the soldier now, thinking back to before he had been a Dragon King, when his life had seemed so simple. When the only things that had mattered were training and his friends. Longing for that time hit him so hard, Merrill couldn't breathe for a moment.

Tomar slammed his wooden tankard on the table and wiped his mouth with the back of his hand, pulling Merrill from his thoughts. Then the soldier bellowed for the serving girl, who was entirely too young to be working in a pub full of rowdy men eyeing her as if she were a morsel they couldn't wait to devour. "Another round!"

Merrill wasn't sure how much more ale he could stomach. He'd already had two pints. He wanted more information on the soldiers, but after he'd spotted Shaw with the woman and then heard Tomar's low whistle, Merrill became intent on learning about the beauty who had ensnared Shaw's interest.

"That woman a little while ago that you whistled at? Who is she?"

Tomar swung his head to him, his eyes blinking as he tried to focus on Merrill. "Nia. A rare beauty in this city. There isn't a man or woman here that wouldn't do anything to be with her."

"And her husband?"

Tomar chuckled and then winked at the serving girl who delivered two more pints. "She doesn't have a husband."

"She doesn't need one," the girl replied before sauntering away.

Merrill frowned. "What does that mean?"

Tomar's eyes were on the girl's swaying hips when he said, "Nia has her own estate on the sixth level."

"She's wealthy, then?"

Tomar nodded as he took a long drink of ale.

Merrill leaned back in his chair, thankful that Shaw wouldn't have to contend with a jealous husband. "Hard to believe that someone of her stature and beauty is single."

"I can honestly say I don't understand half of what the uppers do."

That could be said for the affluent on Earth, as well, but Merrill kept that to himself. "Wealth has a way of doing that."

Tomar grunted and then burped loudly. He placed his forearms on the table. "It's hard sometimes when I see how many riches they have. It could save someone's life down here a hundred times over."

"Is it normal for the uppers to come down to the lower levels?"

"Usually only for religious services."

Merrill noticed Tomar eyeing his still-full pint, so he took a drink. "There's only one temple? I would've thought there would be two."

"I'm sure the uppers would rather that instead of coming down to us, but it's just one level lower from theirs. Besides," he said with a sneer, "they go inside the temple while the rest of us have to wait outside."

That explained the large area outside the place of worship. It had to be big enough to hold a lot of people. "Everyone fits?"

"Not even close. Many of us get there hours early just to claim a spot. Otherwise, you have to sit in the streets and hope you can hear the priest."

"Everyone attends service?"

"Everyone," Tomar said with a solemn nod. His brows drew together. "We're supposed to be having fun. I don't want to talk about this anymore."

Merrill flashed him a smile and lifted his tankard in a salute. "Apologies, my friend. I'm trying to learn the city."

"I can tell you everything you want to know. Ask me anything."

"What can you tell me about the Divine?"

"Ask me anything but that." Tomar burped again.

Merrill quirked a brow. "You said you knew everything."

"The Divine rules from the citadel that sits on the top level. I've never spoken to anyone who has actually *seen* the Divine."

"So you don't know what he looks like?"

Tomar ran a hand through his hair. "Not a clue."

"Are you sure he rules the city?"

Tomar started laughing. "Without a doubt."

"He's never seen, but the priests are. Some might begin to believe *they* govern Stonemore."

A hard look moved through Tomar's blue eyes. "They would be foolish to think that."

Tomar's happy mood had fled. Merrill needed to change the subject and quickly. "Have you always patrolled the upper levels?"

"That's earned," he said with a cocky grin. "Those patrols aren't just given out. Only the best soldiers, the most loyal, are assigned those duties."

"Do any of you live up there?"

Tomar threw back his head and laughed, drawing the attention of others in the pub. He was still chuckling when he took a drink of ale.

"I take that to mean no," Merrill replied.

"Where did you say you were from again?"

Merrill had been evasive before. Tomar might not have traveled, but that didn't mean others hadn't. "Verra far from here."

Tomar eyed him a moment. "You look like you could hold your own in battle."

"If the need arises."

"It's too bad you aren't one of us. You could join the army. We can always use good men."

Merrill leaned forward on the table. "Is there that much need for soldiers?"

"Not too much anymore. At one time, there were many other cities around. Some near, some far."

"What happened?"

Tomar chuckled. "We happened to them."

"You attacked?"

"We did."

Unease snaked down Merrill's spine. "Why?"

"They were inferior. We are the strongest. We proved that by destroying them. Those who survived the attacks came to Stonemore. We've proven how great the city is."

Merrill wanted to puke. Or punch something. Hitting something would certainly make him feel better. Now he knew why the homeless and starving overran the streets of Stonemore. Whoever had ordered the attack had taken people from their comfortable existences and jobs and forced them into destitution.

"We're a power now," Tomar continued solemnly. "We always were, but we've proven it to others. Those with magic know to stay far from our city. If they come here, they die."

Merrill forced his jaw to unclench. "That's a hard line."

"I take it you come from a place that doesn't mind those kinds of people?"

"As long as they doona harm me, I'm all right with it."

Tomar glanced around before leaning close to whisper, "Keep that thought to yourself. I like you, Merrill, but if others hear you, you'll be punished."

"Because my views are different?"

"Why do you think those other cities were annihilated?"

Merrill held the soldier's gaze. "Do you fear those with magic?"

Tomar slowly sat back and finished the rest of his ale. "Just a week ago, a dragon flew over our city. We've not seen one of those beasts in generations. I was beginning to believe they might not be real. Then, there he was. And he was enormous. I couldn't see what color he was because it was night, but he blocked out the moon as he flew."

"Did the dragon attack anyone?"

Tomar's brows snapped together. "That's the odd thing. He didn't. He just roared a lot and flew back and forth over the city several times before flying away."

"Sounds like a terrifying night."

"That wasn't the only thing that happened, and some are beginning to think there's a connection."

Merrill pushed his ale to the soldier. "What's that?"

"I shouldn't be talking about this," Tomar said in a low voice as he stared at the tankard. Then he lifted it to his mouth and drank deeply. He set it down and leaned forward, his voice low. "As I said, we have no tolerance for magic. Sometimes, the children who are taken from other cities end up having some. The parents inform the priests—just as they're supposed to."

Merrill's stomach tightened. He knew what came next, but he asked anyway. "What do the priests do?"

"They take the children to the temple where they're… they…" Tomar cleared his throat, his face tightening in disgust. "The priests sacrifice those kids."

Merrill closed his eyes. He had heard it from Cullen and the others, but hearing it again was even worse. "They're helpless children."

"It's our way."

"It's wrong," Merrill whispered. The fury he kept buried deep rose to the surface.

Tomar sat back, his eyes downcast.

For all his talk about Stonemore being the greatest city, Merrill could tell that the soldier didn't agree with many of the Divine's policies. And if one person felt that way, then there were others, too.

CHAPTER ELEVEN

Nia drew in a deep breath and slowly released it. Her entire body felt weighted, relaxed. It was such a delicious feeling that she savored every second. Her body was utterly sated. Her mind was calm. Even her soul felt happy.

The magic Shaw was using on her could become addictive. The peace was so soothing, she never wanted it to end.

But it had to.

She had no other choice—despite the enjoyment she felt spending time in Shaw's arms. The dragon knew how to pleasure a woman. There wasn't a single space on her body that he hadn't caressed and licked.

She turned her head to find his eyes closed. His breathing was deep and even. Now would be the perfect time to leave. She could clear her head of his magic, but she would only return. So, what was the point? Besides, she didn't want to leave. She would have to be careful of how much his magic changed her. She couldn't lose sight of her goals or objective.

Nia rose and walked naked to the window. She looked down upon the world she had been born into. Her gaze took in the dirty children with their sunken eyes and cheeks, their skin stretched tight over their bones. She had been that dirty and hungry once. If the Divine hadn't seen her and pulled her from the streets, how long would she have survived? Not long, she wagered.

How long would the children she watched now live?

Only a few months of summer remained. Fall was generally mild, but their winters were severe. She wanted to help them. But how? What could she do? It wasn't as if she were a fine lady with riches to spare. She had no money. The Divine granted her everything she had in exchange for her *skills*.

Nia pulled her hair over one shoulder and began finger-combing it. Her face and body had gotten her the position, but her determination and intellect had allowed her to climb to her current station. Eventually, her beauty would fade. There would be no need for a courtesan with wrinkles and gray hair. If she didn't earn her freedom now, the best she could hope for was to escape before the Divine tossed her out like garbage.

She had dined with rulers of other cities.

She had seduced those the Divine felt threatened by.

She had pulled so many secrets from her targets that she'd passed on to the Divine.

It was those that frightened her. They meant nothing to her, but would anyone else believe that? Once she had her freedom, would the ones she had taken to her bed seek her out to mete out punishment? If she were in their shoes, she would. Would the Divine allow her to leave with everything she knew? That was something she hadn't considered. She had been so intent on the prospect of the offer of her freedom that she hadn't looked at all the angles.

Some of the secrets she had gathered had destroyed lives, careers, and even families. It wasn't as if it gave her pleasure to do such things. But she had a job. If she hadn't done it, someone else would have. Nia had learned to lock away her feelings during each assignment. It was the only way she could successfully do her job. She couldn't feel. Couldn't concern herself with the lies she told.

Because she never failed. No matter what, she found a way.

Awareness stole over her. She looked over her shoulder to find Shaw on his side, his head propped up in his hand as he watched her with a smile that made her insides turn to mush.

"Lass, do you have any idea how stunning you are?"

Instead of answering him, she returned her gaze to the residents out the window. "What do you think of Stonemore?"

"I've told you. It's overcrowded, smelly, and noisy." The bed creaked as he got to his feet and came up behind her.

The feel of his heat suffusing her as he wrapped his arms around her was bliss. She stopped combing her hair and laid her hands on his arms. "That's not what I meant."

"Ah." He sighed and rested his chin atop her head. "I doona know much about the city, but the fact that those in charge doona help the ones in need says a lot."

"I know."

"Does no one help?"

She thought of the few times she had managed to steal some coins from her assignments to pass them on to children. She felt a sharp pain of regret for not doing more. "The priests teach that we're on whatever path the gods have deemed we must walk. We are meant to walk it ourselves without the aid of others."

"That's shite."

Nia agreed, but she had learned a long time ago to keep her thoughts to herself. The only way to survive was to follow the rules—but to think for yourself, and plot to get away. She leaned her head against his chest. He was so tall, she didn't even reach his shoulders. If he had wanted to hurt her—anyone, really—he could have. Not that she ever forgot for a second what he really was. "Stonemore didn't always look like this."

"What changed?"

"The city has taken in residents from other villages that Stonemore attacked. With each conquest, the soldiers brought the survivors and integrated them into society."

Shaw tightened his arms around her. "Except there wasna jobs for these people."

She nodded slowly. "With every city we conquered, our army grew, and our streets swelled with people who had lost their homes and their ways of life. We didn't help them find it again. Instead, the army looked to the next target and how to destroy it."

"Were the other cities threatening Stonemore?"

She shrugged, wishing she had some answers. "I have no idea. It didn't happen all at once. Over the last decade, the army has wiped out city after city."

"When someone conquers others in such a way, it's because they want to dominate everyone and everything. Is that what the Divine is doing?"

"I couldn't begin to guess. I just know what I see."

It felt odd to be looking out at the people as she was. She

might walk the streets, but that was different than feeling as if she once more lived on the lower levels. She had left that world behind when they brought her to the citadel.

And she didn't like being reminded that she could be forced back into such conditions again.

"Let's go to my villa."

He pressed his lips to the top of her head. "If that is your wish."

"I could show you the upper levels so you can see the difference."

"Does being down here make you uncomfortable?"

More than he could know. Each time she came, she still searched the sea of faces in case she spotted her mother. Nia turned in his arms to face him. "You found me down here, remember?"

"That isna what I asked."

His eyes held hers, forcing her to acknowledge the question. "I don't like to see anyone hungry."

"Then do something about it."

"I do. When I can."

His black brows briefly drew together. "What does that mean?"

"It means that I can't hand out coins at will."

"Do you no' live on the upper levels?"

She glanced away. "Yes."

"Then explain to me what I'm missing."

How could she, though? The only way she could, would be to tell him exactly who and what she was. And that wouldn't exactly go over well. He would be furious—and have every right to be. But then she would lose her only shot at freedom.

So, she told the only truth she could.

"I live comfortably, but the money is held by another."

Shaw face relaxed. "Ah. Until you reach a certain age, I gather?"

"Yes." How she hated lying to him. Odd, since it had never bothered her before.

He lowered his head and gently kissed her. "I shouldna have pried. I'm sorry."

Tears stung her eyes at his apology. She pulled out of his arms and walked to her clothes to hide her distress. "I've already forgotten about it."

"You've no' asked about my life," he said as he went to his clothes.

Nia occupied herself with dressing. "We've been otherwise engaged."

His deep chuckle filled the room. "Aye. How could I forget? The only reason we're no' still in that bed is that I'm giving your body time to rest."

She laughed and met his gaze. It was so easy to be with him. To talk, listen. Enjoy. Why did he have to be a Dragon King? Why did he have to be the one the Divine wanted? It wasn't as if she could go after the other King now. She had chosen Shaw, which meant she had to make do with the path she had selected.

"What's going on in that head of yours?" he asked in a soft voice.

Nia realized she had been staring at him. She decided on the truth this time. "I'm thinking about you."

"Good thoughts, I hope."

"Only the best."

He winked at her and sat on the bench before the bed to tug on his boots.

Nia fastened her skirt and slid her feet into her sandals. Then she quickly braided her hair and let it hang over one shoulder. When she looked up, she saw that Shaw was watching her again. "What are *you* thinking?"

"That I think it's verra fortuitous that I saw you last night."

"Verra," she said, mimicking his accent.

He laughed and stood, lifting her into his arms as he did. She was at eye level with him when he kissed her before setting her back on her feet. "The accent sounds good on you."

"I like it better on you. It's sexy."

Shaw quirked a brow and shot her a crooked grin. "You think so, aye? Then you should know that I think your hair is unbelievably sexy."

Now that surprised her. Others had told her it was her smile, her eyes, her face, or some part of her body. No one had ever said her hair. She kept it long because she liked it. The unexpected compliment made her belly tremble with some unnamed emotion. "Thank you."

She took his hand, and they left his room. Nia remembered the rip she'd heard when he had undressed, but she couldn't see anything wrong with his clothing. Maybe she had only thought she'd heard it. Perhaps he had used magic to fix it. That was the most likely explanation. She had no idea how magic worked. Did he have to say something? Wave his hands? There were so many questions she wanted to ask, but she couldn't.

He kept hold of her hand as they left the pub behind and walked through the people along the street. Shaw wasn't in a hurry anymore, but he still made sure that no one ran into her.

He was never rude or angry about it. He simply used his body or his arm to shield her from others.

She had a smile on her face—a true smile. Was this what it felt like to be happy? At the very least, content. It was a new experience. She wanted to talk to someone about it, but she didn't have anyone she could confide in. The worst part was that she wanted to tell Shaw. How silly was that? She barely knew him, but she wanted to share something private with him.

That *had* to be his magic.

She wanted to hate it, but she couldn't. The more time she spent with him, the more she wondered why everyone feared the Dragon Kings so much. They hadn't attacked any cities in…well, she couldn't recall a time when they had. Which begged the question of where had the fear of the Kings come from?

Shaw drew her to a halt and stepped in front of her when two men came barreling out of a pub, fighting. One of the men's fists struck Shaw's shoulder. Instead of getting angry and throwing a punch, he drew the two men apart and simply stared at them. Both seemed to come to their senses. They glared at each other but walked away without anyone coming to harm.

"How did you do that?" she asked.

Shaw shrugged and took her hand once more.

She shook her head at him. As they walked, a tall man with dark blue eyes and chestnut blond hair snagged her attention. He didn't look their way, but something about him reminded her of Shaw. Her stomach dropped to her feet, causing her to stumble. Had she just seen the other Dragon King?

Nia's head snapped to Shaw, but he was staring at her. When she swung her head back to the man, he had disappeared behind some others.

"Are you all right?" Shaw asked as he steadied her.

She forced a smile. "I wasn't watching where I was going."

Before long, they passed through the gate to the fifth level. Nia couldn't help but look back over her shoulder, but she didn't see the other man.

Shaw was quiet as they walked to the seventh level. His eyes didn't miss anything, from the soldiers, to the homes that steadily got bigger and bigger, nor the cleanliness. When they reached her villa, he paused at the gated entrance. He gazed up at the arch of pink roses that ran along a trellis before smiling at her.

She walked through the gate first and waited for him to follow. He stopped once more and took in her home. It was made of the same red sandstone as the rest of Stonemore, but she had softened the harshness of it with the gardens.

"This suits you," he said.

Nia's heart swelled. The villa wasn't hers, and she knew it was foolish to think otherwise, but she couldn't help it.

CHAPTER TWELVE

After the basic structures Shaw had seen on the first four levels of
Stonemore, he was unprepared for the detail of the architecture
of the elite homes. Though he shouldn't have been. Whereas the
buildings had sat on either side of the winding street on levels
one through four, things were far different the moment he
stepped foot onto the fifth tier.

The homes were only on the side against the mountain,
giving the illusion of more space. While the structures were
multi-level, a decent amount of space existed between each
estate. They were all made of red sandstone, but they set
themselves apart with unique entrances.

Shaw's gaze was drawn to the pink roses long before he knew
it was Nia's home. A few other estates had large pots of greenery,
but no one had anything quite like the climbing roses. At least,
not on the fifth or sixth level.

The flowers' scent was heady, as was their size. He had
never seen roses as large as his thigh before. He didn't get to

look at them long before following Nia through the short
wooden gate.

Grass might not cover the ground, but he didn't even realize
it because his gaze moved from the different-sized raised planters
to the various pots. The path separated, forcing each of them to
go around a pedestal where a shallow bowl sat. It was easily six
feet wide and housed a plant similar to an aloe vera, though the
stalks were a pale, silvery blue. Off to the right were more of the
large roses, these in a deep purple shade. On the left were roses of
the most beautiful turquoise hue he had ever seen.

As he continued after Nia, they approached the house. Two
tall, round, red sandstone pots that came about even with his
waist flanked the steps to the portico. In each was a variety of
plants. Tall, ornamental grass rested in the center with other
plants with different-colored flowers that trailed down the
planters' sides surrounding it.

He looked up at her home and nodded at the magnificent
arches that made up the porch. The same curve had been used
for the paneled wooden door. Despite the size, it moved easily
and quietly when Nia opened it.

The smell of roses followed him inside. There were vases of
different-colored blooms set about the house. Some
arrangements were a single color, while others had been mixed,
creating a beautiful design. Then he caught sight of the floor. The
builders had smoothed and leveled the mountain to create it. It
would have been pretty on its own, but the crafters had carved
designs into certain sections, like at the entrance.

The walls were made of sandstone carved and cut into
rectangles. The simplicity of it worked because of the extra
attention to detail around the windows and doorways. They

weren't plain windows. Each had a design similar to those on the floor. In addition, the same dark wood as the front door had been used to outline each window with more artwork carved into the surfaces.

Shaw's gaze clashed with Nia's as she stood, watching him. "Well?" she asked.

Was it his imagination, or did she seem anxious about what he thought? Shaw grinned at her. "I love what I've seen so far."

"There are two more floors above us, but let me take you to one of my favorite spots first," she said excitedly.

Without a doubt, she loved her home. Nia's estate wasn't the largest, but it wasn't tiny, either. Still, it ran on the narrow side, using the floors above to allow more room. He was curious to explore each. He followed her through the back of the house, noting that all the doorways were arches.

She led him through an opened doorway and back outside. Even before he stepped out of the house, the smell of roses struck him again. His eyes locked on the raised flowerbeds that butted up to the mountain where roses climbed what looked like a mesh of rope that connected to the house's top. The flower cover gave not only shade but also privacy, something that was needed so the houses on the seventh level couldn't see into her estate.

The climbing roses weren't the only grand thing to see. There were more raised planters with other beautiful flowers, along with a table and four chairs beneath the roses. It created a quiet, tranquil ambiance that Shaw appreciated.

"This suits you," he told her.

She smiled and gazed up at her roses. "Mountain roses are difficult to grow."

"How did you do it?"

Her head swung to him. "What makes you think I did?"

"Call it a hunch," he said with a grin.

She returned it and nodded. "Yes, I grew all of the flowers you see. When I came into possession of this place, it was barren. No plants or greenery at all. It just takes time, the right kind of soil, and water for any plant to thrive."

"You seem to have a gift."

"I love everything about plants. They all need something different. Even with the mountain roses, you would think they were the same, but they aren't. The climbing ones need more care than the others. Really, it's just listening and learning what the plant needs."

His brows shot up. "Listening?"

She chuckled and glanced at him. "Believe it or not, plants can communicate. Most people just can't see it."

"But you do?"

Honey eyes met his. "Yes."

"Like I said, lass, you have a gift."

"I've never told anyone that I can see what the plants need." Her smile was gone, replaced by unease and fear.

He walked to her and touched her arm. "I willna share that with anyone."

She nodded, but her expression said she didn't believe him.

Shaw moved in front of her and waited until she looked at him before he said, "I know there's no tolerance for magic here, but what you do isna magic. Where I come from, we call it a green thumb. Some people have a natural affinity for growing plants. Just like there are people who can't keep a plant alive if their life depended on it. That's called having a black thumb."

That made Nia giggle. "Are you serious?"

"Verra." He then released her and sank into one of the chairs. "I'm no' sure I'd ever leave this spot. The breeze moving through the roses spreads their scent, yet it isna overwhelming. The sun breaking through the vines is beautiful."

"This is my haven."

"You're lucky to have such a place."

"Do you have one?"

Shaw met her gaze. He was surprised to discover that he wanted to tell her about Dreagan in Scotland. But that wasn't possible. Or was it? She didn't know where he was from. As long as he didn't name anything, he could be safe. "Aye," he answered. "One that I've never wanted to leave."

"Yet you did."

He glanced down and nodded. "That I did."

"Tell me of this place," she urged as she took the chair beside him.

Shaw closed his eyes and pictured his beloved Scotland. "The weather is wildly unpredictable. You can have all four seasons in one day. When the skies are free of storm clouds, it's the brightest, prettiest blue you could ever imagine. Mountains that take your breath away, they're so dramatic, from the bright green grass to the deep green of the trees to the craggy rocks protruding from the earth. Glens fertile and lush. And forests so ancient, and the trees so tall you wish they could tell you all they've seen. But more than anything, the woods beg to be explored. Then there's the coastline with water in every blue imaginable. It's as wild and untamed a place as you'll ever find."

"You miss it."

He opened his eyes and turned his head to her. "Aye."

"Will you return?"

"Without a doubt."

She let out a long breath. "I could picture your home just from your words. I envy your love of such a place."

"You have a special place here."

"For the moment."

Something about her words didn't sit well with him. "What does that mean?"

"Things change. I live here now, but who knows what will happen tomorrow or next month?"

"Surely, there's a way to ensure you can no' be made to leave."

She smiled softly. "Maybe I want to leave."

"To travel. But surely you doona want to give up your home."

Her gaze lifted briefly to the cream-colored roses. "It's just a place to live."

One she'd clearly put her heart and soul into, but he didn't mention that. There was something about the house that she didn't want to tell him. He didn't press her on it now, but eventually, he would find out. It could be that it wasn't hers. Shaw still found it weird that she didn't have control of her money. Stonemore was backward in many ways, so there might be something about women handling money. He would have to ask the woman who ran the pub the next time he saw her.

The day was warm, but the shade from the rose canopy kept them cool. Her design was ingenious, really. The happiness that had been on her face when she had shown him the grounds was gone. He saw a tightness around her eyes and mouth now. She had something on her mind, and he suspected that his questions had stirred things up.

"Do you have siblings?" she suddenly asked.

Shaw was gutted for a moment. It had been a long time since he'd thought of his brothers. "I was the middle brother of three. Both are gone now. You?"

"A younger sister and baby brother."

"Do you see them often? Do they live in Stonemore?"

She turned her head to him, her eyes sad. "They died many, many years ago."

"That must have been a hard loss."

"It was. Just as yours must have been."

He nodded slowly. It had been the worst kind of pain. "What of your parents?"

She got to her feet and showered him with a big smile. "Let me show you the rest of the estate. The gardens might be my favorite, but there are other parts I enjoy, as well."

He didn't press her as he rose and followed her inside. They walked up a switchback staircase to the second level. She showed him the three bedrooms before taking him up the final flight. A small hallway branched off in two different directions. To one side was a door that led to what appeared to be an office with a beautiful wooden desk that matched the windows. To the other side was her bedroom.

Shaw walked beneath the arched doorway and stared in wonder at the spacious chamber. The two large windows facing the back of the house were open to let in the breeze. The windows on the other side of the room were also open so the air flowed freely. Cream-colored curtains billowed in the wind.

A large clothes armoire that showed incredible craftsmanship with its detailing on the wood rested to one side. It complemented the headboard of the bed. A simple coverlet of cream brought out the deep, rich color of the wood. A wooden bench sat at the foot of the bed, a padded chair with cream covering rested in a corner, and dozens of white candles were everywhere.

He found Nia at the windows overlooking the back of the house. She had released her hair from its braid, the deep brown locks lifting in the breeze. Her feet were bare. He stared at her in wonder, much as he had done when he'd found her naked before his window earlier.

She looked like someone desperate to get free. But surely, that was wrong. Nia lived in the wealthy part of Stonemore. She wanted for nothing.

Everyone has secrets.

Her words from the night before returned. Just what secrets did she have? Even if Shaw wanted to know them, he wouldn't ask.

Because he had secrets of his own.

CHAPTER THIRTEEN

Nia turned and discovered Shaw staring at her once again. He wore a peculiar expression. It was on the tip of her tongue to tell him that she had been thinking of his description of his home. She was curious to know its name. A part of her had almost asked what it was called, but she didn't want him to lie. So, she didn't ask.

Secrets. She had so many, but they'd never felt as heavy as they did now. Did they feel the same to him? What would happen if they shared everything? Would the world come to an end? Nothing so drastic, surely. Shaw might want nothing to do with her. He could become incensed and storm out. Then again, he might offer…

Her thoughts trailed off as she inwardly laughed. What did she think Shaw would do? Offer to help her escape? To take her away from everything? That would never happen. He was charming and looked after her as no other had, but that didn't mean he was some savior.

He was a Dragon King.

She was a courtesan.

Together, they were nothing.

"I doona like the sadness in your eyes."

She smiled and walked to him. "I'll only be sad if you have to leave."

"I wouldna dream of it."

"You aren't afraid of water, are you?"

He chuckled and raised a brow. "I'm no'."

"Perfect. Relax here for a moment. I'll return shortly."

She walked into the hall and found Sadie waiting.

"I made sure everyone was out of sight," the woman said with a grin. "He's very handsome. And that accent."

Nia nodded in agreement. "It is rather nice to hear, isn't it?"

"Do you want food, ma'am?"

"I do, but I'd also like the water drawn."

Sadie's eyes widened. "Ohhh. That will be nice with the windows open. Some honey wine, too?"

"Please."

"I'll get it all sorted right away."

Nia smiled her thanks and detoured to her office. She made sure the missive from the Divine was put away just in case Shaw decided to investigate the room. With his magic, he could most likely get into any drawer, so she didn't bother to lock it. But she couldn't leave it out, either. The safe thing would be for her to burn it, but something urged her not to.

This wasn't the first time she had brought someone to her home. In fact, she preferred it, because she could control when and where her servants were, and if she needed help, they would give her assistance. Which meant she had hidden documents before. Nia reached under the desk and pressed a hidden panel that quietly slid open. She rolled the note tightly and placed it inside before closing the panel once more.

She straightened and looked around the room. Then she hurried down the stairs to check on her surprise. She saw Sadie holding a jar of onyx oil. Nia stopped her. "Save this one. Bring the amber instead."

Nia then used a hidden door in the hallway to see how the bath was coming. The three walls of windows were open wide. The bathing tub had been constructed using the more durable marble from a nearby quarry. The material was so costly that it was used sparingly, even by the wealthiest of Stonemore. She had been overjoyed to find some at the estate.

She sat on the raised edge of the sunken tub and let her fingers dip into the heated water. The mountain's thermal spring had been altered long ago so that the elite of Stonemore could have hot water instantly. The tub itself was a large square and could easily fit four people. Today, it would be perfect for her and the handsome Dragon King in her room.

Nia double-checked the jar Sadie carried. Then she went upstairs. When she walked into her room, Shaw was on her bed, his hands behind his head, and his legs crossed at the ankles. His eyes were closed, but she suspected that he wasn't asleep.

She moved to the edge of the bed and stared down at him. He really was gorgeous. She wondered if they might have been friends, lovers, or…possibly more had they met under different circumstances. It was something she would never know. At least, when everything was over, she would have the memories of their time together.

And know how much he hates you for betraying him to the Divine.

Nia winced at the voice in her head. Shaw *would* hate her, but she couldn't help that. If he was as powerful as everyone thought, then he would be able to get away. This was her one—and possibly only—shot at freedom. Only a fool would let that go.

The only way she had survived for as long as she had, the simple reason she had prospered, was because she hadn't trusted anyone. She kept her true feelings locked deep inside, only daring to let the thoughts drift through her mind when she was alone deep in the night. Even then she feared that someone might reach into her head and pluck them out, exposing her. If the Divine or the priests ever learned how she wanted to kill every last one of them for harming innocent children, they would plunge a sword through her heart.

Or worse.

She despised the priests. Hated the religion that was forced down the people's throats. Nia blamed it on her mother, who used to tell her to think for herself. Her mother had also said no one was as righteous as the priests claimed to be. That had stuck with Nia long after the memory of her mother's face had faded.

But now wasn't the time for her to think about her mother, the past, or things that no one would ever change about Stonemore. She had a man with a mouthwatering body at her disposal, one who also showered her with pleasure. Since the only way she had ever climaxed before was by her hand, she wasn't nearly finished with Shaw.

She put her hand atop his. Shaw's eyes opened instantly. She didn't say anything as she tugged him to sit up. When he swung his legs over the side of the bed, she squatted before him and unlaced his boots before pulling them off his feet and setting them off to the side. Then she straightened and held out her hand to him.

He didn't demand to know what was going on. Others always had. Maybe it was because he knew his magic would get him out of any predicament. Oh, to have magic at her fingertips. The things she would change would be numerous. And she would start with the damned priests who made her skin crawl.

She pulled Shaw after her out of her chamber and down the stairs to the main floor. Nia glanced at him to see his gaze on her. Her stomach fluttered in response. He grinned as if he knew how he made her feel. She tugged him to the left and to the doorway hidden by the stairs. Once inside, she stared at him, waiting for him to see the room.

Shaw's gaze lingered on her before he finally looked away. His eyes widened, and his lips turned up in a smile full of pleasure. There was astonishment there, as well. She nearly burst with happiness. She didn't know why it pleased her so much that she could surprise him. Nor did she allow herself to linger on that thought for too long.

Sadie and the other servants had laid out the food and mead along one side of the tub, leaving it within easy reach for when they wanted to snack. Steam rose in fat tendrils from the water. Orange rose petals floated on the surface as the scent of the flowers, along with the amber oil, filled the room.

Nia walked to Shaw and began removing his clothes one item at a time. She didn't allow him to move. When he was nude, she walked him to the tub, where a couple of buckets and soap sat. She washed every part of his amazing body, lingering on his tattoo because it intrigued her so. When his cock hardened in her hand, she remained, teasing him until he reached for her. She maneuvered away from him, but he snagged her—and the soap.

"My turn," he said in a low voice filled with desire.

Her heart skipped a beat. It wasn't the first time she had been undressed and bathed, but it *was* the first time anyone had done so with such relish. By the time he finished, her body thrummed with need. He grinned, knowing full well what he had done to her.

Nia took a bucket and made him kneel. Then she dumped it over his head, washing away the soap. He repeated the process for her. She motioned him into the tub. Her eyes lingered on his fine body and the tattoo that labeled him a Dragon King as he stepped into the tub.

The water came to the tops of his thighs. A sigh escaped him when he found one of the benches and sank down. She couldn't tear her eyes away from his face. He had his eyes closed, and his contentment was so great that she could almost reach out and touch it.

As he enjoyed the heated water, she quickly got in on the other side of the tub. She walked slowly to him. His lids cracked open when she stopped before him.

"Lass, you keep this up, and I'm never leaving," he said with a grin.

It was said in jest, but a little thrill went through her all the same. Nia chided herself. It was his magic. That was the only reason she felt such…fondness…for him. It was probably his magic that made him an incredible lover and brought her so many orgasms, too.

"Perhaps that's my plan," she replied with a grin.

His arm snaked out and wrapped around her, pulling her to him. He opened his eyes to look at her. "You're doing a verra good job."

"Then let me finish."

"I think it's my turn."

She shook her head and reached between them for his arousal. It pulsed in her hand. She ran her hand up and down his length. "Stand," she told him, the word coming out in a voice rough with need.

He held her gaze as he stood, the water sluicing off him. She got on her knees and brought his cock to her mouth. A low moan rumbled in his chest as his hands tangled in her hair.

CHAPTER FOURTEEN

Shaw relaxed on the bed next to Nia with his gaze out the open windows facing the front of the estate, giving him a beautiful view of the night sky. She had fallen asleep on her stomach, her wealth of hair spread around her.

He'd lost count of the number of times they had made love. After hours in the bathing chamber, either in the water or lying on the warm tiles, Shaw had to remind himself that she was human and needed to keep up her strength. He had forced himself to give her breaks so she could eat and rest.

The day had passed quickly—too quickly if he were honest. He was loath for it to end. Not only because Nia was an amazing lover, but because he liked being with her. She didn't badger him for not talking. Though, now that he thought about it, she hadn't asked him questions either, perhaps because she didn't want to answer any.

He didn't know much more than he had before he'd come to her home. Normally, that wouldn't bother him, but since his entire objective in Stonemore was to gain information, he needed to get more than what he had—which wasn't much.

Shaw turned his head on the pillow and looked at her. The sheet was down near her waist, giving him a view of her beautiful back. One of her legs was outside the covers. She was well and truly sated.

But his hunger for her had yet to be slaked.

He closed his eyes and listened to the sounds of the house. It was quiet. No one was up. The only sound he heard was a small animal out back. The noise of the lower levels of Stonemore could still be heard, but it was weak enough that it could be ignored.

Shaw lifted his lids and focused his gaze back out the window to the stars. One of the reasons he had wanted to come to Zora was to be able to fly whenever and wherever he wanted. Now, however, he was once more prevented from turning to his true self. It was only while he was in Stonemore, though. He could handle his need to fly until he left.

His thoughts turned to Merrill. He wondered how his friend was getting on. Shaw opened the link and called Merrill's name.

"How are the upper levels of Stonemore?"

Shaw smiled. *"Verra nice, actually. The breeze keeps the stench from the lower tiers away."*

"And the woman?"

"Sleeping, if you must know."

"That isna what I meant."

Shaw sighed. *"She's no' outright refused to tell me anything, but she hasna been an open book, either."*

"I doubt either of you have had much time to talk. I saw that look in your eye earlier this morn."

"*What did you find out?*"

"*That no' everyone in the city is as gung-ho about the religion, the priests, or the killing of children as others.*"

"*Impressive. Who is your source?*"

Merrill chuckled. "*A sergeant. His station is the upper levels.*"

"*So, he sees a lot.*"

"*Aye. Like the woman you're with.*"

Shaw didn't like the implication. "*Meaning?*"

"*He wasna the only one watching Nia. He knew her name, and by the way everyone around us looked at her, they did, too.*"

"*She's well known. What's wrong with that?*"

"*I can no' put my finger on it, brother. Just a feeling that something isna right.*"

"*I've felt that way since we got here.*"

Merrill sighed loudly. "*I've no' sensed anything watching us. No' how Cullen described it. No shimmering out of the corner of my eyes. You?*"

"*Nothing.*" Then again, he hadn't been looking for it. Perhaps his time with Nia hadn't been the wisest. He wasn't getting information, and he wasn't paying attention as he should.

"*You're getting to see how the uppers live. That is information we have no' had before. Any chance you get to see inside the citadel?*"

"*I'll try. Can you find out if a woman can control her own money?*"

"*Aye. What's going on?*"

Shaw crossed his ankles. "*Maybe nothing, but Nia told me that she doesna have access to her money. She also alluded to the fact that she could lose her estate at any time.*"

"*That should be easy enough to find out. I've seen several female shop owners, so I doona think they couldna control their funds."*

"That's what I was thinking. A woman runs the pub I'm renting a room in. She doesna seem the type to allow anyone but herself to manage her money."

Merrill grunted. *"Which means there is more than Nia is telling you."*

"The first night we met, she told me that everyone had secrets. I'm keeping a big one. So are you. Who am I to push for her to reveal hers?"

"I doubt her secrets have anything to do with us. Besides Tomar, the soldier, I'm flirting with a woman and playing a card game with a group of men. Everyone is friendly enough, but no one wants to talk about the Divine, the religion, or how children with magic are being murdered."

Shaw knew he should be out there with Merrill, but he also knew that Nia would have different knowledge than the people Merrill was dealing with. *"I doona have to remind you to be careful."*

"The worst these people could do would be to send the soldier priests after us. I'd almost like to see that."

They shared a chuckle. *"For a city to claim they're the greatest ever, they have no defenses against anyone with magic. They doona even know if anyone with magic enters. It would be easy for those with magic to take Stonemore."*

"Then why have they no'?"

"Fear has kept them running, but that fear willna always be there. They will fight back, and my money is on sooner rather than later."

The thought of Nia getting caught in the middle of a war

made a knot of worry form in Shaw's gut. *"I'll find out more tomorrow. Con, Brandr, and Eurwen are going to want an update."*

"I'll pass on the information to the others. Press her, brother. She has answers that could get us back to Cairnkeep quickly."

"I will."

Shaw severed the link and clasped his hands behind his head. His lust had steered him to Nia. There was no reason he couldn't continue to slake his need, but when dawn broke, he would start asking questions.

Now would be a perfect time for him to investigate the house, or at the very least, the top floor, which was Nia's. Shaw had never liked lying, and he didn't like sneaking around, either. Then again, someone or something had attacked and killed dragons. It didn't matter if he knew the dragons or not, they were kin. And that was all that mattered.

Shaw sat and softly swung his legs over the side of the bed. The frame creaked slightly when his weight shifted and he stood, but Nia didn't stir. He walked to her wardrobe and used his magic to quiet any creaking hinges as he opened the doors. After rifling through the clothing and putting everything back exactly as it had been, he shut the doors. He hadn't expected to find anything in the wardrobe, but he was disappointed, nonetheless.

Nia's minimalist decorating style made it easy for him to know where to look. It also made his job harder since there were few places for things to be hidden. His lips flattened when he saw the only other place to look in the chamber was the small table beside the bed and its narrow drawer.

Once more Shaw used his magic to silence any sound so as not to wake Nia. When he looked in the drawer, he found it empty. He shut it and rose, more annoyed than ever. Maybe there wasn't anything to find on the estate.

He faced the closed door of the bedroom and made his way to it. His enhanced hearing told him that the servants were still abed. He wrapped his fingers around the knob and turned at the same time he used his magic. The door swung open soundlessly. He slipped through and pulled it to him without closing it fully.

Shaw strode to the door that led to her office. Just like her bedchamber, the office area had minimal furniture. Besides the desk, there were two decorative tables, each holding a vase of roses. There was the chair behind the desk, and another filling an empty corner. Several rugs in various sizes and colors gave an eclectic look to the room that fit with the rest of the house while also setting this room apart. Nia's bedchamber was comfortable and soothing. This room was vibrant and energetic.

The desk was neat and orderly, just like everything else in the house. He sank into the chair and looked about the desk, trying to put himself in Nia's shoes. She favored her right hand, which meant that the more important things would be on that side.

The desk had two drawers on either one. The top ones were only a few inches deep. The bottom ones were significantly deeper. He went through each one, careful to put things back into place. And, once again, he came up empty-handed.

He was about to give up when he recalled the certainty with which Nia had said that everyone had secrets. She wasn't foolish enough to keep anything around that would connect her to a secret. At least, he didn't think she would. Then again, he didn't know her.

He knew her body. But that was different.

Just as she didn't know him.

He'd been fine with that before. Now, he wondered why she hadn't pushed to know more about him. He needed to be prepared because he intended to get answers, and she would likely ask the same ones that he posed.

Shaw rose to his feet, but he didn't leave. Something held him here. He frowned as his gaze slowly moved around the spacious room. He stopped at the desk again and surveyed it closely as he walked all around it.

He squatted and leaned on one hand to look underneath the desk. If she had a hiding nook, this was likely where it would be. Close enough that she could get to it, but not invading her room, which was the place she relaxed.

It took him looking twice before he saw it. His lips flattened as he stared at the hidden panel. A part of him wanted to walk away, to forget what he had found, but he couldn't. He drew in a steadying breath, then reached up with his free hand and began pressing on the wood until it slid open.

Slowly, he withdrew a rolled piece of paper from the slot and then lowered his butt to the floor. He held the note for several moments just staring at it. An uneasy feeling spread through him as he unrolled it. Then, he began to read.

MY DEAREST NIA,

I KNOW I SAID THAT YOU HAD A MONTH OFF, BUT SOMETHING HAS COME UP. SOMETHING, I DARESAY, THAT WILL INTEREST YOU. TWO DRAGON KINGS ARE IN STONEMORE. MERRILL AND SHAW. THERE IS NO MISTAKING

THEM. THEY AREN'T DRESSED AS ONE OF US. SEARCH THEM
OUT. PICK ONE—YOUR CHOICE. USE ALL YOUR SKILLS TO
SEDUCE HIM UNTIL HE IS IN LOVE WITH YOU.

THEN, BRING HIM TO ME.

IF YOU SUCCEED, I'LL GRANT YOUR GREATEST DESIRE:
YOUR FREEDOM.

D

Shaw didn't need to ask who D was. Obviously, it was the
Divine. The bastard knew he and Merrill were there, but *how?*
He immediately called Merrill's name through the link.

"*What's wrong?*" Merrill asked.

"*He knows we're here.*"

"*Who?*"

"*The Divine,*" Shaw spat. "*I'm reading a letter he sent Nia,
telling her we were in the city and instructing her to find us. He
know our bloody names! Told her to pick one of us and seduce
us and make sure we fall in love with her. She's supposed to bring
one of us in to exchange for her freedom.*"

"*Fuck me,*" Merrill said, shock coloring his words.

Anger filled Shaw. He was being used. But, just as quickly,
his ire dissipated. Because he was using Nia, too.

"*What are you going to do?*" Merrill asked.

"*I doona know.*"

"*Well, now you have your answer about the estate and
money. It sounds as if the Divine owns Nia.*"

"Find out who she is. I need to know everything, and she willna tell me."

"I'm on it. You may no' want to hear this, but now that we have this knowledge, you can use it to your advantage."

Shaw closed his eyes and let out a sigh. *"My thoughts exactly. Nia knows the Divine. And the wanker knows about us. We need that information."*

"You focus on that. I'll pass on this information to Con and the others. Every King needs to know they'll be discovered if they enter."

"But that doesna make sense. If the Divine knows when anyone with magic enters the city, then he would know which children have magic."

"Maybe he does," Merrill said. *"Maybe he keeps tabs on the families to make sure they report the children."*

"That doesna explain Tamlyn. She's a Banshee and entered the city numerous times to save the children about to be killed. If they knew about her, then they—"

"Would've stopped her," Merrill said over him.

Shaw shook his head as he opened his eyes. *"Stonemore is built on a no-tolerance rule of magic. If the Divine has this kind of knowledge, then he would enforce it."*

"You're missing one important part."

"What's that?"

"It also means that either he has magic or is using someone who does."

"Bloody hell."

Merrill blew out a breath. *"I couldna have said it better."*

CHAPTER FIFTEEN

"Well?"

Daelya winced at the grating voice of Amsden, the Divine's steward. She hated being yanked out of observing someone else's magic. She also hated that she had turned the two Dragon Kings into the Divine. If she'd had any choice, she would've kept the information to herself.

"Now!"

It took everything she had not to spin around at the steward yelling in her ear and spit in his face. Her days of doing whatever she wanted were long gone. She was a prisoner now, a slave to be commanded by none other than the Divine. Too bad she couldn't do magic herself, because she wanted nothing more than to unleash all her hatred and anger on those responsible for her current predicament.

"I'm not going to tell you again."

Her head turned to look the steward in the eyes as he walked to stand in front of her. If she thought the soldiers would kill her for acting out, she would do it in a heartbeat. Death would be better than this. Instead, the brutes took it out on a young boy who looked no older than twelve.

"The Dragon King is still with her," Daelya replied.

Amsden looked behind her. They forbade her from turning to look at the Divine. Daelya had dared a side-glance when they'd brought her in, but the Divine sat in shadows, revealing nothing. That was fine with Daelya. She got to look out over Stonemore, which she would rather see than the face of the bastard holding her captive.

"Did the dragon do magic?" Amsden demanded.

Daelya turned to look back at the city, her gaze lowering to the roses that indicated Nia's house. "He did."

"Don't make me keep asking questions. Spit it out."

"He searched her house."

There was a pause as the steward looked at the Divine once more. Then, he asked, "Did the dragon find anything?"

"No." Daelya hadn't intended to lie. The word simply fell from her lips before she had time to think about it. But once she'd said it, she was glad she had.

Amsden moved closer to her, lowering his face to hers, his nostrils flaring as he glared at her as if she were shite on the bottom of his shoe. "Are you lying? We'll find out if you are, and the repercussions for the boy will be severe."

Oh, yes. When she got free—because she *would* escape one day—she would find a way to unleash her vengeance on everyone in the citadel. Most especially this buffoon of a steward. "I learned my lesson. I won't lie again."

Two lies in succession. Daelya needed to be careful. She had been captured and bought for the sole purpose of locating magic in Stonemore. Who was to say they didn't have someone who could tell when another was lying?

After a moment, the steward moved back and looked over her head. She allowed her gaze to shift beyond him to the bodies that glowed with a whitish light. It was what she had always seen when she looked at those with magic. There were dozens of people with magic in Stonemore. Most were children or babies who had yet to come into their gifts. Some were attempting to hide them. How long until the Divine made her seek the children out?

Daeyla's stomach roiled violently. She wouldn't be able to do that. She *wouldn't* do that. It was one thing to point out a Dragon King. She knew to respect such powerful creatures, but she also knew the Kings could take care of themselves. Whatever the Divine had in store for the Kings wouldn't be enough to hold them.

Her blood ran cold suddenly. The Divine despised magic and anyone who had it, yet they had bought her. The Divine had found a way to bring Daeyla to her knees and command her. She had dismissed leaders like him before, but she had underestimated him. Her entire tribe had paid the price with their lives.

And she was a slave, doing the bidding of the very person she had once laughed about. The irony wasn't lost on her.

Cruel fingers grabbed her upper arm and squeezed. "Continue," Amsden ordered.

Daelya drew in a breath and slowly released it. She bit her tongue so hard she drew blood. She closed her eyes and shifted her focus to the other Dragon King.

Waking up with a man in her bed wasn't unusual. But it was the first time Nia actually *wanted* someone there. She sighed as Shaw pressed his body against her back. His hand drew her to him so that she laid her head on his arm.

"Hmm. This is nice," she murmured.

He pressed soft kisses to her neck. "Aye, it is."

She turned to face him. For the first time, she didn't have to fake a smile. She was genuinely excited to see Shaw. So happy, in fact, that she leaned forward and kissed him.

"Keep that up and we willna leave this bed," he said in a husky timbre.

"That's fine with me."

He gave her a flat look. "It isna. You're sore."

"Maybe a little." When he quirked a brow, she rolled her eyes. "Fine. I'm sore. You're a very thorough lover."

His crooked grin made her heart miss a beat. "I aim to please."

Her stomach rumbled. She chuckled. "Apparently, I'm also hungry."

"Never say I got between anyone and a meal."

Nia was disappointed when Shaw rose and began to dress. She had thought he would attempt to keep her in bed. The difference in her feelings toward him compared to the others she had seduced were like night and day. Even though she knew his magic caused the feelings, she couldn't stop thinking about it.

With the others, she had counted down the hours until her job was finished. Not that all of them were horrid, but few of them were people she wanted to spend time with. If they had come to the Divine's attention, then they were generally individuals who had done something, knew something, or knew someone the Divine wanted information about. From her experience, few in leadership roles were decent people. Most became enamored with the power they received. The same could be said for the wealthy. Those with money always believed they were better than those without. When, in reality, it was simply a matter of Fate what family you were born into.

"Something wrong?"

She stirred at Shaw's words. Nia smiled as she shoved away the covers and rose. "I got lost in thought."

His eyes darkened as his gaze ran over her nude body. She walked past him to her dressing robe. Nia purposefully turned herself to show her breasts while slowly drawing on the garment and belting it at her waist.

The desire that flared in Shaw's eyes was just what she needed to see. She wasn't sure what the emotion was that tightened her chest. A memory in the back of her mind suggested that it might be nervousness. But...surely, that couldn't be right. Not since her first few times as a courtesan had she been anxious about someone wanting her.

"Nia?"

There was concern in Shaw's eyes when she looked at him. She carefully schooled her features. What was wrong with her? She never let anyone see what she was thinking or feeling. Why had she let anything show with him?

But she knew—his magic.

Maybe being with him too long was having an effect on her. Perhaps she needed some time to herself to regroup and focus, to remind herself what was at stake.

"My apologies. I'm still waking up," she lied.

She watched Shaw closely to see if he bought her lie. Deceits and falsehoods came easily to her, mostly because she didn't care about the people she was sent to seduce. That wasn't the case with Shaw. She didn't like lying to him. Each time she did, the words stuck in her throat. The only reasoning behind it was his magic. Nia had never imagined enchantments would affect her in such a way.

"Shall I call one of your servants?" he asked.

Before Nia could answer, a knock sounded on the door. "Enter, Sadie," she bade.

The door slowly cracked. Shaw rushed forward and opened it so Sadie could walk inside with a food tray. Another servant was behind her with a second meal for Shaw. The women placed the food on the table near the window.

Sadie remained and looked at Nia. "Will there be anything else, ma'am?"

"That'll be all." When she left, Nia found Shaw's gaze on her. "Hungry?"

He walked to the trays and looked over the food. "I could eat."

"I hope it isn't too different from what you're used to."

Shaw smiled and shot her a wink. "My palate isna too picky."

Nia poured herself some jasmine rose tea and offered some to Shaw. She expected him to refuse, so when he nodded in acceptance, a little thrill went through her.

"You look surprised," he said.

She chuckled as she poured. "In my experience, men don't like tea."

"Where I'm from, everyone drinks it. I drink tea often. We

have a variety of flavors." He lifted the cup to his nose and sniffed. "I smell hints of rose."

"It's jasmine rose. My own special blend."

He held her gaze as he brought the cup to his lips and took a sip. Delight spread over his face. "It's light with just the right amount of flavor. The rose doesna overpower the jasmine or vice versa. Did you use green or black tea leaves?"

Once more he surprised her. "Green. You know your tea."

"Like I said, it's a staple where I'm from. Do you have other blends?"

"I do. I like to try different things."

"Where do you get the leaves?"

She speared a bit of butter and spread it over her toast. "I bartered some of my roses for the plants. I grow my own tea plants."

"Have you ever thought of selling your blends?"

Nia glanced outside. No one had ever asked about her tea before. Shaw's interest seemed genuine, but she was too used to hiding things. In her experience, when people pried, it was because they wanted something.

"You should consider it," he said as he set down the cup and reached for some food.

Nia wished she could tell him that it was her dream to get as far from Stonemore as possible and then set up somewhere where she could create and sell her teas. She wanted to fend for herself. She knew the ache of hunger, the fear of freezing to death. She never wanted to be in that position again.

"One day, maybe," she whispered.

It was the first time she had given voice to her dreams. Even whispered, she feared they might be snatched from her.

Shaw swallowed his food. "You have a way with plants and tea blends. You could do verra well for yourself with both."

She didn't want wealth. She wanted to live somewhere that was hers, a place that no one could take from her. She wanted to surround herself with flowers. A simple life. That's all she had ever wanted. The fine clothes, servants, and beautiful estate were nice, but they were all a reminder that she was beholden to someone.

And that individual could take her life in an instant.

"Can I see you later today?"

Nia's head swung to Shaw. She had considered spending some time alone to get some distance from his magic, but she hadn't planned to say anything until after they had eaten. It seemed he had beaten her to it. That stung a little.

A lot, actually.

She made sure her smile was cordial. "What time were you thinking?"

"We could meet for the noon meal."

Nia was free, but she didn't want it to appear as if she were too eager for him. Even though she was supposed to be spending all her time with him. "I'm otherwise engaged. How about after?"

He nodded once. "Shall I come to you?"

"I'll find you."

CHAPTER SIXTEEN

As he walked from Nia's estate, Shaw looked up and caught a glimpse of the citadel. He could get up to the top level and confront the Divine, but that wasn't his mission. That event would come, but it would likely be Brandr or Eurwen who faced Stonemore's ruler.

Merrill had been trying to talk to him all morning, but Shaw hadn't been able to hold a conversation with Nia and communicate with Merrill. Now that he was alone, he opened the mental link and said his friend's name.

Merrill replied instantly. *"About fucking time."*

The exasperation in his voice told Shaw that Merrill had something important to say. *"What is it?"*

"Are you still with Nia?"

"Nay. I'm returning to the lower levels. Though, I am tempted to have a chat with the Divine."

"You and me both," Merrill replied with a snort. *"I updated*

those at Cairnkeep last night. As you can expect, their reactions ranged from shock to anger."

"I'm no' concerned for my safety."

"Are you daft? Zora may look like Earth, but it isna anything like our realm. There are beings here we doona have. Need I remind you that there is an old woman here with enough power to pull a Dragon King from our world?"

The hairs on the back of Shaw's neck stood on end. Someone was watching him. *"Varek got out of that situation just fine."*

"He was lucky. We both know that. A lot was because of Jeyra. We had no idea where he had gone."

Shaw slowed his steps until he stopped. He pretended he was looking at the horizon while trying to determine where the person was.

"Then there is this invisible antagonist that can kill dragons," Merrill continued.

"It's always possibile that we'll encounter a being more powerful than us. That doesna stop me from doing what I do."

There was a pause, then Merrill asked, *"What's happening?"*

"Someone is watching me."

"Can you locate them?"

"Aye."

Merrill released a long sigh. *"It's from the citadel."*

"It is. Do you think whoever can sense magic knows when we're communicating?"

"Anything is possible, but I doubt it."

Shaw fought the need to turn toward the imposing structure where the Divine hid. The bastard wanted to play dirty, then Shaw was willing. *"I need to know what the Divine wants with us."*

"What does anyone want with a Dragon King? They either want our help or to kill us. I think the Divine arse is leaning towards killing. Sorry bugger has no idea he can no' do it."

Shaw started walking again before he did something he'd later regret. *"Everyone on this realm fears us, but no one knows anything about us. How can people hold such dread and contempt without knowing the cause?"*

"It's all they've been told, Shaw. They've never had a reason to learn."

"Then perhaps we should show them."

Merrill issued a long-suffering sigh. *"That isna why we're here."*

"Maybe no', but I'm no' letting my guard down. Did you find out what I asked about Nia?"

"I did," Merrill answered hesitantly.

Shaw didn't like that tone because it meant he wouldn't like the news Merrill had. *"Where are you?"*

"I'm no' sure we should meet."

"Bloody hell. They already know we're here. They know who we are. Why no' meet?"

"Well, when you put it like that…"

Shaw glanced at the sky and fought the prick of anger. He shouldn't take it out on Merrill since Shaw's fury was directed at himself, Nia, and the Divine. *"Where are you?"*

"I'll meet you at The Full Fiddler." Merrill severed the link before Shaw could respond.

Shaw's strides were long and purposeful as he made his way down to the gate that led to the lower levels. He didn't look back again. By the time he reached the gate, he no longer felt that someone was watching him.

Shaw took in every detail around him. And every face. It irritated him that he had fallen so easily into Nia's trap. When he found her, he'd believed her to be afraid of the priests. Now, he realized that it had just been a ploy to get his attention. Everything she had said and done had been to get him to fall in love.

It was a good thing that he didn't allow himself such emotions.

When he entered the pub, he paused and looked to the bar area. Jane was pouring ale and gave him a nod. He returned it before looking around the establishment and spotting Merrill in the back. Shaw made his way to him.

"You look like you're about to take someone's head off," Merrill stated as Shaw sat.

"I'm fine."

Merrill snorted. "You're a terrible liar."

Shaw wasn't fine. He was as far from fine as anyone could get. "Tell me about her." He couldn't even say Nia's name. The anger inside that had begun when he found the note had continued to grow.

"Perhaps now isna a good time," Merrill cautioned.

Shaw glared at him. "I need to know."

Merrill blew out a breath and raked his hands through his blend of brown and blond hair. His dark blue eyes held Shaw's as he shook his head. "She's a courtesan. Tomar was the one who told me. No one else knew about that. They know her face and her name, but nothing else."

"If a guard for the uppers knows what she is, that means her occupation is kept quiet so word doesna get out." Shaw propped an elbow on the table and lowered his voice. "That tells me she's special to the Divine."

"My thoughts, as well. How did you meet her?"

"I thought it was purely by accident. I doona like being fooled."

"We know now. That gives us the upper hand."

Shaw fisted his hands. "We'll never get what we came for, no' now. We should leave."

"So more of us can come and be put through this?" Merrill shook his head. "We stay. I have your back, and you have a way in. Use it."

"I can no'. I'm too angry."

Merrill's brows drew together before his face smoothed out. "Why?"

"Why?" Shaw repeated. "Are you really asking me that?"

"What upsets you more, brother? That you like Nia, and she's using you? Or that the Divine knows about us?"

Shaw stared at him, unable to decide on an answer.

Merrill flattened his lips. "That's what I thought."

"I had a nice time with her. I have a nice time with other women, too. But they doona use me."

"That's shite," Merrill spat in an uncharacteristic show of anger. "Every time you sleep with a woman, you're using her, and she's using you. How is that any different than Nia? Unless you're falling for her."

"Doona be daft." Shaw couldn't believe Merrill would even suggest such a thing.

Merrill shrugged. "Why no'? I saw her. She's stunning. Everyone watched her. Including the children. She commands attention."

Shaw sat back. His temper was usually easy to keep in check, but he was having a difficult time containing it.

"Doona look at me like that. You know I'm right, or you wouldna have spent time with her."

"So what if I was attracted to her? I know what lust is. That's all it was."

"Then why are you still angry?"

Shaw was going to punch Merrill. He looked down and saw he fisted his hands so tightly, his knuckles were white. Immediately, he flexed his fingers. Why was he so furious? Despite not wanting to hear it, Merrill was right. He had used Nia for sex, and she had been willing. It wasn't as if they had sat down and spoken of a relationship. They had both stated what they wanted, and they had both gone into it with their eyes wide open.

Except she had an ulterior motive.

And that's what infuriated him.

Shaw lifted his head to look at Merrill. "She used me for more than sex."

"Aye," Merrill replied in a soft voice. "And it appears she did it to gain her freedom."

To his disgust, Shaw had forgotten that part. "She has a lot of freedom for a prisoner."

"How do you know that? She told you she doesna control her money. I think it's because she doesna have any. The Divine pays for everything she has. Her home, her clothes, her food."

"Her servants," Shaw added.

Merrill nodded and leaned both forearms on the table. "What would you do to gain your freedom if someone held you against your will?"

"Anything."

"We both would. Anyone would."

Shaw breathed deeply and slowly released it. "I blamed her for something that isna her fault."

"That doesna matter now. Like I said, we have the upper hand."

Shaw let his gaze move slowly around the pub. He recognized several from before. There were a couple of new faces, but no one seemed to be paying them any attention. "Someone can discern magic. That means we need to be careful."

"Cullen and Tamlyn have already been warned. Let's just hope that no children are set to be killed while we're here. Cullen will have a hell of a time keeping Tamlyn out of the city."

"He needs to tell us if that happens. We'll rescue them."

"For fuck's sake," Merrill whispered as he looked to the ceiling. "Are you trying to bring everyone's attention to us?"

Shaw quirked a brow. "Do you really expect me to believe you'd allow bairns to die simply because they have magic?"

"Hell, no. I just wanted to give you a hard time." Merrill flashed him a grin.

"I still might hit you."

Merrill's brows snapped together. "Still? When did you want to hit me?"

"This entire time."

"I do have that effect on people."

Shaw rolled his eyes. Then he grew serious. "Thank you for helping me see reason. I was too wrapped in my anger to do it."

"You would've gotten there eventually."

"I think you have more faith in me than I do."

Merrill grinned. "Now that we have that out of the way, let's talk about what we're going to do next."

"That's simple. I'm going back to Nia."

CHAPTER SEVENTEEN

Somewhere on Zora

She hobbled over the rocky terrain, careful where she placed her cane so she didn't lose her balance. The wind whipped around her, threatening to topple her down the steep incline. Then again, it was always trying to knock her down. One day, it would win.

But it wasn't this day.

When she finally reached the top of the mountain, she paused and looked into the distance. Dark clouds approached, a stark contrast to the bright, clear skies around her. Lightning streaked in beautiful displays behind the clouds, and thunder rumbled menacingly, harkening the impending storm. A deep boom of thunder, even from the current distance, told her the storm would be fierce.

She had been through rougher storms and was still standing. She had prayed for death once. Begged for it. To no avail. This was her punishment, and she had no choice but to carry on.

Magic had pulled her from the warmth and safety of her home this day. She knew better than to ignore such an invitation. The realm pulsed with magic. It ran in the water, sprouted in the leaves of plants and trees, wove its way through the ground, and hung in the air. Zora had been created with magic, which meant that the supernatural was at its very core.

Ignorant, bigoted humans who couldn't do magic themselves took it out on others who could. That had been the way for many, many generations. But things were changing. The storm that approached wasn't just about the weather. It warned of something unfolding through the realm that couldn't be stopped now. At the very center of everything was none other than the Dragon Kings.

She wondered if she had done the right thing by pulling that Dragon King from his world to Zora. He had found himself in a fine mess but had gotten out of it. Then, more Kings came. She had expected that, however.

Their arrival had shifted something on Zora. She wasn't yet sure if it was fortuitous or not. She may never know—until it was too late. Not that she could reverse time and undo what she had already done. No, she had set things in motion. All she could do now was watch.

She wasn't the only one on Zora taking note of the change. The others felt it, too. They wouldn't do anything. They never did. The one time she had, she had been punished severely. She'd learned her lesson. Not that it did much good. She was stuck in this hell and would be for eternity.

Her eyes closed as she felt the humidity drench the air. The storm was approaching fast. She thought about staying on top of the mountain. A memory surged from the deepest recesses of her mind. Her running through a thunderstorm, reaching for the lightning.

When she opened her eyes, a phenomenal display of lightning that lit up the sky, allowing her a brief glimpse into the frothy configurations of the clouds. The sun fell behind the storm clouds and blanketed the world in dark gray. The Dragon Kings were magnificently powerful, but she didn't know if they were ready for what awaited them. The universe had granted them absolute supremacy in their domain, and it would be tested on Zora.

Many wanted the Kings to fall.

She was anxious to see how everything settled once all was said and done. Not a soul on Zora wouldn't be affected in some way.

Change was coming. Whether it was good or bad had yet to be determined.

She had seen what the magic wanted her to see. She slowly turned and began the long descent to her cottage. There were those who sought her, but they would never find her unless she wanted to be located. And she had no interest in being found.

Halfway down, she set her cane atop a loose rock. She tried to catch her balance, but the ground soon rushed up to meet her. She rolled several times before using her magic to bring herself to a stop.

Her hands were slashed from the sharp rocks sticking up through the verdant grass. She lay on her side and gingerly pushed herself up into a sitting position. Her head pounded as something dripped onto her neck. The coppery scent of blood filled the air. Her entire body ached. There would no doubt be bruising. It would take a lot of power to heal her wounds, both internally and externally. She looked around for her cane and saw it a few feet away, just out of reach.

She extended her hand for the stick. Magic rushed down her arm and through her hand. The cane vibrated before flying to her. It landed in her palm, and she wrapped her fingers around it, ignoring the pain. She took her time getting her feet under her, and fat raindrops began to intermittently land. By the time she stood, the skies had opened.

She lifted her face to the rain. Once, long, long ago, she had danced in it. There was nothing to dance about now. But still, the memory lingered.

It was better not to dwell on the past. It was gone forever with only a long, lonely eternity before her. She had made her bed. She would willingly lay in it.

She opened her eyes and blinked against the downpour. Her face lowered. She regretted much, but the one thing she didn't feel remorse for was what had landed her in this isolation.

Nia checked the hidden compartment of her desk, but the missive was still there. Nothing was out of place or appeared to have been moved. She didn't usually sleep deeply when someone stayed at her home, but she had never been made love to so thoroughly so many times in a day, either.

Her body hummed from the multiple orgasms. She hadn't realized she could have so many. She wasn't even upset that Shaw had used his magic to give her pleasure. The fact that she was able to find release with him was shocking, no matter how he'd achieved it. She had learned to fake a climax before she learned how to seduce.

Nia returned to her bedroom and found her gaze on the bed. She was still sorting through the turbulent feelings that had been swirling within her. She wanted to know what Shaw was doing. And who he was doing it with.

She wrinkled her nose. It made her sound jealous.

"I'm not," she stated.

Yet a voice inside her head snorted as if to say, "*Liar.*"

Since becoming a courtesan, Nia had never had reason to be jealous. Not over a person. But the more she tried to deny the emotion within her, the stronger—and louder—it became.

The minutes since Shaw had left were passing with agonizing slowness. She had taken a leisurely bath, washed her hair, dressed for the day, and sat beneath the roses out back. She'd had several cups of tea while attempting to read, and it was still hours before she was to meet Shaw. How would she ever make it?

She walked to the window and looked out over Stonemore. He was somewhere in the first four levels. She had to admit that he looked at home there just as he did in her estate. He didn't seem to mind the dingy quarters of the pub where he had a room. He was a Dragon King. He could have anything he wanted. And yet, Shaw walked among the poor and the wealthy as if he were one of them.

He was an enigma.

She had spent considerable time with him, but she didn't know anything about him. The questions she had were forgotten the moment he touched or kissed her. When they weren't having sex, they were simply enjoying each other's company in silence. She hadn't realized how unusual that was until now.

Her targets generally asked dozens of questions in an attempt to get to know her. He hadn't.

Neither had she.

The Divine didn't want answers or secrets from Shaw. The Divine merely wanted *him*. Nia had no idea what Stonemore's ruler would do with a Dragon King. Shaw hadn't been aggressive, but she knew he had it in him. She had seen it banked behind his beautiful fern green eyes.

The lethal dragon within could tear them all apart in a matter of seconds. Why would the Divine want to push Shaw or his friend to such a place?

Unless…the Divine had something else planned. But what could that be? If the Divine wanted to speak to the Dragon Kings, then the Kings could be brought to the citadel to do just that. Since that hadn't happened, Nia believed that the Divine had something else in store for the Kings.

She knew very little about the workings of the citadel or those within it. For all she knew, the Divine could have a weapon to use against the Dragon Kings. But if that were the case, why hadn't they used it already?

Nia squeezed her eyes closed. She was going round and round and not coming up with an answer. A pain behind her eyes had begun. She rubbed her forehead. How she hated not figuring out a problem. Though, she wasn't sure why she wanted to. It wasn't as if she were anything but a pawn in a game that Shaw had no idea he was playing.

Maybe that was what upset her.

She could argue that the Divine needed the advantage

because the Dragon Kings had magic. Then again, she could argue that the Kings had done nothing to warrant such a move by the Divine.

The pain intensified behind her eyes.

Bells tolled from the citadel, announcing the noon hour. She opened her eyes. Nia should eat and forget the thoughts that troubled her, but she knew she wouldn't. Shaw's magic must need more than a few hours to wear off. She couldn't stop thinking about him or how it had felt to be in his arms.

He'd made her feel as if she were the only woman in the entire city. He had touched her as if he cherished her. Had kissed her as if his very soul needed to be quenched by her taste. And he had held her in his arms tenderly and securely.

Not once in her life had she felt as safe and protected as she had with him. Even knowing it was due to magic didn't dampen her yearning to be with him again. It was silly, the need within her to have him beside her.

So what if he could bring her to orgasm easily? She could do that for herself.

Never the way he does it.

So what if he offered her protection? She would get it herself soon enough.

Never like he does it.

Nia wanted to scream at the voice in her head. She was trying to distance herself from Shaw. She had never been in this quandary before, and she didn't know what she was doing. Normally, she'd be setting up ways to get a target out of her house and life without them realizing it. This all came down to Shaw's power. If only she could tell him that she knew who he was, then ask him to stop using his magic on her. That way, she could think clearly again.

What if he isn't using magic?

She frowned at the thought. What else could it be? She had no answer, which meant it was his power. She had earned her position as the favorite courtesan to the Divine because she used her wits as well as her body. She wouldn't let anyone, not even someone like Shaw, ruin everything simply because she couldn't control her body around him.

"I can do this," she declared. She drew in a breath and said in a firmer tone, "I can *do* this." Then, a smile turned up her lips. "I *will* do this. I'm Nia of Stonemore. I went from the streets to living in a grand estate with my freedom close enough to touch. I don't know the meaning of failure."

CHAPTER EIGHTEEN

Shaw didn't wait for Nia at the pub. Instead, he waited for her at the gate to the fifth level. He didn't reveal himself to her as he had the day before. He wanted to see if anyone followed her, or if she might be working with anyone on the lower levels.

It wasn't easy for him to hide. He stood out because of his height, but he managed to stay hidden well enough. Sure enough, it was just as Merrill had said. Everyone watched her. Some stared at her in awe, others with unadulterated lust. Even a group of children pickpockets halted their thievery to ogle her.

Nia rarely made eye contact with anyone. She kept her head up and her back straight. Most got out of the way before she neared them. Shaw didn't know if it was because of her beauty, her status, or her perceived wealth—or a combination thereof—but they gave her deference.

He had watched enough of the uppers coming down to the lower levels to know that they expected to be treated differently.

The people of the lower levels did as requested, mostly out of fear but also because it was just the way things were.

Shaw caught sight of a couple of soldiers standing beside Nia's carriage that'd let her off at the gate. The men lingered behind the gate. Once she was through, Shaw followed her. She was easy to track. She didn't look behind her or alternate her walking speed. Her steps took her from the gate straight to his pub.

He remained outside the building, his gaze roaming from face to face. He knew soldiers watched her. There had to be. Whether in uniform or undercover, they were there. Rulers like the Divine didn't allow their property loose without some sort of leash. Shaw needed to find these people so he could determine what to look for in the future and alert Merrill.

He should've done it yesterday, but he'd let his cock rule him —something that wouldn't happen again.

"One headed your way from the fourth," Merrill said, his voice filling Shaw's head.

Shaw clenched his teeth.

"Make that two," Merrill corrected.

"We're likely being followed, too."

"Probably."

"Watch your arse."

Merrill chuckled. *"I'm the one who should be telling you to do that. Do you see them?"*

Shaw turned his head to look back the way he'd come. The crush of people filling the street didn't make it easy. Most milled about, moving between the shops and outside vendors or just talking. Few moved with purposeful steps, but that's how he spotted the two.

"The soldiers out of uniform," Shaw stated.

Merrill snorted. *"And no' doing a verra good job of disguising it."*

"Those watching us will be more careful."

"I would in their shoes."

"Be careful."

"Aww. Are you worried about me?"

Shaw rolled his eyes and severed the link. He then walked into The Full Fiddler. Nia stood at the bar, talking to Jane. The pub owner nodded his way. Nia's head swiveled to him, and their gazes locked. For a heartbeat, she didn't move. Then she glanced at Jane and said something before making her way over.

"Hi," she said with a welcoming smile.

"Hi."

She studied his face, a small frown creasing the spot above her nose. "Is everything okay?"

"It's noisy. I need to get out of the city. Are you up for another walk in the forest?"

She only hesitated a moment before saying, "All right."

They turned in unison and walked from the pub. Shaw spotted the two men who had been following Nia not so subtly fall into step behind them. No doubt if Shaw turned around, he would see more men that had likely been tasked with watching him.

No words were exchanged until he and Nia were out of the city. When the large wooden gates closed behind them, they trapped most of the noise—and the people following them. It would be too obvious if the soldiers left the city, but they were no doubt on the battlements, trying to keep him and Nia within sight. Shaw didn't care about that. He just didn't want anyone listening.

"It would be easy to just keep walking, would it no'?" he asked.

Her eyes moved about, searching for dangerous animals. "I suppose."

"How often do you come out here?"

"Not very." She shrugged. "I'm too afraid of what's out here to find the comfort that you obviously do."

That was because he wasn't afraid of any animals. He was a dragon. There were few things he feared.

"For some time, they had patrols set up on either end of the road, as well as one in the middle," Nia said.

"Why did they stop?"

Her honey eyes met his. "A brineling attacked the soldiers. Then a second attack happened. That time a wildcat. All within days of each other. Everyone was terrified of the animals. It's safer inside the city walls."

"Yet, you come with me?"

"We won't be going far, and it's daylight. I can see if anything is near." She faced forward as if her words made it so.

He almost smiled at her naiveté. Numerous wild animals were all around her. Some might be small, but they were just as threatening. "You left out the dragon."

Her head snapped to his, her eyes wide with shock as if she had just gotten caught at something. "That's right. I told you about the dragon. How could I forget about that?" she asked with a forced laugh.

"Were you scared?"

"Everyone was. We had no idea what its intention was. Its roar shook the mountain. I've never heard anything like it."

"But it didna harm anyone?"

She shook her head, refusing to look at him.

"The brineling and the wildcat killed the soldiers who were out here, but you hold more fear for dragons?"

"Dragons have magic."

And there was the source. "Ah. I see."

She halted and turned to him. "I don't think you do."

"Explain it to me, then."

Her lips parted, but she hesitated. "Why aren't you afraid?"

"Who says I'm no'?"

"You have a dragon tattoo on your body."

He grinned and shrugged. "Where I come from, people have all sorts of tattoos on their bodies. The designs could have meaning, or could be they just liked the design and wanted it on themselves. Doona read too much into it."

"You aren't scared to be out here."

Shaw gazed into her eyes. He thought about stating who he was. Would she pretend to be shocked, or would she admit that she knew? "As I told you before, there is peril everywhere. You may no' perceive it, but it's there. Even in the city."

"I know exactly what kind of dangers are in the city."

Something in her tone gave him pause. Almost as if she had suffered something. He wanted to ask, but he didn't want to deviate from his current track. "I'm talking about the two men following you."

Nia looked at the ground before turning to the side. "I know about them."

"Why are they there?"

"A precaution."

Getting anything from her was like pulling teeth. Shaw sighed, reining in his irritation. "For what?"

"Anything."

Shaw clenched his teeth. He had to remind himself that she had been taught to fear him and magic. If he was going to get anything from her, he would have to push. "Walk with me through the forest. Then, let's keep going."

"I can't," she said in a soft voice.

But he heard the longing to do just that. "Why no'? Is family holding you here?"

"I'm not like you." She faced him, anger flashing in her eyes. "I can't just pick up and travel when I want."

"Is it the money? Are you afraid of being without?"

"Everyone is afraid of being without, be it shelter or food," she snapped.

There was something there, a stark fear that had flashed for just a moment in her eyes. Had she known hunger? "I'm no' without funds. I could ensure you have both. Just a wee trip."

Her eyes narrowed as she regarded him silently. "Why are you pushing this now?"

"Why are you resisting?"

"I told you."

"Actually, you didna. You've no' said much of anything other than nay."

"That should be enough."

Shaw wasn't going to give up. "We doona have to stay the night. Let's just walk through the forest to the other side. There's a beautiful canyon. I'll show you, and then we can return if you want."

"I can't leave yet."

Yet. A reminder that she was a prisoner. He hated that he was pushing her toward the revelation, but he had a feeling she wouldn't do it any other way. "Why? Is there a deadline you have to meet?"

Exasperation filled her face. "Of course, not. There are things I have to do."

"You didn't mind putting anything off yesterday while we were having sex. But taking a walk to see something that isna far from the city is too much?"

"Yes," she cried, her anger, exasperation, and anxiety letting loose in that one word.

He was getting somewhere now. It pained him to have to keep going. "Why?"

"Because." She had composed herself once more.

"Does it have anything to do with the men following you?"

Her nostrils flared. "Yes."

"I can take care of them. I'll make sure they doona follow you anymore."

"More will just take their place." Her lips were pinched, and her hands clenched at her sides.

"Who is having you followed?"

"It doesn't matter. Leave it alone, Shaw."

That's exactly what he *wouldn't* do. "Who is it?"

"Stop," she said softly, her anger and fear gone, replaced by acceptance.

"I'll go ask the men, then. They'll tell me."

She reached for him when he acted as if he were going to turn away. "Don't you dare."

He caught her gaze and held it. "What are you afraid of?"

"Everything."

Finally. Some truth. "Who controls you? Who holds your money? Who tells you what to do? Who lends you the estate? Who is doing this to you?"

She threw up her hands and covered her ears as she bent over. "The Divine!"

Even though Shaw had read the letter, hearing it from her lips was like a kick to the bollocks. He released a breath. Nia's entire body shook. He touched her, but she jerked away and dropped her hands as she straightened and glared at him. Tears trailed down her face, and he hated himself for forcing the words from her.

Her chest heaved as those beautiful eyes narrowed dangerously. "You don't look surprised. Because…oh, my gods, you *knew*." She stumbled back, her face contorting with betrayal. "How could you?"

"I could ask the same of you. You were the one sent to seduce me and make me fall in love so you could bring me to your ruler."

Her gaze darted toward the city. "How long have you known?"

"It doesna matter."

"It does to me."

"Since last night."

She closed her eyes as her face tightened. When she looked at him, there was fury there. "You found the missive."

"Aye." He wasn't going to lie.

"You could've left the city. Why did you stay? Just to force me to admit to this?" she demanded indignantly.

Shaw crossed his arms over his chest. "I'm here for information. That's all."

"I'm supposed to believe that?"

"The one thing I've no' done is lie to you. I can no' say the same about you."

She flipped her long hair over her shoulder. "I didn't lie, either."

"You just left out the part about seducing me."

"Just as you left out the part about being a Dragon King."

She had him there. "Touché."

"What?" she asked in confusion.

"It means that you're right." He dropped his arms. "I can help you, Nia. If you'll let me. You want your freedom. It's right here. I can take you anywhere you want to go."

She swallowed and glanced at the ground. "Why would you make me that offer? You don't know me."

"Everyone on this realm fears Dragon Kings, but you doona. Why?"

"You say that as if you aren't from here."

What was the point of keeping it from her? "I'm no'."

Her lips parted in shock as she put a hand to her chest. "Well. I wasn't expecting that."

"Why weren't you scared of me?" he pressed.

She licked her lips and lowered her arm. "The Divine has never dangled freedom in front of me before. I was intent on doing whatever I needed to get it. If that meant taking a Dragon King to my bed, then I'd do it. Then, I met you. You weren't at all what I thought you would be." She paused, her brow furrowed. "You were kind. Are kind. And the attraction, it took me by surprise. I was overwhelmed by it."

"Let me help you," he urged.

Nia drew in a steadying breath. "If we leave, the Divine will hunt me down."

"No' if you go over the border with the dragons."

"What information do you need?"

"Anything. Everything. We want to stop the children with magic from being murdered, and I think it all begins and ends with the Divine."

A shiver went through her. She wrapped her arms around her middle. "The Divine has utter control of everything in the city. Everything."

"Those with magic have every right to live. Just as anyone does. No one has the authority to take another's life simply because they're different."

"The Divine would disagree." Nia walked to him and put a hand on his chest. "Get Merrill and leave Stonemore. Nothing will change this city."

"I'm no' going anywhere without you."

CHAPTER NINETEEN

Nia stared at Shaw in dismay as her arms loosened and fell to her sides. "Have you lost your mind?"

"I know what I'm doing."

"You don't know the Divine."

"I know arses like him. It doesna matter what realm it is, there is always someone like that."

She shook her head as she squeezed her eyes closed. When she looked at Shaw, he wore the same determined expression as before. "Where are you from?"

"A place called Earth. It's home to the dragons. Or it was. Until humans arrived."

Now that got her attention. "What do you mean?"

Shaw sighed, resignation tightening his face. "It's a long story."

"I like long stories. Will you tell me? Please? There are dragons and humans on this realm."

"And you fear dragons enough that you want to know what the humans did to make them leave?"

She jerked back, his words like a slap. They had been said softly, but the meaning was clear. "No."

"How do you know that isna what the Divine wants?"

"I have no idea what the Divine wants with you or anyone."

"You, more than anyone would."

Nia took offense to that. Anger spiked through her, shoving aside the hurt he'd inflicted before. "Because I got a missive?"

"Because you're his courtesan."

While she had never been exactly proud of what she was, she had never been embarrassed by it. Not until now. She couldn't explain why she suddenly had the urge to cry. Shaw had known that she'd been sent to seduce him. She'd been fine with that, but nowhere in the note had it declared her a courtesan. Now that he knew her true station, she wanted to forget everything about him —including how it felt to be in his arms.

"So, that means I know the Divine?"

"Don't you? You got a personal letter from him."

She wanted to rip away his quirked brow. That know-it-all attitude grated on her nerves. Though she knew it was because he had stated a fact, one she hadn't realized she didn't want him to know until it had been out in the open. "No."

"You've never met the Divine?"

"No. How many times do I need to say it for you to believe me?"

He stared at her with those green eyes. She couldn't tell what he was thinking, but oh, how she wished she could. Then again, maybe she really didn't want to know what he thought of her.

"How is it you can live in Stonemore for your entire life and be a courtesan without seeing the person who rules you?"

She shrugged. "I don't speculate on the Divine. My goal is to get free."

"The freedom you want is standing right before you. All you have to do is grasp it."

He made it sound so simple. It never was. "What's the catch?"

"There is none."

"Now who's lying?"

He threw up his arms in defeat and let them fall back to his sides. Then he released a long sigh. "You have no reason to trust me. In your shoes, I'd be just as cautious."

She had expected another argument, not for him to yield so easily. Nia looked away. She had waited all morning to get to see him again, and now all she wanted to do was get away, to lick her hurt pride, and yes, even embarrassment. It was wishful thinking that she could have two good days. She should be grateful she had been given one.

"What does the Divine have over you?" Shaw asked into the silence.

Nia looked at him and shook her head. "What do you mean?"

"What does he have that keeps you here?"

"The Divine owns me."

Shaw didn't move a muscle, but she saw the fury that rolled through him just the same. "No individual owns another. *Ever.*"

"What an amazing world you must live in."

"It has its benefits, but we've been through a lot to get there."

How she wished she could see his realm. She had once only

dreamed of finding freedom. Now, she wished to not just get away from Stonemore, but also to escape Zora altogether. "Slavery is a way of life in Stonemore. The Divine will never get rid of it."

"Why have you no' escaped? You have some freedom."

"You saw the men following me. Even now, they're at the wall, waiting for my return."

Shaw tilted his head to the side. "You didna answer my question."

"When they first took me as a slave, I worked in the citadel. I was a small child and was given the dirtiest jobs. It was the first time I had three meals a day, though. I was thankful for that."

"Did you no' have parents?"

She shrugged, her mind drifting back. She tried not to think about those days much. She was so far removed from it now, it seemed as if it had happened to another person. "I never knew my father. Mum did what she could to feed my siblings and me. I was the oldest."

"She must have leaned on you a lot."

Nia swallowed and smiled as she remembered how her mother had praised her for taking care of her brother and sister. "She did. I was happy to help. It gave me something to do."

"You were a child. You should've been playing. Having fun."

Her gaze slid to him. "Do you see many children playing in Stonemore? The ones on the lower levels are barely surviving. They steal because they have no other choice. Otherwise, they starve."

"Did *you* starve?"

She looked away at the compassion in his eyes and his soft

voice. Damn him for showing her kindness. "We weren't any different than anyone else."

"I didna ask about everyone else. I asked about you."

Nia closed her eyes. The sound of Chanler's shrill cries filled her head. She hadn't understood then that it was hunger that made her brother scream. Myria had shed silent tears, and those had been even harder to bear. "Sometimes, Mum came home with food. I never saw her eat. She gave it to me and my younger sister. Chanler was still nursing, but it wasn't long after that Mum's milk dried up. That night, she cried and cried. Even at my young age, I knew things weren't just bad, they were the worst. To make matters worse, it was winter."

She blinked open her eyes. Tears clouded her vision and spilled onto her cheeks. "She would go out and leave me in charge of my siblings, but she always returned. Then, one day, she didn't. We waited anxiously. Two days passed, and I knew I had to do something. I was so hungry. I got us water, but Chanler didn't want it. He kept shoving it away. Myria wouldn't get out of bed. She kept telling me how hungry she was. I got so angry with her. I was just as hungry, but they looked to me to solve things." Nia turned her head to him. "Mum told me to never leave our rooms. By the third day, I had no choice. Our water was gone, and we had to get something in our stomachs.

"I debated for hours what to do. I kept hoping and praying that Mum would return. Finally, Chanler stopped crying. I thought he was asleep. Myria was curled beside him, so I knew they would keep each other warm. I took the opportunity to sneak out. I remember how cold the stones were on my bare feet. The smell of food hit me. I wanted all of it, but I settled for the bread vendor. He was the closest to our home. I was so terrified, but I promised Mum that I would keep my siblings safe.

"Miraculously, I was able to steal a loaf of bread without being seen. I was on my way back to my siblings when some soldiers grabbed and hauled me up. Stonemore's leader was there, though I never saw a face or heard a voice. The Divine had seen me and wanted me as a slave, so the soldiers took me. When I said something about my brother and sister, they went up to our rooms and brought them out. The sight of their lifeless bodies sucked all the fight out of me." Nia tried to recall her brother's and sister's faces, but they had long since faded. "They brought me to the citadel, cleaned me from head to toe, gave me warm clothes and the first meal I'd had in days. It didn't matter that I was a slave, not when I knew I would have food."

Shaw caught her gaze. "And your mum?"

"I never saw her again. I don't know if she returned to find us gone or not."

"You never went looking for her?"

Nia lifted her chin. "I used to walk past our old place, but I've never gone inside. Sometimes, it's better to leave the past where it is and move on."

"Aye, lass. That is certainly true."

She couldn't handle his sympathy right now. Not when reliving the second-worst day of her life. The worst had happened years later. "That's how I became a slave. Some might think it a horrible fate, but I'm alive. Not many who came from my poor beginnings can say that."

"You're a fighter."

She had been called many things, but never that. "I've done what I have to do to survive."

"Like I said, a fighter. You take whatever life gives you and you use it to claw your way out of whatever situation you find yourself in and want out of."

The smile that accompanied his words made her reevaluate his statement. Was that how he saw her? She had never thought of herself as such, but perhaps she should give it a try.

"Every decision you made, every action you took led you right here," Shaw said. "Never be embarrassed or ashamed about anything. Look at where you started. Then look where you are now. That's bloody impressive."

"Even though I use my body?"

He shrugged. "You chose a way to take another step to freedom. What's wrong with that?"

"I didn't choose it."

She noted that he was careful to keep his expression neutral, but she had begun to learn to read Shaw. She saw the slight tightening of his lips, and the way he stilled. She wasn't sure why she had made that statement. Maybe because she didn't want him to think less of her.

"You were forced?" he asked carefully.

Nia almost laughed at how he was handling her like some broken thing. But that was because she *was* broken. And right now, it felt as if the only thing holding her together was sheer will. No one knew her story. No one had asked. And even if they had, she never would've told them.

So, why Shaw?

It had to be his magic breaking down the barriers she always kept to ensure she never got close to anyone. Never trusted. Because to trust anyone in the citadel was tantamount to signing your own death warrant.

Yet, she wanted to tell Shaw. The old hurts that she'd believed were tucked so far down they could never harm her again broke open as if they were freshly made. She wanted that wound healed. She didn't know if telling him would begin the process, but the urge was there—and she followed it.

CHAPTER TWENTY

"It was a soldier priest."

Shaw forced himself to remain still as Nia's softly spoken words reached him. With five words, he knew exactly what had happened to her. The anxiety he had seen the first night he'd met her had been all too real. He hadn't liked the priests before.

Now, he loathed them.

Nia smiled, but there was no humor there. "He said it was my beauty that'd caught his attention. He couldn't help himself after that."

Shaw wasn't sure he could hear details and not take it out on the priests and the Divine. But he wouldn't stop Nia, either.

"The entire time, he kept telling me that it was my fault," Nia continued. "I still remember how his fingers dug into my arm as he grabbed me and shoved me into a room. I wasn't stupid. I knew what he wanted, what he planned to do."

Shaw saw the shiver go through her. His hands itched to pull her to him and offer comfort, but he wasn't sure it was what she wanted or needed. Nia was a survivor—she was strong mentally and emotionally. Her standing before him now proved that after everything she had endured.

She walked to a tree that grew alongside the road and leaned back against it. Her palms flattened against the bark as she looked up through the limbs and leaves to the sky above. "I didn't fight him, even though I wanted to. The priests are revered. You are to submit if one chooses you. Inside, I screamed for help. No one would've come if I had yelled."

"Are your priests celibate?"

Nia's soft laugh danced around him. "No. Fortunately for me, one of the citadel soldiers happened to walk in. For some reason, that made the priest release me before he could finish. But the damage had already been done. The priest withdrew from my body, told me once more that what had happened was my fault, and left."

"He wasn't punished?"

She shot him a dry look and curled her fingers against the bark. "You did hear the part where I said the priests get whatever they want, right? I knew he wouldn't be punished. The priests get away with whatever they want, especially against those on the lower levels. I wasn't the first one raped by a priest, and I wasn't the last. The soldier who found us ordered me to clean myself up. The next morning, as I was doing my chores, a woman came for me. She was dressed as finely as the wealthy. I thought perhaps the Divine had sold me. In fact, I was simply being given another vocation—that of courtesan. I began my training that very day."

Shock ran through Shaw. "They didna give you time to deal with your assault?"

"I'm a slave. My feelings don't matter," she said as she looked at him. Her eyes sharpened. "I didn't dwell on what had been done to me. If I had, I would've died there, and I refused to let that happen. Instead, I used the opportunity that I'd been given to my advantage. I've done very well for myself. I'm the one the Divine turns to for important matters because I never fail. I always get whatever is needed, be it secrets, items, or…people."

Shaw still had so many questions about her assault, but it was obvious that she didn't want to dwell on it. She had done what she needed to move past it enough to keep living. She hadn't addressed it, though, and she would have to, sooner or later.

"All right," he replied.

Her shoulders rose as she inhaled. On the exhale, she released the tree but didn't move away from it. "All right, what?"

"We'll go in front of the Divine. You'll win your freedom, and I'll get the face-to-face I want."

"Did you hit your head recently?" she asked, her brow furrowed. "Because that's the only reason anyone would say that."

"It's a win-win for both of us. You said you never fail. And since you willna take the opportunity I'm giving you for freedom, what other choice do I have?"

She turned her attention forward and looked through the thick forest. "If I leave, the Divine will go after Merrill."

"Trust me, Merrill can take care of himself. Just as I can."

Nia snorted as she shook her head. "You might have magic, but the last thing you should do is underestimate an opponent. The Divine has been ruling for a long time."

Those were wise words, ones he would heed. "He must be an

old man then. He detests magic, but he doesna mind using it to
his advantage."

Her head snapped to him.

"He knew about Merrill and me, Nia. How could he unless
he had someone with the ability to locate those in Stonemore
with magic?"

She pushed away from the tree to face him. "It has to be
something new. Otherwise, the city would know of it. The
priests would be rounding up all the children with magic instead
of waiting for the parents to report them."

"What happens if the parents don't inform the priests?"

"They're killed along with the one they're hiding."

Shaw really wanted to meet the Divine so he could toss him
over the side of the mountain. "Which proves my point. He
willna tolerate magic being used unless it's for himself. Talk
about a hypocrite."

"I've heard that some parents don't mind magic, and as long
as the children keep it hidden, they won't report it. It's just a
rumor, mind you, but it wouldn't surprise me if some in
Stonemore do that."

"How does everyone react when the children are murdered?"

She shrugged and looked away. "It's a part of life. No one
says or does anything because it's simply the way things are."

"Do you like it?"

Her fury was instant as she met his gaze. "Of course, not,"
she snapped.

"Then help me stop it."

She cut him a look before she gave a bark of laughter. "That
will never happen."

"Several have been lately."

Nia shook her head. "Impossible."

"A fellow Dragon King stumbled upon a Banshee who had been sneaking into Stonemore to save the children about to die after hearing their screams. The last time Cullen was here, he and Tamlyn saved seven."

Her lips parted as the truth dawned on her. "That's why the dragon was here."

"Aye. That was Cullen. If he had wanted to destroy the city, he could have. All he did was provide a diversion so Tamlyn could get away with the bairns."

"Nothing was ever said," she murmured. "The priests informed the city that the ceremony had been done the night after the dragon was here."

He saw that she was absorbing everything and trying to come to terms with it. "I could take you to see Tamlyn. Have you ever met a Banshee?"

"I don't even know what that is."

"They see death coming. For Tamlyn, she specifically sees the death approaching the children with magic."

Nia pressed her lips together. "I see."

"Do you want to meet them?"

"It wouldn't matter if I did. I can't leave."

Shaw wanted to bellow his fury. "You can. You have the power. The only hold the Divine has over you are the words he's put into your head all these years."

"If I left with you, I'd be beholden to you."

"Nay," Shaw said with a shake of his head.

She smiled sadly. "It's true, and you know it. I will have my freedom, but I'll do it my way. With you."

"What?" he asked, taken aback.

"You want to save the children, don't you?"

"Aye, but—"

"And meet the Divine?"

"True, b—"

"Then you're going to need my help," she stated.

Shaw started to argue, but damn if she wasn't right. "Just until you're to bring me to him. Then you leave."

"We'll work out the details later."

"No," he said flatly. "Whatever we're doing, we discuss it now where there are no' any ears to overhear anything."

She wrinkled her nose. "Good point. The plan is simple. We keep up what we've been doing. The spies will think you're falling for me just as it's supposed to happen. The soldiers will report that to the Divine. Then, it's simply a matter of going to the citadel."

"Which you willna accompany me to."

Nia rolled her eyes. "I'm the only way you'll get in."

"No' if I say you're ill. It'll happen at the last moment. Food poisoning, perhaps. You *willna* be there," he repeated, letting her know in no uncertain terms that this was the only way he would proceed with the plan.

"All right."

Her quick agreement didn't fool him, but she wouldn't change his mind. "You'll have safely left the city with a King before I meet the Divine."

"You mean Merrill?"

"He'll remain in Stonemore. We're being watched, too. We doona want to give anyone any ideas that we know what's going on. It'll probably be Cullen. He's the closest, and he knows the city and woods."

Nia released a breath. "That might work."

"It *will* work. The Divine will try to use you against me. As long as you are no' in the city, everything will work perfectly."

"You sound very sure of yourself," she said, perturbed.

He shrugged. "I am."

"If this is going to work, then you have to stop using your magic on me."

Shaw blinked, not sure he'd heard her correctly. "Lass, I've no' used any magic on you."

Nia stared at him for a long time before looking away and shrugging nonchalantly. "Just make sure you don't."

He was more confused than before. Why did she think he had been using magic? He wanted to ask, but she had already moved on.

"We're going to have to be careful when we return. Not a word about any of this. You can't act as if you know about my encounter with the priest. Nothing can change in how it was before we walked out of the city."

Shaw nodded because he couldn't form words as his rage enveloped him when he thought of the priests and Nia's assault. He would be hard-pressed not to take out every priest and soldier who called the temple home.

"I'm serious, Shaw."

He focused on Nia's face when she said his name. He liked the sound of it on her lips. "You doona have to worry. I willna do anything that would harm you."

"You recently discovered I was sent to seduce you, and now you're protecting me?"

He grinned as he shrugged. "I'm a complicated man."

"You also need to tell Merrill to be careful with who he talks to. Some are fanatical about the Divine, the priests, and the religion."

"And their hatred of those with magic."

"That, too. If they hear anything, they'll report it."

Shaw nodded his thanks. "I appreciate the heads-up. We've been through this enough times to know how it plays out."

"How many times?"

"I've lost count."

Her gaze raked him up and down. "You don't look that old. You must have started early."

"Something like that."

Her brow furrowed. "How old are you?"

"A lot older than you think."

She shot him a tired look.

"Think in the millions."

Nia stumbled back, shock making her face go slack. "H-how?"

"Dragon Kings are essentially immortal."

She stared at him numbly.

Shaw had to admit that he could've handled that better. He didn't want Nia afraid of him. For someone who had been told that dragons and magic were to be feared, she hadn't shown him a single ounce of it. "Let's stay out here a wee bit longer. I'll tell you anything you want to know about me."

"Anything?" she asked hesitantly.

He nodded. "Aye."

"Even why the dragons left your world?"

Shaw briefly closed his eyes. "Even that."

Nia wavered as she bit her lip. She glanced toward the city, then faced him with determination. "Tell me everything."

CHAPTER TWENTY-ONE

A Dragon King stood before her, pledging to keep her safe. It left Nia befuddled. Shaw had said that he was complicated, but she thought that was putting it mildly.

"Where do you want me to start?" he asked.

She shrugged. She wanted to know every detail he would share. Somewhere in his words, there had to be the reason everyone feared the Kings and magic. If she could just uncover what that was, then perhaps she could…what? What could *she* do? She was nothing more than a courtesan with a pretty face.

"The beginning," she finally said.

Regardless, knowledge was knowledge. The more she had, the better off she would be. Maybe she could pass things on to others. It wasn't much, but it was a start.

That was if she learned anything from Shaw.

He reached for her hand. She didn't stop him when he led her away from the road to a secluded place in the trees where no one could see them. She glanced around, looking for anything that might attack them.

"Nothing is near."

She swung her head to him. "How do you know?"

"Enhanced senses. I can see, hear, and smell far better than humans. There's a brineling you described that way," he said and pointed in the opposite direction. "Even if it does come near us, I'll stop it."

He said it with such conviction that she had no choice but to believe him. And, oddly, she realized that she felt safe. Nia watched as he sat and motioned for her to do the same. She found a place near one of the large trees and sank to the ground, facing him.

Shaw took a deep breath, his eyes on her. "Our world is called Earth. Dragons ruled for eons. Every color, every size. We inhabited every part of our realm. The frozen lands, deep in the waters, the harshest deserts, the tallest mountains, and the rolling hills. We had clans, and a King ruled each clan."

"A Dragon King," she said.

He nodded. "The magic in our realm chose the Kings. It looked deep within each dragon, learning its heart and power. The magic chooses that dragon to become a King."

"What if there's already a King?"

"The one constant in the universe is change. Every King knows he will only hold that position for a certain amount of time. Some hold it for a verra short period. Others, long. Sometimes, a King dies in battle, so the new King steps into the role easily. Then there's the other way. The way most take the throne."

Nia swallowed. "And what way is that?"

"By combat. To the death."

"Is that how you came to be King?"

He glanced away. "Aye."

"You felt the magic, then?"

"I did. It was undeniable. I heard it talking to me. I didna want to rule my clan."

Given everyone Nia had come into contact with, everyone wanted power. So, it came as a shock to hear Shaw say that he didn't. "Why not?"

"I didna come from a good home. My father was injured during a skirmish with another clan, and he was never the same afterward. He became mean and angry. My eldest brother, Rollon, had enough and left. That left only me to look after my younger brother, Ross."

"What of your mother?"

"She died shortly after Ross's birth."

Nia licked her lips. She knew the pain of not having a mother. "I'm sorry."

He shrugged. "It was what it was. Da's rages were so severe that others in our clan began stepping in. Da liked to focus his fury on Ross. Anyone was fair game, really, but he usually turned to Ross first. Ross was just a youngling. He had barely learned to fly. Every time I saw him flinch at the sight of our father, I knew the time was coming for us to leave. Then, one day, I returned to find Ross lying unconscious and bleeding on the ground. I was so angry. I could've killed my father right then." Shaw's gaze lowered as his brows furrowed. "I wanted to. Had he been there, I might have." He shook his head slowly. "Ross moaned, pulling me out of that haze. I was so scared to move him in case I caused more pain. I called for help. Others

came and took us away. While Ross healed from his wounds, I
planned."

"To get revenge?"

Shaw's green eyes lifted to hers. "For a better life. I found
Rollon. The three of us then went as far away from Da as we
could. We struggled, but we looked out for one another. Da had
bitten through a part of Ross's wing. Every time Ross flew, it
caused him tremendous pain. Can you imagine what it would be
like for a dragon who can no' fly?"

"Yes," she said with a nod.

He briefly squeezed his eyes closed. "That's when I began
hearing the magic telling me I had been chosen to lead the
Sapphires. I wanted to ignore it, but there was no ignoring the
call of the magic." He paused, a small smile on his lips. "I told
my brothers. They were as shocked as I, but they were excited
about the prospect. All I had to do was challenge the current
King."

"I don't understand the challenge. If the magic chooses you,
then why doesn't the old King step down? Obviously, his time is
over."

"Because some think they hear the magic and really doona.
Kings were challenged often. Most times, the dragons only
believed they heard the magic because they wanted to rule so
desperately."

Her stomach clenched. "The King doesn't kill them,
does he?"

"It's our way. Every dragon who issues a challenge knows
what's at stake."

"But...that isn't fair to those the magic didn't choose."

Shaw shrugged. "When is anything in life ever fair?"

She had to admit that he was right. "Clearly, you challenged him."

"Aye," he said softly. "The fight was brutal for both of us. It went on for hours. It was worse because I actually liked him. He'd been a good clan leader. A couple of times, I didna think I would win. Even when the tides turned, and it was clear that I would, he didna give up. He fought like the noble King he was until the verra end."

Nia asked, "How do dragons fight? Is it in the air? On the ground?"

"Aye, to both. We use our wings, tail, claws, and teeth."

"Not fire?"

"Dragon fire can incinerate everything but a King."

She frowned in confusion. "Wait. You said Dragon Kings are immortal. That means they shouldn't be able to be killed."

"I said they are *essentially* immortal. A Dragon King can only be killed by another Dragon King."

"And since the magic chose you, you were basically a King."

He nodded his head of black hair. "We can be hurt, but we heal instantly."

That was an interesting fact. Maybe that was why everyone feared the Kings. They couldn't be killed by anyone or anything but another King. "How long have you ruled?"

"I'm no' sure I can count these last few millennia. The dragons were here and no' with us. I was a King in name only."

The pain in his words gave her pause. She wanted him to continue talking, but she didn't want to push him after hearing the torment in his voice.

Shaw rose to his feet and turned away. "Bloody hell. This is harder than I thought."

"You don't have to continue."

He shook his head and faced her. "It isna as if I doona relive it. It's always there. What is the difference in telling you?"

"I'm a stranger who knows nothing of what you endured."

Shaw attempted to smile before sighing and looking away. "Being King of Sapphires was hard. I was pulled in hundreds of directions every day. I hated it. And I loved it. I didna see my brothers as much as I wanted, but they were with me. Ross was well cared for at all times. It took a while, but I settled into a routine of sorts. I'd meet the other Dragon Kings, and, of course, Constantine, King of Dragon Kings."

"What?" she asked in shock.

A soft chuckle fell from his lips as he looked at her. "Did you think we wouldna be governed? The magic of our realm is specific. Only the very strongest of the Kings, the one with the greatest power, can be King of Dragon Kings. Con is the perfect person for the position. He puts us and the dragons above all else. I'm no' sure I could've done the same in his position."

"I'm sure you could." As a matter of fact, she knew he would. They shared a long look. She was the first to look away.

Shaw cleared his throat. "It was a normal day when we first learned that new beings had arrived on our realm. Humans. The Kings approached them together, and it was there that we shifted for the first time. I'm no' too proud to admit that it scared the shite out of me. None of us knew what was happening. Just this awful pain that consumed us. Then, it was gone. Leaving us in these new bodies."

She almost asked what he looked like as a dragon, but her attention was drawn to him as he lifted his hands and flipped them back and forth, gazing at them as if for the first time.

"My talons were gone. My tail and wings were gone. I was in a body I didn't know how to move or use." Shaw slowly lowered his arms to his sides as he met her gaze. "The humans talked amongst themselves, shocked and scared. We pick up languages quickly. Con was the first to speak. Dragons communicate telepathically, so to hear his voice outside of our heads stunned us all. We quickly realized that the humans had no magic. They had no way to protect themselves or even find shelter. We offered them sanctuary on our realm. We taught them how to hunt and what locations would be safe for them."

Nia was speechless. To have such powerful beings like the dragons open their home to those they could've wiped out in an instant was astounding, to say the least.

Shaw continued. "Our new bodies were no' the only things we got. The tattoo you see? Each of us has one. Some say we've always had them, but that our scales hid the design. I think it's something the magic gave us when we shifted. From then on, we've been able to shift back and forth at will."

"And the humans?" She swallowed hard when his face went taut.

"Things began all right. Humans breed quickly, though. It wasna long before every dragon gave up land so the mortals could spread out and grow. Then came the time when the dragons snacked on mortals that crossed boundaries. Humans also hunted the smaller dragons for food—and sometimes for sport."

Her stomach knotted. This was where the hatred and fear stemmed from. It had to be.

"Still, we took mortal females as lovers. Some dragons had an issue with it. More humans had a problem with it, though."

"Were there children?"

Shaw shook his head. "Two different species. In some instances, the females became pregnant, but most miscarried quickly. Few rarely carried to term. Those who did birthed stillborns."

Nia had never wanted children, but she couldn't imagine the pain the women or the Dragon Kings must have endured.

"Until recently, no child between a Dragon King and human has ever lived."

Her mouth fell open.

"I'm getting ahead of myself," Shaw said. "First, you need to know about the war. Ulrik, King of Silvers, who was more of a brother to Con than anything, fell in love with a mortal. Dragons mate for life. We know when we find our mates. Ulrik believed he had found his with Nala. Ulrik's uncle, angry that he wasna King, turned Nala against Ulrik. Mikkel told her that she needed to kill Ulrik on their wedding night. Con noticed Mikkel acting weirdly and overheard what was being plotted. Con gathered us and told us."

"Ulrik was furious, I suspect."

"He told everyone but Ulrik. Con wanted to spare him any pain."

Nia snorted. "That didn't work out, did it?"

Shaw shook his head. "We hunted Nala down and killed her. When we told Ulrik, he was devastated. And furious. He didna lash out at us as he should have. Instead, he gathered his Silvers and began attacking the humans. There was verra tenuous peace between us as it was, and that severed it. The Kings were divided. Some went with Ulrik because they were tired of seeing their world destroyed by ungrateful mortals. Others remained with Con."

"Which side did you fall on?" She was almost afraid to ask, but she had to know.

He held her gaze and said, "Ulrik. I watched the mortals hunt down the Pinks. They were the smallest of the dragons. No' much taller than my knee. I saw humans encroach more and more past the boundaries of their land and onto my clan's and other clans' land. They were never satisfied with what they had. They always wanted more, and they didna care how they got it."

His words made her ashamed to be a human.

Shaw ran a hand through his hair and blew out a breath. "I wanted them gone. We had made a vow to protect them, and Con held to that. He was the one that reminded us of who we were. Of why the magic chose us. But I saw the mortals as bullies, just as my father was. The Pinks? They were slaughtered. I heard Con. I knew he was right. I also knew that if I kept with Ulrik, if I allowed my Sapphires to kill the mortals, the magic would choose a new King. And I didna care."

The resentment and rage were so thick, Nia thought she could reach out and touch it. Had he never spoken of this before? Had he kept it bottled up all this time? She feared the answer was yes.

He made a sound in the back of his throat. "Con and the others made me see reason, even though I knew the only way for us to have our realm again was to wipe out the mortals once and for all. Con kept saying, '*That isna who we are.*' It wasna who we were, but we had reached a tipping point. It was all-out war then. None of us could stop Ulrik. He and his Silvers continued their destruction. The worst part of all was the Kings who told their dragons to guard human cities against Ulrik and his Silvers."

"What was wrong with that?" she asked when he didn't continue. He was silent for a long time before he blew out a shaky breath and fisted his hands.

"The mortals killed the dragons."

She was aghast. "What? I don't understand. Didn't the dragons fight back?"

"They had been ordered by their Kings to guard and protect the humans."

Nia brought her hand to her mouth as tears filled her eyes.

"They were slaughtered," he said as he shook his head. "Screamed in pain. We couldna get to all of them. That was when we all knew. The war would continue. We would either turn into the verra killers Con had brought us back from, or we could let the humans win. There would be no middle ground. The smaller dragons would continue to be hunted, and the larger ones would retaliate every time. Whatever peace we'd had was gone forever."

She closed her eyes as the tears fell down her cheeks. The words Shaw said painted a vivid picture that she would never forget.

"We had to stop Ulrik," Shaw said. "His Silvers were some of the largest of the dragons, and they were doing a lot of damage. Con, with the aid of our magic, stripped Ulrik of his powers, bound him in human form, and banished him from our home: Dreagan."

Nia frowned.

"You think that was extreme?"

She nodded.

He shrugged. "Perhaps it was, but Con was our King. And Ulrik refused to listen. Con begged him to stop before he took action. Ulrik never did. Once Ulrik was no longer King of Silvers, Con bade them to return to him. All but four of the Silvers heeded him. We had to trap those four on Dreagan, deep in a mountain. Then, we combined our magic to open a dragon bridge from our world to another. We sent our dragons away, hoping they would be able to return someday. Seeing my Sapphires leave the realm was devastating."

"Did you fight the humans then?"

"We set up a barrier around Dreagan, much like the one around the dragon land here. We hid there for centuries, waiting until dragons became myth and legend. Only then did we begin to venture out. We saw that the humans had spread to every corner of the globe—and destroyed everything in the process. We live among them now, but we hide who we are. We only shift at night or during thunderstorms."

Nia climbed to her feet. "How did you know where the dragons went?"

"We didna until recently."

CHAPTER TWENTY-TWO

Fuck. Shaw felt as if dragons had trampled him. Replaying his history had been challenging. Yet, somehow, he had gotten through it.

"You sent the dragons away without knowing where they were going?" Nia asked incredulously.

"If they had remained on Earth, their lives would've been constant war. At least we gave them a chance."

She rolled her eyes. "That's shite. Dragons have magic. They, at the very least, could've killed the humans and taken back their world."

"Were we to allow them to become killers?"

"Every one of you had a right to make a stand for your home."

He twisted his lips. "We told the mortals that Earth was also *their* home. Were we supposed to go back on our word? Trust me, I've looked at it every way there is, and it all comes back to the vow we made—and the dragons we are."

"You lost your world. Your dragons. Your very way of life," she said in a soft voice.

"Aye."

She licked her lips, confusion marring her brow. "How do you walk among them? Us, I mean."

"I did it to one day see the dragons again. We soon realized that there wasna a place for our kind on Earth. It is the humans' now. But the Kings are still the realm's protectors."

Nia looked away, digesting his words. "That's a tremendous story." Her gaze slid back to him. "But you aren't finished, are you?"

"For millions of years, we prayed the dragons had found a home. Unbeknownst to us, a goddess named Erith created Zora for the dragons. She had befriended Con, though he had no idea who she was. Erith's part in the story doesna end there, however. Con fell in love with a Light Fae, Rhi."

"A Fae?"

Shaw frowned at her puzzled look. "Do you no' know of the Fae?"

"Of course, I've heard of them, but they're a myth."

He grinned, thinking of all the Fae he knew. "Och, lass, they're verra real. Rhi is on Zora now. She looks just like any other mortal. She's verra powerful."

"I-I…"

Shaw let her adjust to that knowledge and continued. "Con and Rhi are mates, but they fell in love during a time when the rest of the Kings were still dealing with our new lives. Con made the decision to end his relationship with Rhi because of us."

"I don't think Con is as intelligent as you think he is. I hope he at least told Rhi what he was doing and why."

"As a matter of fact, he didna."

Nia rolled her eyes. "Men. I swear."

Shaw fought not to laugh. Rhi would love Nia. "The breakup didna go well, as you can imagine."

"Obviously."

"Neither of them knew that Rhi was pregnant."

"I thought you said humans and dragons can't have children."

"I did. But Fae are no' exactly human."

Nia nodded and motioned for him to continue.

"The Fae came to our world because of a civil war that caused their realm to die. Rhi returned to the Fae Realm because she was distraught, and was attacked and left for dead. Fae live verra long lives, no' as long as dragons but much longer than humans. They can be killed, however. Erith found Rhi. She knew that Rhi wouldna survive long enough for Con to find her, and she couldna save Rhi and the babies."

"Babies?"

"Rhi was pregnant with twins. Erith used magic to remove the embryos, which allowed Rhi's body to begin mending itself. Con found Rhi and used his magic to heal her. She was still unconscious when he returned her to Earth and left her."

A sound like a growl came from Nia. "He didn't wait to talk to her?"

"Meanwhile," Shaw said to get her attention, "Erith followed them and tried to return the babies to Rhi's body, but they wouldna go. Erith ended up taking them to her realm until they were born. Then, when they were old enough, they left her and came here. They knew all along where the dragons were. The twins, Eurwen and Brandr, rule this realm. And they've only recently set aside their anger at their parents and allowed them to venture here."

Nia crossed her arms over her chest. "I hope Rhi found someone else."

"Actually, she and Con are happily mated now." Shaw didn't bother to hide his smile. He liked how Nia had immediately taken a liking to Rhi.

"I bet she made him grovel."

"Oh, she did."

Nia smiled as she dropped her arms, but the grin died. "When did you get here?"

"A few weeks ago. Con and Rhi only came a couple of months earlier. What some call an old crone somehow brought one of our Kings here. He was then captured by humans from Orgate and held there for a while. He freed himself, as well as two other dragons that had been imprisoned and tortured there for years."

"So, the rumors were true," she said, her forehead wrinkling.

Shaw nodded. "Varek was pulled here before Eurwen opened the Fae doorway and let Con and Rhi in. Vaughn came with them. Then, dragons started getting killed. Whoever did it attacked Brandr and Eurwen, too. That's when the rest of us came to help look for the new enemy."

"And that's what brought you to Stonemore?"

"Cullen and Tamlyn alerted us to what was going on here. Merrill and I were sent to find out more about the city and the Divine."

Nia blew out a breath and walked a few paces away. She stopped and turned back to him. "If Eurwen and Brandr wanted, they could wipe us out, just as you could've done with the humans on Earth, right?"

"Aye. But they willna. They know what happened on my realm, which is why they've set up land for all of you and willna give any more."

"I can't blame them for that." She bit her lip as she thought. "You said that Erith created this world. Is she the one who brings the babies here?"

"No one knows why that is happening. Or why none of you can procreate."

Nia cut him a look. "That's probably for the best, actually. Can you imagine how many more of us there would be if we could have children?"

"I can, actually."

She visibly winced. "Do the humans on your world have magic?"

"Some. They're called Druids. We doona have Banshees, though. Tamlyn is the first I've met."

"I know very little of what types of magic are on this realm. I had hoped that I would discover why we're so terrified of dragons, especially Kings, somewhere in your story."

He raised his brows. "And did you?"

"Nothing," she said as she threw up her hands.

"We're hoping to find the source, as well. It had to have come from somewhere."

She quirked a brow. "Or someone."

"We're no' here to take over. We're no' here to hurt anyone unless they attack us first. But we will stop the children from being murdered, whether they have magic or not."

"You've come to the right place."

Shaw watched as she came to stand before him. She had listened intently, even shedding a few tears. He hadn't expected that.

"I feel safe with you," she said.

"Because you are."

"If we work together, there's a chance we'll be found out."

He reached for her, shocked by his need to touch her. Shaw rested his hands on her arms. "No one will harm you."

"I'll do this on one condition."

He imagined she'd ask that he help her escape, which he had already offered. So, he nodded before she finished.

"If I'm caught, don't save me."

"Have you los–?"

"It will only make others more fearful of dragons," she said over him. "Look what's happened since Cullen was here. All he did was fly over the city, and people keep looking up, expecting there to be another dragon ready to attack."

Shaw shook his head. "I can no' give you that promise."

"It's the only way I'll do this. I lived my life in fear of dragons and magic. It wasn't until I met you that I realized I have no basis for that feeling. Others need to learn the same thing."

"That willna happen anytime soon."

"It has to start somewhere."

Shaw stared at her, trying to find a way to thwart what she asked.

"Take it or leave it," Nia replied.

CHAPTER TWENTY-THREE

"You're being unreasonable."

Nia hid her smile as they walked the streets of Stonemore. Shaw had yet to bend to her request. And she had no plans to yield. "I'm not."

He leaned close so his breath fanned her ear. "I'm no' leaving this bloody city without you."

Before she could answer, he pulled her away from two drunken men staggering down the street. For just a moment, she allowed herself to lean in to him, to accept the safety and protection he offered. His large hand slid down her arm. Their fingers twined. Her mind was a whirlwind of information he had shared, most of which she had yet to absorb fully. What she kept tripping over was that the Dragon Kings had given their world to humans without magic.

If his story were true—and she suspected it was—then why did everyone fear the Kings? Why was there such distress and apprehension about magic? There had to be some kind of link.

For humans to just show up on Earth *and* Zora? That wasn't a coincidence. It couldn't be. She might not be a scholar, but it seemed logical that they were connected. If someone could find how, then there was a chance for peace.

Or maybe that was just wishful thinking.

Shaw turned her toward a building and jerked Nia out of her thoughts. She recognized it as The Full Fiddler when they entered. They went straight to his room. Shaw opened the door, and she stepped inside to find another man. The same one she had spotted on the street the day before. So, this was Merrill. He was tall and broad-shouldered and dressed similarly to Shaw. That's where the likenesses ended, though. The man had a mix of brown and blond hair that was on the longer side. Dark blue eyes studied her as he sat in the chair and stretched out his legs to cross them at the ankles.

A slow smile pulled at his lips. "You're no' surprised to find me here?"

"Not especially," she said.

Shaw grunted as he closed the door behind him. "Talk some sense into her."

"I'm Merrill," he said and bowed his head.

"Nia, as you well know."

Merrill chuckled. "You're taking all of this in stride."

"Knowledge tends to change things," she said.

Shaw braced his hands on the window. "Merrill," he growled.

Merrill glanced at Shaw before motioning for Nia to take the other chair. "Shaw informed me of your request."

"It wasn't a request. It was a stipulation." She wasn't surprised that Shaw had turned to Merrill. If she were able to speak to someone telepathically, she would, too. "All three of us are being followed. Are you sure it was a good idea to come here?"

Merrill linked his fingers over his stomach. "No one saw me."

"I did say we've been in situations like these before," Shaw said, his gaze still out the window.

Nia looked at him. She had thought he would balk at her condition, but she hadn't imagined that he would react so harshly. Her gaze slid back to Merrill to find him watching her. She let out a sigh. "Do you have any idea what it's like to have something ingrained in you from birth, only to learn it isn't true? Magic. Dragons. Dragon Kings. I knew of the world but knew very little about it. I've always had a healthy respect for those with magic. Just as I do with anyone who has skills with weapons. They can do things I can't fathom. I never believed anyone should die simply because they have magic, but I learned quickly at the citadel that to speak my opinions would get me killed. I've only ever thought them to myself. Until now."

Shaw slightly turned his head to her, but neither he nor Merrill replied.

She swallowed, shrugging. "When I received the missive informing me of my mission to seduce a Dragon King, I didn't know what to think. I was scared, of course. What was a King doing in the city? How did the Divine know about it? Why had I been chosen? The offer of freedom sealed it." Nia paused and glanced at Shaw. "The last person I imagined to offer me protection was a Dragon King. It didn't take me long to realize that was exactly who Shaw was. The very man I had been sent to seduce had stepped out of the shadows and calmed me. I learned a lot about him that night."

Merrill raised a brow. "Did you? He doesna like to talk."

"He talked to me," she said with a smile.

Merrill's lips twitched as if he were fighting a grin. He crossed his arms over his chest. "Did he, now?"

Her gaze dropped to her lap. "I've been trained to seduce, to entice secrets and information from others. But I didn't ask Shaw anything. I'm not sure why, other than he kept surprising me. I tried to think of what we had been told about Kings, but I couldn't pinpoint anything. Just an overall feeling of fear and hatred. The more time I spent with him, the more I wanted to know." And all that time, she had thought Shaw used magic on her, but he hadn't. Had everything she'd experienced and felt been real?

Nia looked at Merrill. "I asked him to tell me everything about the Dragon Kings. I know there's some correlation between your world and ours. That isn't why I'm holding firm to my condition, however."

"Then why are you?" Merrill asked.

Shaw lowered his arms and turned to her. Nia felt his gaze on her, and she was powerless to ignore him. She looked into his fern green eyes. "The information we can share with others in the city and around Zora is bigger than me. This is something that can begin to heal the divide between those with magic and those without."

"You doona need to sacrifice your life for it," Shaw stated.

She swiveled on the chair to face him and then stood. "Children are being sacrificed. Anyone who comes here with magic is killed. It's bad enough that other cities run those with magic out. Those people will be pushed to the breaking point, and a lot more will die. I turned a blind eye to all of it for too long. I told myself there was nothing I could do. That it didn't concern me. I'm ashamed that I haven't done more, but I can now."

"There are ways you can help without putting yourself in danger."

Nia wanted to reach for him. She had always stood on her own. Now, all she wanted was to have Shaw's arms around her. It must be because he could actually protect her. "You and Merrill were sent to gather information without letting anyone know who you are so a war won't be started."

"Aye," Shaw said as his brow furrowed deeply.

"We're being watched. I've lived like this for long enough that I have ways of hiding myself for short periods."

Merrill sat up and said, "That will bring attention to you."

"I already have that attention." She glanced at Merrill before returning her focus to Shaw. "Fate brought us together. I've spent most of my life thinking of only myself. I've had my eyes opened. I see the big picture. You do, too, or you wouldn't be here. You know I'm right."

"It was Fate." Shaw took her hand and rubbed his thumb over her knuckles. "We're going to come up with a way that doesna put you in danger. I'll no' discuss this further."

It was pointless to argue. Nia knew Stonemore better than Shaw or Merrill. She alone knew what dangers awaited, especially at the citadel. And she accepted each and every one, because she saw her purpose for the first time in her life. She had sat by and done nothing for too long. It was her time to make a difference.

Merrill cleared his throat and rubbed his hands on his thighs. "Well. That was certainly eye-opening."

Shaw shot him a dark look.

Nia wondered if they were conversing mentally. What she wouldn't do to hear what was being said.

Finally, Merrill held up his hands as if in surrender. "Fine," he snapped to Shaw. "You're being cranky."

"I'm no'," Shaw replied gruffly.

Merrill turned his blue eyes to her. "What's your plan?"

"We go to my villa," she said as she looked to Shaw. "It'll be easier access for me there while I impart everything I know about the city, the priests, and the soldiers."

Shaw's face hardened. "What are you planning?"

"Depends on what you need."

"Everything," Merrill said.

Nia looked between the two men. "You mean the Divine."

"Aye," Merrill said.

A muscle jumped in Shaw's jaw. "She's never met him. We can no' expect her to walk in and talk to him."

"The Divine doesn't see anyone," she answered. "Even if I wanted to, it wouldn't happen."

"That's no' true." Merrill smiled as he got to his feet.

Shaw's face relaxed as he nodded. "That's right. He wants one of us brought to him."

That was the one thing she wouldn't do. Nia didn't know what the Divine had planned, but whatever it was, it couldn't be good. Otherwise, the Divine would've invited the Kings to the citadel instead of sending her to seduce one of them.

"You can no' go to the citadel anytime soon," Merrill cautioned. "It has to look as if the two of you have fallen in love."

Shaw shrugged as he swung his gaze to Nia and grinned. "It

isna a hardship being together. We'll spend time at Nia's estate. We'll make sure those watching see what is needed."

"I'll remain in the lower levels, watching things on this end." Merrill nodded slowly. "It's a sound plan."

Nia smiled, even though her blood had turned to ice. The Kings knew magic. They knew how to fight Fae and other magical beings. But they knew nothing of the treachery within the Divine's court. She did. The humans ruling the cities on Zora were beyond cruel. They needed to be stopped from attacking and killing those with magic. That's where the Kings came in.

She saw her path now. She knew what she had to do, and she would do it willingly.

CHAPTER TWENTY-FOUR

Brandr stood at the border, looking out over the canyon to the forest and then beyond to Stonemore. He couldn't shake the irritation that had plagued him these last weeks. Ever since the unknown foe had attacked him, he'd been agitated and restless. The only problem that he and his sister, Eurwen, had had on Zora previously were the humans.

What had changed?

Because something evidently had. He wanted to blame it on Varek being brought to Zora. Had Jeyra not been so intent on revenge, she wouldn't have sought out the crone. Then again, if she hadn't been able to do the magic to pull Varek from Earth to their realm, then the peace of Zora would've continued.

"I'm surprised to find you here."

Brandr forced himself to remain relaxed as Cullen walked up. "I didna come to chat."

"A wee bit testy today, aye?"

Brandr had been biting everyone's head off lately. It was why he'd been out flying on his own. He had intentionally landed far from the canyon and the underground ruins of Iron Hall.

Cullen blew out a breath. "I know what you're feeling."

"I doubt it," Brandr snapped.

"You and Eurwen watched everything we did on Earth. You know the foes we battled. You know how they attacked. Doona be a wanker and act as if you're the only one who feels anything."

Fuck. Brandr hated when any of the Kings was right. About anything. "Point taken."

"Why are you here?"

Could Cullen not leave anything alone? "I doona know."

"That's shite. You doona want to tell me? Fine. But doona lie to yourself."

Brandr turned his head to look into Cullen's light brown eyes. "I'm no'."

"Clearly," he replied sarcastically.

Brandr looked back toward Stonemore. "Eurwen and I focused all our attention on the dragons. We wanted a safe place for them. They had lost one home. We were going to make sure they didna lose another. We couldna stop the humans from arriving here. Nor the children. So, we set up the boundaries. We gave the dragons room to breathe, to roam, to be themselves. We could tell you everything happening on our side of the border. How did we miss what was happening on the other side?"

"Because you didna care." Cullen shrugged. "I doona blame you. None of us do. I would've done the same. You can no' carry the sins of others on your shoulders."

Brandr frowned as he faced Cullen. "Innocents died."

"Unfortunately, that happens everywhere. Innocent dragons die every day. Do you carry that?"

"No."

"Then doona carry others." Cullen's jaw tightened as he crossed his arms over his chest. "Humans doona have a monopoly on being cruel. Every being in the universe shares that. The mortals just have a way of doling it out in particularly vicious ways."

Brandr looked down into the canyon. He spotted a few of the children playing right outside the hidden door to the city. "Had you no' helped Tamlyn, we wouldna know what was happening at Stonemore. Those kids would be dead."

"But they're verra much alive."

"I didna want you helping Tamlyn."

Cullen shrugged. "If you think Con never made a bad decision, you're mistaken. We all have. There's no shame in it. You learn from it."

It was good advice. Brandr hadn't wanted to like any of the Kings, but damn if a few hadn't begun to grow on him. "Have Merrill and Shaw still no' seen our new adversary?"

"They've no'. I'm no' sure whether to be happy about it or worried. Whatever it is moves quickly, and its near-invisibility caught me unawares."

Brandr nodded. "It's difficult to explain to others what to look for. I only saw it for a second out of the corner of my eye. I didna feel it's approach or sense anything."

"That puts us on the defensive. I doona like that."

"Me, either."

Cullen dropped his arms. "It could come at us at any time."

"At least it hasna killed any more dragons."

"Did it cross onto your land?"

Brandr shook his head. "I can no' be certain. If it did, neither I nor Eurwen were aware of it."

"It might just have sent its magic."

"True." Brandr watched him. "You really think it's another Dragon King we doona know about?"

Cullen sighed as he shook his head. "What else could it be?"

"We have beings here that I was unaware of before. A Banshee." Brandr blew out a frustrated breath. "What else is there? If Eurwen and I had spent more time with the mortals, we would've learned everything."

"We're learning now."

It was a step. Brandr should feel good about that, but something still niggled. He couldn't put his finger on it. He remembered the first time he and Eurwen had found humans on Zora. They'd been stunned and aghast. They had taken the humans to another realm, but the next day, the mortals were back. No matter how many times he and his sister took them away, they always returned.

Eurwen had been sure the mortals were using magic. So, the two of them had hidden and watched the small group for weeks. If any of them had magic, they kept it to themselves. With nothing else to do, he and Eurwen let the humans know where the boundaries were, and what would happen if they crossed onto dragon land.

They took steps not to repeat the mistakes the Kings on Earth had done with the mortals. He and Eurwen had been so confident they had found the answer. Instead, they had created other problems. They might have been able to foresee some, but they would've had no way of knowing about others.

"It isna good to stay in your head too much," Cullen said, breaking into Brandr's thoughts.

He ran a hand over his jaw. He was tired, and the fight was only getting started. Eurwen was mated to Vaughn now. They were happy. He wanted them to remain that way. A war would jeopardize that—it would threaten everything.

"You're more like your father than you care to admit," Cullen said with a snort.

Brandr shot him an apologetic look. "I have to sort this out."

"Like I said, just like Con. Take a lesson from him. Con knew he had to make decisions as King of Dragon Kings, but he always wanted our input. The more heads you have working a problem, the easier it is to solve it."

They had been rehashing the problem for weeks—to no avail. Something drastic had to be done—and Brandr knew what that was.

The sound of children's laughter reached him. Brandr observed the kids for a moment. Tamlyn and the Alchemist, Sian, were watching over them. At the top of the canyon, the black-spotted fur of a lounging wildcat could be seen.

"That's Nari," Cullen said.

Brandr smiled. "The same cat who went after the invisible foe who attacked you?"

"The verra one. She keeps coming back. She walks with me in the evenings."

"Looks like you have a new friend then."

Cullen ran a hand over his blond beard. "I know your parents well. You have Con's sense of justice, and Rhi's headstrong nature. Your mother is an amazing woman, but she's prone to making hasty decisions. I hope you're no' planning something stupid."

"If you were in my shoes, what would you do?"

"Something stupid," Cullen replied with a grin. "Doona be me."

Brandr looked across the border. "I'm never stupid."

"Good. I doona want your parents and your sister turning their fury on me."

Brandr nodded before turning and leaping into the air. He shifted instantly and flapped his wings to take him higher. He flew far from Cullen's eyes before landing and returning to human form. Brandr made sure the clothes he produced with his magic were plain. Then he crossed the border onto the human side.

Everything going on with Zora was happening on this side. The dragons were safe. Eurwen, his parents, and the other Kings would make sure that didn't change. This was where he needed to be. Whatever hunted dragons, whatever had gone after him and Eurwen was out here.

And he was going to find it.

CHAPTER TWENTY-FIVE

Shaw wasn't fooled by Nia ceasing her arguments. There had been too much determination in her words and voice. It didn't matter what she decided. He wouldn't allow her to sacrifice herself. There was always another way.

And he was going to prove that.

After Merrill had departed, Shaw gathered his few items, and the two of them set out to Nia's. This time, a horse and cart were waiting for them. Shaw eyed the conveyance suspiciously. It looked like only one person would fit inside.

"It'll hold us," Nia said with a smile in her voice.

Shaw wasn't so sure, but he helped her inside before squeezing himself into the tight confines. The cart creaked ominously with his added weight, and Shaw thought it might break right then. Curtains hung to prevent others from seeing inside, but that was their only privacy.

"I like Merrill," Nia said.

Shaw glanced at his hands as he chuckled. "Everyone likes Merrill. He has a way about him that puts people at ease."

"And you don't?"

He quirked a brow and gave her a flat look. "Merrill has always had a gift for knowing what to say to lift others up. I'm no' a talker."

"You talk to me."

That he did. And he still wasn't sure why. Shaw shrugged since he had no answer.

Nia grinned and shifted so that her knee brushed his. "You have your own qualities."

"Oh?" He shouldn't want to know, but damn if he didn't.

"When you look at someone, you're focused solely on them. I know when you're looking at me, that you hear what I say. Then there's how you hold my hand. It isn't done in a possessive manner. Instead, you hold me gently and protectively. Everything about you speaks of a guardian. I know why the magic of your realm chose you as a Dragon King."

He was taken aback by her words. "You think of me like that?"

"Oh, yes. I like your qualities. Quite a lot."

His hands itched to pull her to him. The only reason he didn't was that he wasn't sure the cart could take it.

"Does my carriage make you uneasy?"

He didn't comment on how her lips twitched when she spoke. "This isna a carriage. This is a buggy, at best."

"I assure you that it'll take our weight."

Shaw shifted, and the vehicle moaned again. "Really?"

Her laughter drifted around him as they came to a halt. Shaw wasted no time in getting out. He helped Nia out and slung his pack over his shoulder as they faced her estate.

"Are you ready?" she asked.

He turned his head to her. "I was about to ask you that."

"The knowledge you've shared has changed everything. I'm just one person. Wait until everyone knows."

"Things will no' go as you expect. Especially those who are fanatics. They willna appreciate their faith being called into question."

She squared her shoulders. "That's the only way change comes about."

Shaw wished that everyone thought as she did. He squeezed her hand.

"I'm prepared for this," she said. "I know you don't think so, but I am."

He smiled, unwilling and unable to tell her that nothing could prepare someone for what was coming. Nia was strong. She would survive in the end. "Doona trust anyone."

"I never have," she said with a wink.

They walked beneath the rose entrance and down the path to the villa. Sadie was there to greet them when they walked through the door.

"Ma'am," the servant said with a smile. Then her gaze slid to him. "Sir."

Nia greeted Sadie with a smile. "Shaw is our guest now. Please make sure there is enough food for him at every meal."

"Of course," Sadie said before bowing her head and walking away.

Nia tugged Shaw after her toward the steps. He didn't see any other servants as they went up to her chambers. She sighed once inside and rushed to the windows to open them. He walked slower into the room and glanced around. He didn't look for anything in particular, just followed his instinct. He set his bag near the bed and inhaled the scent of roses that drifted through the windows.

"We're very fortunate to have such temperate weather during the summer," she said as she turned to him.

"How is autumn?"

She shrugged indifferently. "Lots of bright, sunny days with the temperature dipping. We have our first snowfall then. Winters can be harsh with the wind and snow."

"Do you get a lot of snow?"

"The upper levels get much more than the lower."

"What about ice?"

Her brow furrowed slightly. "Occasionally. We get more wind than anything. Many times, it pushes the clouds away to keep the snow from falling. Unfortunately, it doesn't stop the frigid temperatures."

He grinned at her response. "You don't like the cold?"

"I'd rather have this weather."

Shaw had to agree. It was warm without being hot.

She looked out the window. "This is my favorite season. Spring is nice because everything is budding and green again, but nothing is quite like the summer." When she looked at him, he met her gaze. She walked to him and asked in a low voice, "What about the weather at Dreagan?"

"Dreagan is in the Highlands of Scotland. Many regions get rain every day. Our weather is unpredictable."

"The winters?"

"Harsh, wet, and cold," he told her frankly.

Her face scrunched up. "That doesn't sound appealing."

"It's beautiful when everything is covered in white. The evergreens are coated so you only see a little of the green. The crunch of the snow while walking through the Dragonwood is calming. For me, I love to watch the snow fall. I love the flurries as they dance upon the air just as much as I love the blizzards where the snow is so thick you can no' see much before you."

"Despite my aversion to cold, you make me want to see it."

"Then I'll take you."

She gave him a shocked look. "You would really take me to your world?"

"Why no'?" Why not, indeed? Now that he'd said it, he wanted to take her right now. Merrill or someone else could continue the mission.

That thought drew him up short. He'd never put anyone before an assignment. It wasn't pity that had him offering, but he wasn't sure what had caused him to even propose such an outing.

Nia's shoulders lifted as she drew in a breath. "Maybe when things are finished here."

"It's a verra different world."

"You miss it?"

"I miss Dreagan. And Scotland."

She kicked off her sandals and crawled onto the bed to lie on her side. She propped her head on her hand and rested her other arm along her waist and hip. "I wouldn't miss a single thing about this place." She patted the bed beside her.

Shaw eyed the seductive position she had struck. His cock twitched as desire began to grow. He walked to the bed and sank onto it, shifting so he rested against the headboard. He held out his arm and waited until she was nestled in the crook of his arm, her head on his shoulder, before he lowered his arm. "Doona think badly of the entire realm because of one city."

"It isn't just one city, though, is it?"

"We're still figuring that out."

She made a sound. "You know it isn't. There's no reason to try and soften my views of Stonemore and Zora. My eyes are wide open now. I see everything clearly."

"Nothing is ever black or white," he cautioned. "Few are truly good or evil. Everything is various shades of gray. I've known good people who do bad things. I've watched an evil person do something good."

"Stonemore is soaked in the blood of children. Those in power have had the chance to change things."

"True, but you doona know their reasoning."

"Fear," she replied instantly. "You even said it."

Shaw squeezed his eyes closed for a heartbeat. "All I'm saying is you shouldna see people or things as either good or bad."

"It's difficult not to," she admitted in a soft voice.

"You thought I was firmly in the evil column until you met me."

There was a slight pause before she said, "True."

"Remember that there are a hundred different sides to every story."

"And Merrill said you never talk."

That made Shaw chuckle. He ran his hand up and down her back. "He isna jesting. I prefer no' to speak. There's just something about you that loosens my lips."

"I'm glad, since you seem to have some kind of spell over me."

He frowned. That was the second time she'd said something like that. Earlier, she had asked him to stop using his magic on her. "What do you mean?"

"Nothing."

"Nay, lass. It's something. I've never used magic on you. I swear."

She released a sigh and hesitated a long minute. "It seemed the only explanation."

"For what?" he pressed.

"How you make me feel."

Shaw stared at the far wall. He wished he were looking into her eyes. When he tried to move so he could do just that, she refused to budge. He didn't push her, even though he wanted to. "What is that, exactly?"

"Free, happy, content. Protected."

His chest ached when he thought of everything she had endured: starvation, abandonment, slavery, assault. "I will always protect you, lass."

"You don't have to say that."

"I doona make vows I'm unwilling or unable to keep. I say it because I want to, and because I mean it."

She lifted her head so their eyes met. He'd seen a dozen different emotions in them in the time he'd known her, but the vulnerability reflected in her honey-colored eyes now made something shift inside him. He lowered his head to hers. The instant their lips fused, need swept through him. He rolled her onto her back. Nia sighed and grabbed his hips to grind herself against his hard cock.

With a thought, he removed their clothes. She gasped, pleased at how quickly they were naked. He would have to do that trick again. Her hand slid between them and around his rod. He paused in his kisses to look down at her as she guided him to her entrance. The pleasure that crossed her face when he pushed inside her only made him burn hotter for her.

CHAPTER TWENTY-SIX

All Nia wanted to do was make love to Shaw. Each time they were together, he brought her to different heights of pleasure. She lay spent in his arms for the last hour. Her thoughts were on anything but their task.

Partly because the quicker Shaw completed his mission, the sooner he'd be gone from her life. He'd given her a glimpse of how things could have been, had she been born to another family. Many said her mother had abandoned her, but Nia knew her mother would never do that.

Shaw idly traced designs on her back with the tips of his fingers. It was so enthralling that she never wanted him to stop. She didn't need to look at him to know that he was as lost in his thoughts as she was in hers. For a little while, she wanted to pretend that she wasn't a courtesan or a slave. For just a moment, she wanted to believe that she was free and with a man who would do anything for her.

Because that's how Shaw made her feel.

She knew better than to let herself get too wrapped up in such delusions. But, oh, what beautiful things they were.

Nia inwardly shook herself. If she remained in that daydream for an instant longer, she might chicken out and ask Shaw to take her away to freedom, uncaring what might happen to Stonemore and its people. That would be the easy way out. Besides, she had never failed in anything. She wasn't about to start now.

"You being here will solidify that I've caught you in my web," she said.

Shaw drew in a breath and kissed her forehead. "I was just thinking that. I've no doubt at least one spy is here and reporting to the citadel. We'll have to be careful when we talk."

Nia wanted to defend her servants. Then she remembered that they weren't her servants. They were also slaves—and owned by the Divine. Of course, they would spy. "We should be fine here."

"No' with the windows open. Voices carry farther than you think. If we're in your chamber, we should talk like this—in low voices."

She nodded. "And not discuss anything of importance outside of this room."

"Agreed."

"How long does it take people to fall in love?"

"I've no idea."

That shocked her enough that she rose on her elbow. She searched his eyes. "You told me you're millions of years old. Are you saying you've never been in love?"

"Aye."

"How is that even possible?" She had no inkling about love, but even she knew she could fall for him if she allowed herself.

Shaw shrugged and moved a strand of hair from her face. "After I became King, my focus was my clan. Then it shifted to living with the mortals, with war following on its heels. After that, we hid on Dreagan, and I went to my mountain and slept."

"You make it sound as if you were asleep for a long time."

"Aye. Dragons can do that. Dreagan is a big place, and each King has his own mountain. Each of us dealt with anger, heartache, and thoughts of revenge. Con did the right thing in gathering us on Dreagan. Otherwise, I've no doubt we would've wiped out the humans. Instead, we sought our mountains to help us deal with everything. I slept for thousands of years, deep inside my mountain. Most of us did. The only two who didna were Con and Ulrik. Ulrik because hatred for us and the mortals consumed him. And Con because he watched the humans and oversaw their advancements. He visited each of us every ten years to update us on things. Some of us would wake then, but most of us remained asleep."

Just when she thought she knew everything about the Dragon Kings, Shaw told her more. "When did you wake?"

"The first time was five thousand years after the war. I was awake for about four months before I returned to my mountain. It took another millennium before I woke again. That time, I was awake for about forty years when I'd finally had enough. I kept doing that until Con woke all of us this last time a handful of years ago."

Surely, no one in all the universe was as fascinating as Shaw. It was more than the sound of his voice or his protective nature.

It was every molecule of his being. "Will you return to your mountain again?"

"Now that we found the dragons, I doona know. Brandr isna thrilled we're here. Eurwen doesna mind since she married one of us."

Nia's brows shot up. "So, is she a Dragon Queen?"

"Aye."

"Were there none on your realm?"

"There wasna, but only because males are much larger than females. That already puts us at an advantage. The magic chooses the strongest dragon in both might and magic."

Interesting. "Can I assume that Eurwen has both?"

"The twins are different from us. This realm has magic because magic created it, but it isna like Earth. Our magic is a living, breathing entity. There isna anything like that here. The dragon clans no longer had Kings to lead them. There was no magic to pick a leader, so, initially, there was chaos. Until Brandr and Eurwen came. They are half-dragon, half-Fae, and no' just any Fae. Rhi is a royal Light Fae. She could have the Light throne if she wanted it, but she doesna. Combine someone with her magic with Constantine, and their children are extremely powerful."

Nia's arm grew tired. She returned to her position lying against Shaw. "Can they shift like you?"

"They can. They also got a big perk of Fae magic— teleportation. They can no' travel as far as a full-blooded Fae can, but they can still teleport, and that isna something the Kings can do without the aid of Fae magic," he told her.

"You said you're King of Sapphires. What color is that?"

He tapped the sleeve of her dark blue shirt. "Similar to this. It's a deep blue, no' quite as dark as your shirt."

"What do you look like? How big are you?"

"Each color dragon looks different. It's more than just the scales. Some have horns, some spikes, some tendrils. Even our tails are different. I could describe myself, but I doona think I'd do it justice. You saw Cullen fly over the city, right?"

She shook her head. "I heard him and saw his shadow, but it was night. I couldn't even make out his color. You'll just have to show me."

"I wouldna want to scare you. Besides, I couldna do it without drawing attention to myself."

"Does that mean you wouldn't fit in here?"

He chuckled. "Och, no."

Nia looked at the height of her ceiling. She couldn't fathom how big Shaw would be in his dragon form, but she really wanted to see him. "What color is Con?"

"Gold. The Golds and Silvers, like Ulrik, are the largest of our species."

"The smallest were the Pinks."

"That's right," he said, surprise in his voice. "You remembered."

She glanced up at him. "Of course."

"We thought the Pinks dead since they had been hunted on Earth, but some of the eggs were brought to Zora. There are Pinks again. It makes me smile every time I see one of them flying."

Nia tried to picture dragons flying, putting colors to different-sized ones, but she couldn't envision it. She had little

knowledge of dragon shapes, sizes, or hues. It just wasn't
something she had seen in Stonemore—until recently.

How would it be to see the dragons, to hear their roars all
around her? Since she knew that Shaw would protect her, she
wasn't as afraid as she had been when Cullen had flown over the
city. Her thoughts took her in another direction.

"If Eurwen and Brandr are rulers here, what color are they?"

"A mix. It's no' something that was done before. Everyone
mated within their clans. With the twins being half-Fae, they each
took part of Con's gold color. Eurwen is peach with gold wings.
Brandr is gold, but his underside fades to beige. They are no' the
only multi-colored dragons now, either. The clans are gone. The
dragons now mingle where and with whoever they want."

That made Nia's head hurt, trying to envision the mixing and
matching of different colors. She would just have to wait and see
it for herself. "Does that upset you or the other Kings?"

"It doesna me. And I've no' heard anyone else say anything
about it."

She tapped her finger on his stomach. "I'm still confused
about how Eurwen is a Queen if there were none before."

"It's because of her parents and the power they gave her. She
isna the only Queen. There's also Melisse, who was the very first
part-dragon, part-Fae."

"So, there *can* be Queens?"

He laughed, the sound bouncing off the walls. "Aye, lass."

Her smile died as she thought about what Shaw would tell
everyone about her. She had never given any thought to how
others saw her, but now, it mattered. She didn't like the anxiety
that caused, or the fear that came along with it.

"You'll get to meet everyone and see everything," Shaw said.

She blinked against the tears that suddenly pricked her eyes. "I hope so."

"I can take you away right now. Just say the word."

Her heart melted even more. "Not yet. We've work to do. Speaking of which, that brings me back to my original question. How long before I tell the Divine that you've fallen in love with me?"

Shaw was quiet for a long time. She was beginning to think he wouldn't answer when his voice reached her. "With as much time as we'll spend together, I'd say about a week. If we do it sooner, he might question things. We'll only have one shot at this."

"We'll have to make sure we appear in love when we're seen together."

"Aye. Thankfully, that willna be hard with you."

She heard the smile in his voice but couldn't quite muster her own. Mostly because she'd scared herself with her daydream. She would be living with Shaw, acting as if she were in love. What frightened her the most was that she might find herself actually falling for him.

"I promise to make it enjoyable," he murmured as he rolled her onto her back and nuzzled her neck in the spot that always drove her wild.

She wrapped her arms around his neck and closed her eyes. The feel of his lips on her skin, his hard body against hers, was seductive. She had set out to charm him, but he was the one who had seduced her. What would she do when he was gone? How would she ever be able to take anyone else to her bed? She wouldn't. She was certain of that.

Falling? Are you sure you don't already love him?

The thing was, Nia didn't know. Shaw was like a raging fire, and she a bug, unable to turn away from the beguiling, enticing flame—or the tantalizing promise of untold pleasure.

"I'll fill your hours with this," Shaw said as he kissed down her neck and wrapped his lips around her nipple.

Nia arched her back as he pulled. She sank her nails into his back, her body already clenching and ready. It knew what awaited. He'd given her a taste of pleasure, and she was starved for it now. Greedy and ravenous, she couldn't get enough of him.

He rose and looked at her with eyes darkened by desire. "I'm going to make you scream."

A thrill went through her. She reached to bring his head back down for another kiss, but he flipped her onto her stomach and lifted her hips. He slid inside her from behind. A gasp fell from her lips. She looked over her shoulder at him. His jaw was clenched, his face tight as his hands gripped her hips and held her still as he began to move.

The sight of him made her entire body weak. Scream? She screamed every time he made her orgasm.

CHAPTER TWENTY-SEVEN

The sun had already set when Shaw descended the stairs to look for Nia. He looked out back first. His gaze immediately lifted. He could see only small slivers of the night sky through the thick vines of the climbing roses. Their scent hung heavy in the air while torches placed strategically around the perimeter offered light.

Shaw appreciated beauty like anyone, but he had to admit that he had never looked too hard at flowers before. He enjoyed them as anyone would, but now he viewed them differently. He would like to say it was because they were a different variety than he knew, or that it was because they grew on the mountain. But the real reason was because of how Nia's face lit up whenever she saw them.

He could've sank into one of the chairs and remained outside, utterly content. There was a part of himself that demanded he do just that, but it was the other part of them, the more insistent one that urged him to find Nia. This was a dangerous game they played. The estate didn't belong to Nia, nor were the servants hers. Everything they said and did was under scrutiny.

Shaw was used to this. Nia, too, to an extent. But that didn't calm his worry or ease any of his concerns. In fact, it heightened both. One wrong move could cost Nia her life. That was what had him seeking her out. He needed to know she was all right.

He had to continue to remind himself that he was on another realm and that none of the Kings knew if they were the most powerful beings on the planet. The Divine might hate anyone with magic, but that didn't necessarily mean he didn't have magic himself. The council leader in Orgate had said the same thing, and he had been able to do magic. The Kings were wading into dark, turbulent waters with vicious currents that kept trying to knock them off their feet.

And this didn't even include the new foe they sought.

Shaw crossed his arms over his chest and shook his head as he thought of the adversary—an invisible one, at that. He fought the urge not to call out to Erith and demand an explanation from her. But Death and her Reapers had their own issues at the moment. Still, Shaw suspected there would come a time where Erith would have to come to Zora.

Would she, though, was the question.

She had created the realm for the dragons, as a favor to the Kings. In his mind, she was responsible for the realm. No doubt others would argue that just because Erith created the realm didn't mean she had any say in what went on with its occupants.

The hairs on the back of Shaw's neck rose in warning. His

advanced hearing picked up the sound of breathing. He recognized it as Sadie's. Shaw dropped his arms to his sides and waited for the servant to come to him. He didn't have to wait long.

"Sir?" she said as she came from the shadows.

He looked her way and quirked a brow. "Aye?"

"Is there anything I can get you?"

"I'm enjoying the night."

Her brown gaze shifted upward as a smile pulled at her lips. "This is my favorite place on the entire estate."

"I can see why. Have you always worked here?"

She glanced at him nervously. "I have. I was brought when I was very small."

"You've done well for yourself then, working your way up."

"I suppose you could say that."

"Do you get out?"

She wrinkled her nose. "I've gone with ma'am before, but I prefer to stay here."

"It is beautiful." He spotted the moon through the rose leaves.

"She's happy. You make her happy."

Shaw swung his gaze to her. "I'm glad."

"There's a sparkle in her eyes I've never seen before." Sadie smiled and lowered her eyes. "Thank you for that. She deserves happiness."

"Everyone deserves that."

Sadie flashed him a soft smile and turned on her heel to leave.

Shaw watched her depart. Her words surprised him. He returned through the open doors and made his way to the bathing room. He heard the splash of water and smiled as he slowly opened the door to peek inside.

Nia reclined in a smaller tub with her head back and her long length of hair draped over the side as a servant rinsed it. He silently made his way inside. As he drew close, the servant looked up. Shaw put his finger to his lips to silence her. She smiled and nodded. He then motioned with his hand for her to leave. After taking her place on the small stool, Shaw took over rinsing the soap from Nia's hair.

She sighed. He glanced in the tub to see the water coming to her nipples. She had one leg bent and her arms along the edges of the bath. He had never washed anyone's hair but his, and yet he was eager to sink his hands into the brunette strands.

He lifted the small cup from the bucket beside him and poured it over her hair. With his other hand, he followed the water down into a second bucket where her hair hung. Shaw repeated the process until the last of the suds was gone. Then he set aside the cup and wrung out her hair.

"That felt good. Thank you," she murmured.

He grinned but said nothing.

Nia sat up and gathered her hair in her hands. She wrung it out even more as she got to her feet. Shaw watched how the water sluiced from her body. He was tempted to carry her to the large tub they had spent the first day in together. She turned then and spotted him.

Her eyes widened, but a smile pulled at her lips. "How long have you been here?"

"Long enough to rinse your hair."

"You should've told me."

Shaw handed her the towel. "You looked to be enjoying yourself. I didna want to disturb that."

"It was nice."

She started to step out of the tub. He jumped to his feet and took her hand to ensure she didn't slip. Then he walked to the open windows so she could finish drying herself.

"It's a beautiful night," she said.

He nodded. "That, it is."

"Would you like to go out?"

Shaw considered it for a moment before turning to her. "If you want."

"I had something else in mind."

"Is that so?" he asked with a grin.

She laughed and set aside the towel to put on a robe. "All I need you to do is go to the back and get comfortable."

He held her gaze and nodded. "I can do that."

She winked and walked out of the room.

Shaw made his way to the back of the estate. When he'd come to Zora, he'd expected to be in battle. In a way, he was. But this wasn't the type of fighting he had anticipated. It wasn't that he couldn't handle the present battle lining up before him. He just preferred the other kind. There, you knew your enemies. On this battlefield littered with landmines, everyone was an enemy.

Maybe he *did* know who his enemies were then.

"*Merrill?*" he called through their mental link.

"*I'm here.*"

"*Anything new?*"

"*I learned the rotation of the guards at the main gate. I also learned more about the priests and their soldiers.*"

"*Anything useful?*"

Merrill was silent for a moment. *"If we need to save another child, aye."*

"Stay vigilant."

"You, too."

"Always, brother." Shaw severed the link and turned when he heard approaching footsteps.

Nia appeared with her servants in tow. One spread out a large blanket on the ground while others set up food and drink. Shaw let his gaze move over the dark blue kaftan type of garment Nia wore. The soft, flowy material had large, loose sleeves while being gathered at the waist with a plunging neckline. The trim, cuffs, and hem were embroidered with silver climbing roses. Her wet hair had been pulled into a loose plait that fell over one shoulder. She smiled as she walked barefoot onto the blanket and slowly lowered to her knees before leaning to the side. She raised a brow and waited.

Shaw made his way to her. He paused beside the blanket and removed his boots before sitting beside her. "You look dazzling."

She said nothing as she poured mead into two cups and handed one to him. Then she leaned on her free hand and looked up. "The only time I feel a pang of regret about my roses is when I can't see the stars."

"You can still see them, just not as clearly as before." He set aside his cup and lay on his back. Shaw shifted several times until he found a spot through the roses. "Come lay with me. Let me show you."

She stretched out beside him and rested her head on his shoulder.

He used his other hand to point through the thick leaves and vines. "There. Do you see them?"

"I do," she replied softly.

Something changed inside Shaw as they lay in silence, looking up at the night sky. He wasn't sure what it was, but he felt it. Sensed it. His arm tightened around Nia, pulling her close. Out of all of them, she would need protection the most.

"Do you ever regret anything?" she asked.

He watched a rose leaf bend against the breeze. "I try no' to live with regrets."

"That isn't what I asked."

"Everyone looks back on things and finds something they wish they'd done differently. That's life. You learn from the mistake and move on."

Her hand on his chest flattened over his heart. "I regret not helping others. Especially the children."

Shaw rolled her onto her back and looked into her eyes. "You've been busy keeping yourself alive. No one can fault you for that."

"I fault myself. I could've tried to do something."

"It would've gotten you killed. You know that. It's why you didna do it."

She touched his face. "That's an excuse. You wouldn't have hesitated, no matter the cost."

"We're different people, lass. We come from different worlds. I've been bathed in blood and battle my entire life. There are only so many places for people like me. The world needs people who are brave and caring like you. You're the kind who softens the edges and helps everyone heal from war."

"That's not what my role feels like."

"Your *role* is whatever you make it."

Her hand fell away from his jaw. "I want to fight. I'm tired of thinking about only my survival. I might still be living, but I'm no freer than I was as a child. I just didn't see the cage then."

Shaw's heart clenched when he saw a tear fall from the corner of her eye and disappear into the hair at her temple. "If you want to fight, then fight. I'll be standing right beside you."

CHAPTER TWENTY-EIGHT

Nia searched Shaw's eyes for the lie, but she found none. "Most would run."

"I'm no' most."

He certainly wasn't. He was the one who made her reevaluate her life, to take a hard look at what she had been doing—and hadn't.

"I willna let anything harm you."

She wanted to believe him. She wanted to put all her trust in him. He made it seem so easy. Then she remembered how her father had deserted them, how her mother had left her. Even her brother and sister had gone.

"Whatever you're thinking, stop," Shaw demanded in a fierce tone.

Nia held his gaze, daring him to push her.

He shook his head. "Remember what I told you, lass. You're a survivor. There are no' nearly enough people like you. It's easy to give into the things we tell ourselves, the horrible, cruel things. They're no' true. Doona listen to them."

She wanted to shove him away. At the very least, tell him to shut up, but she could barely hold back the tears that suddenly formed.

"I used to tell myself things I would never speak to another, no' even my enemy. You tell yourself something long enough… you start to believe it. No one is as hard on us as we are on ourselves. It took me far longer than I want to admit, but I stopped telling myself those horrid things. You're stronger than I am. You can stop now."

She snorted and rolled her eyes. "I'm not stronger than you."

A muscle twitched near his eye. "I'm no' talking physical strength, and you know it." He tapped the side of her head. "I'm speaking of mental strength. Do you have any idea how tough you had to be to get where you are today? How many others have survived it? How many, Nia?" he asked sharply.

"Two," she answered.

"I can bet there are many courtesans. Am I right?"

"Yes."

"How many have their own estates?"

Damn her eyes for welling up again. "Just me."

"Just you." He shook his head and gently ran his fingers down her cheek. "Never think yourself weak, lass, because you are anything but. You're strong and fierce and have a determination others will never know. That is what's gotten you this far. It's what will keep you going, too. And before you think I'm merely saying this for show, this is the truth. It's what I feel and see."

Then he was on his feet and walking away. She sat up,

thinking that he would leave, but he stopped near one of the torches. His gaze was on the flames. She wondered what he was thinking.

He had made her face things she hadn't dared before. Had said things no one had ever said before, and she had reacted with fear and anger. Shaw might not hold to his promise to stand with her during the battle or to protect her, but that shouldn't determine her decision about what to do.

She was ashamed that she hadn't tried to do more, given more to the children that were starving. She had once been them. She knew that hollow feeling of hunger, the worry of wondering if you would have the strength to steal food. She knew the cold nights when there was only the body heat of her siblings for comfort. She knew the disdain and contempt that others showed her simply because she didn't have coin to buy food, as if it were her fault. She had been a child.

Nia got to her feet. This was supposed to have been a romantic night so the servants could see and report back to the citadel. It was all a ruse. Or it was supposed to have been one, but when her gaze had met Shaw's and she saw the desire in his eyes, it had dawned on her that she wanted this. All of it.

She wanted Shaw.

Not a ruse, not a lie. Him.

All of him.

Even if she somehow managed to get free of Stonemore and the Divine, she couldn't have the life she wanted with Shaw. He was a Dragon King. She was a mortal. He lived forever while her life would be gone in a blink. But that was for her to carry. It wasn't fair that she had taken it out on him.

Nia walked up behind him. She put a hand on his back and felt the tension running through him. "I'm sorry."

He sighed as he turned to her. "You doona have anything to be sorry for."

"I do, actually." She moved closer and lowered her voice to barely a whisper. "I make myself into another person for whoever is my target. I become someone else. I never show myself to anyone. But I can't seem to be anyone but myself around you."

"Good," he said with a smile.

"You—"

"I'm sorry to disturb you, ma'am," Sadie said from behind them.

Nia saw a frown mar Shaw's forehead before she turned around. The instant she looked at Sadie, she stiffened. She had someone with her. Anytime Nia was near him, she felt as if she needed a bath afterward. He was thin with a long, narrow face and dark, beady eyes. His thin, limp brown hair was parted to the side. As usual, he was decked out in the best material money could buy, but it did nothing to hide his skeletal frame. Nia forced herself to remain impassive, but his gaze wasn't on her.

"Forgive the intrusion," he said as he flashed a too-bright smile at Shaw. "I'm Amsden, the Divine's steward. If I had known that Nia had a visitor, I wouldn't have called."

"That's a load of shite," Shaw whispered. Then he nodded. "Shaw."

Nia had to fight to keep from laughing. She lifted her chin and bowed her head. "Good evening, Amsden. What can I do for you?"

"I realized I've not seen you for some time in court. I thought I would stop in and see how you were," he replied.

She wished she could usher Amsden out the door, but his visit was for a reason. The Divine must have sent him. That was good since it would prove that she was doing her job. And it would make the Divine believe that Shaw was falling in love with her.

"Perhaps I should leave," Shaw said.

Amsden blinked before chuckling. "Nonsense. Please, remain. I'll only stay a moment. I just wanted to catch up with Nia."

Shaw's firm hand on her back reminded Nia of their end goal. She smiled and motioned to the chairs. "Please."

Once seated, Amsden asked Shaw, "I take it you aren't from Stonemore?"

"I'm traveling," Shaw answered.

Amsden's brows rose. "I've never heard an accent like that. Where are you from?"

Shaw grinned. "It's verra far away. I've been wandering for some time."

"Alone?"

"Aye. And what is it you do as a steward, Amsden?"

Nia crossed one leg over the other. Shaw was good at this. Amsden was usually composed, but she saw the sweat on his forehead now and noticed how his hands shook slightly. So, he knew he sat across from a Dragon King. A picture of Amsden on the ground curled in a ball as Shaw stood over him in dragon form flashed in her mind. She had to cover her mouth to keep from laughing.

It earned her a glare from Amsden and a raised brow from Shaw. She ignored both.

"I do whatever the Divine asks," Amsden answered.

Shaw stretched out his legs and crossed his ankles. "Anything?"

"Anything," Amsden said with a nod.

"Tell me about the Divine. I've been asking Nia, but she's never seen him."

Nia's heart skipped a beat. She shot Shaw a dark look, but his gaze was locked on the steward.

"The Divine is private," Amsden said.

Shaw nodded as his face scrunched up. "I've never heard of a ruler keeping to themselves. Usually, they like to be front and center."

"The Divine is different."

"Why that name? Why no' some other title? Emperor? King?"

Amsden's eyes narrowed. "Because that is not what the Divine wanted."

"Forgive the questions. I'm just trying to sort things out," Shaw said with a smile.

Amsden relaxed somewhat. "How long are you staying in Stonemore?"

Shaw's head turned as he looked at her. "I had thought to just stay a few nights, but I find I'm quite captivated by Nia. She's been showing me the city. I'm beginning to understand what draws others to Stonemore."

Amsden laughed as he looked between her and Shaw. "Nia is quite the catch. Maybe you'll be the lucky one who captures her heart."

"I can only hope," Shaw replied.

Nia ducked her head because Shaw had never stopped looking at her. She knew all of this had been for show, but to hear Shaw say he wanted her heart had made her pulse race and her stomach flutter in excitement.

Careful, Nia. This is just a game. A dangerous one, but a game all the same. Don't get attached to him.

It was good advice.

Too bad she couldn't take it.

Amsden pushed to his feet. He bowed his head to Shaw. "I'm glad I got to meet you. I'll leave the two of you to get back to your night."

"I'll walk you out," Nia said.

Shaw touched her hand as she walked past him. She kept her back straight as she followed Amsden into the house and toward the front door.

When he reached it, he paused before opening it and then turned to her. "How do you do it?"

"Do what?" she asked.

"Be around him," he snarled as if the thought made him sick. "Be around magic."

She shrugged and placed a serene smile on her lips, the kind she used for her clients. "I do it because the Divine ordered me to. It was obvious you weren't comfortable around him. If you return, try to do a better job."

"Do not dare to tell me how to act."

She drew closer to Amsden and lowered her voice, letting her anger fill her. "I was asked to take him to my bed. You simply had to speak to him. I will tell you how to behave because I won't have you messing this up for the Divine."

At the mention of their ruler, Amsden took a step back. "The Divine doesn't need to know how I reacted."

"I won't need to tell anyone as long as you report back that things are going well here."

"They seem to be, so it won't be a lie."

"They are," she said tightly. "Just make sure the Divine knows that."

Amsden gave a curt nod and walked out. Nia closed the door softly behind him. When she turned around, Sadie was there.

"Is everything all right, ma'am?" the servant asked.

Nia could well understand her question. Amsden had only come to the estate once since it had been given to Nia. She didn't like the man, and she hoped never to see him again. "Yes. I also wanted to thank you and the others for treating Shaw as if he were any other person."

"No one else but me knows who he is," Sadie said. "I didn't want any of them acting strangely around him."

Nia put her hand on Sadie's shoulder and smiled before walking past the servant and returning to Shaw. As soon as he saw her, he opened his arms and met her halfway. Nia closed her eyes when he enveloped her.

"Are you okay?" he asked.

She was now. It felt good to lean on someone. She'd never had that before. But she shouldn't get too used to it.

Don't get attached.

CHAPTER TWENTY-NINE

Once Nia finally fell asleep, Shaw prowled her chamber. Amsden's visit had rattled her. She'd tried to blow it off, but Shaw had seen the concern in her eyes. He wasn't surprised the steward had come. In fact, Shaw had expected someone to pay them a visit. Nia wasn't naïve, so why had she been taken aback?

Was it Amsden? Or was it something more?

Shaw turned his gaze from the window to look at her. She slept deeply. He blew out a breath as he returned his gaze out the window to the city below. He hoped Merrill was watching himself. Something had changed during the night. Shaw couldn't put his finger on it, but it was there, hanging ominously in the air.

"Merrill?"

His friend responded immediately. *"Everything okay?"*

"I'm no' sure. We had a visit this evening. Amsden, steward to the Divine."

"I take it things didna go well?"

"He was nervous around me, but more than that, his arrival upset Nia."

Merrill grunted. "Is that because of the man or the visit?"

"That, I doona know. It could be either. Or both."

"The fact that someone came means they've noticed things are progressing."

Shaw crossed his arms over his chest and glanced at Nia. "Aye. Amsden is a wanker, there's no denying that."

"What's really bothering you?"

"Have you sensed anything?"

Merrill chuckled softly. "You mean other than the utter shite that's already here?"

"Something's changed. I feel it."

"Now that you mention it, I've noticed it more in the soldiers. They added a few more to each station. Regular folks have taken notice, too. It's making them nervous."

Shaw briefly closed his eyes. "Surely they wouldna be stupid enough to try and take us."

"I wouldna think so, but the Divine did want to speak to a Dragon King."

"Nia thinks he wants something more than a few words."

"Like what?" Merrill asked.

"I wish I knew."

"Are you worried?"

"If I say no, then I'm a fool. The Divine is an unknown enemy. Nothing ever good comes from underestimating an adversary. Yet, the Divine isna supposed to have magic."

Merrill sighed loudly. "But we know the bastard is working with someone who does."

"Precisely."

"I'd be happier about this entire situation if I were with you."

That made Shaw grin, but it was gone quickly. "If things do go sideways, get out."

"I'm no' leaving you behind."

"I want you to get out, find Cullen and the others and return. If the Divine wants a fight, then we'll give him one."

Merrill made a sound. "If you're looking for a way to piss off Brandr, that's it."

"It willna be us who starts this."

"I'm no' sure Brandr will see it that way."

"He was the one who wanted us in the city. We'll all have to deal with whatever comes of it. I do have to admit, though, I've got a bad feeling."

Merrill snorted loudly. "I've had one from the beginning. This probably isna the time to bring it up, but what are you going to do about Nia?"

"You're right. It isna the time. Watch your arse."

"I'm no' the one planning to meet the Divine."

"Good point," Shaw replied with a sigh before severing the link.

The sky had gone from black to dark blue to lavender. The clouds were streaked with orange as the sunrise put on a dazzling display. When he looked at the bed again, he saw that Nia's eyes were open and locked on him.

She sat up and shoved her brunette hair over her shoulder. "What is it?"

"I'm no' sure. Just a feeling."

"Should I be worried?"

He dropped his arms and walked to the side of the bed. Shaw looked down at her, wondering if he had missed his last chance to lay beside her. He tucked a strand of hair behind her ear before letting his fingers caress her jaw. "We should be prepared. And stay that way."

"It was Amsden's visit, wasn't it?"

"You tell me. You were upset from the moment you saw him."

Her gaze dropped to her hands on the bed. When she looked back at him, he saw resolve in her eyes. "I knew we were being watched. I also knew that someone would eventually come, or we would be summoned to the citadel."

"But?" he asked when she paused.

"There was something in the way he talked to you. And looked at me."

Shaw forced himself to remain calm. "You know these people. Tell me everything."

"That's just it. I don't know Amsden very well. He's seen around the citadel, and everyone knows his power. He's the Divine's right hand. I've had a few dealings with him, but they've been rare. My assignments come from the Divine and are delivered from the citadel."

"No' from Amsden?"

She shook her head.

"What kind of dealings did you have with him?" Shaw asked.

Nia shrugged and frowned. "I saw him a lot when I was still at the citadel, but he rarely paid us any heed."

"He didna...spend time with you or any of the other courtesans?"

"He visited a couple, but never me. He was never outright rude, but he wasn't exactly agreeable, either."

Shaw rolled his eyes. "I know the type. He likes the power

his position gives him, and he makes sure that others know just what will happen to them if he's displeased."

"Exactly. The first time he spoke to me was when they chose me to be a courtesan. He grabbed my chin and looked me over before shoving me away. He was shocked the first time I completed an assignment and returned with the secrets the Divine wanted."

Shaw's eyes narrowed. "Secrets?"

"I have all kinds. That's why the Divine sends me. I'm very good at learning things from my lovers."

"And you share all of it with him?"

She nodded. "Why do you think I have this estate? Amsden wasn't happy about it. He was furious, in fact. He told me my face would only be pretty for so long."

"He's jealous of the power you wield," Shaw said with a grin.

"He isn't interested in me."

"The hell he isna. He couldna stop looking at you. He wants you, Nia. Badly. It's why he's never gone to you. Because if he does, if he gives in, he knows you'll pull some secret from him. Because he knows he's that weak when it comes to you."

She blinked up at him. "I thought he hated me."

"He does. Because he wants you so badly. He hates anything he can't control or win with power, and he can do neither with you. Because you're no' his."

"No, I belong to the Divine."

"For the moment." Shaw didn't like hearing those words. And he sure as hell wasn't going to let them be real for too much longer.

Nia took his hand and smiled. "No matter what happens, I wouldn't trade these days I've had with you for anything."

"Let me take you from here today. You never have to see any of this again. You never have to belong to anyone again."

She smiled and squeezed his hand. "I've made my decision. Everyone who calls Stonemore home is part of the problem. That includes me. Someone has to do something. An outsider did. Tamlyn risked her life to save those children while the rest of us did nothing. It's my time to do my part. Don't take that from me."

Every fiber of his being wanted to throw her over his shoulder and fly her out of Stonemore to somewhere safe. He would do it in an instant if she asked, but that wasn't what she wanted of him. As he stared into her honey-colored eyes, he remembered a time when Ross had asked something similar of him.

Shaw had wanted to keep him safe, but he'd wanted to fight alongside everyone else in the clan against the Silvers. If Shaw had refused, Ross might have been safe, but it would've crushed his soul. His little brother had been through enough. So, Shaw had let him go. Ross had died that day, but he'd done so a warrior for his clan.

Nia had been forced into slavery after starving on the streets. Her willpower and mental strength had helped her rise to her current station, but she was still a slave. This was her way of breaking those chains. Once again, Shaw found himself in an impossible situation.

He could force Nia away, but she would hate him forever.

Or he could stand beside her with the possibility that he might not be able to save her.

The choice was harder than he wanted to acknowledge.

"I know what you want of me," she said with a smile. "I want it, too. It's all I've ever thought about. If I leave now, I'll be a coward. I'm not that."

He shook his head. "Nay, lass. No one could ever call you that."

"I've never been in battle, though. I don't know what to do."

"This willna be the kind of battle you think," he warned. "This will be another kind altogether. And this kind is infinitely more dangerous."

She briefly looked at their joined hands. "How?"

"This kind of warfare is the kind most think they're ready for, but they're no'. On the battlefield, you can see your enemy coming. You know who they are, and you can prepare. In this arena, everyone is a potential enemy. They'll close in and surround you without you even realizing it."

"I've never trusted anyone at the citadel."

He held her gaze. "Doona start now. It doesna matter how long you've known them. Their loyalties are to themselves and what will keep them alive."

"You make it sound as if the Divine will win."

"I state the facts. Your leader is smart. He dangles the one thing a person wants more than anything in front of them and tells them it can be theirs if they do what he wants."

She swallowed. "Like my freedom."

Shaw nodded slowly. "Like your freedom. The soldiers will guard him because that's their job. The servants are slaves and do it because, if they doona, and the Divine wins, he'll kill them."

"Then we don't go to the citadel."

He grinned. "That isna an option."

"That puts us on the Divine's territory."

"Lass, we're already on his territory. I can almost guarantee that if we tried to take a walk in the forest today, they would stop us."

She lifted her chin. "Then what do we do?"

"We prepare."

CHAPTER THIRTY

The churning in Nia's stomach was so bad, she couldn't look at food. All she could manage to keep down was her lemon ginger tea. Ever since her talk with Shaw, fear had quietly taken up residence in her stomach.

They spent the day in her chamber with the curtains drawn over the windows. The servants likely thought they were making love when they were, in fact, making plans. She had ink and paper, as well as anything else she could find in her room to draw and lay out the parts of the citadel that she knew. Shaw studied them relentlessly.

"They'll take us to a section you doona know," he said, drawing her from her thoughts.

She looked at him with a frown. "Why do you say that?"

"In case you turn on them and tell me what you know. And because we'll be in front of your ruler."

"You actually think we'll get to see the Divine?"

Shaw's fern green eyes lifted to her. "Aye. I suspect they'll keep you in another room to separate us."

As if things couldn't get any worse.

"I can teach you a few things in case anyone attacks you."

What had she been thinking? To say that she had to stay and fight. She knew nothing about battle, nothing about the warfare that Shaw and Merrill prepared for. She should've run when she had the chance.

"Nia."

She pressed her lips together. "Do you think I'm being irrational?"

"For wanting to fight for your city and its people? Never," he replied.

"I'm scared."

"I'd be concerned if you were no'."

She looked at the ceiling in irritation. "Do you have an answer for everything?"

"Nay," he said with a chuckle. "Normally, I doona speak."

Nia looked at him and gave him the best smile she could muster under the circumstances. "I'm glad you're here."

"Me, too, lass." He walked to her and took her hands in his. "I know I said doona trust anyone, but I need you to trust me. It's the only way this will work."

"I do trust you."

He gave her a lopsided grin. "Good. Now, when they separate us, they'll take you far from me."

"Why?"

"For a couple of reasons. They'll want to make sure you're still with the Divine, and they'll ask you questions and probably make you prove what you say. You'll have to give them something about me."

Nia shook her head. "That's the last thing I should do."

"It's a way to keep you safe. We have spent a lot of time together, and they're going to be told that you seem taken with me. They'll fear I've used magic on you, so expect all sorts of queries. That's why you're going to tell them that the Kings learned children with magic are being murdered. That's why we're here."

"I think it's a bad idea."

"It'll demonstrate to them that you've done your job."

She wanted to refuse, but she knew that Shaw was right. They would question her relentlessly. She nodded, though it turned her stomach to give the Divine anything about the Dragon Kings. "You said a couple of reasons."

"Taking you makes it difficult for me to find you if I do anything to the Divine. They'll threaten you to keep me in check."

"Only because they're going to believe you're in love with me."

He stared at her for a long, silent moment. "Aye."

"I'm one person, Shaw. Just one. And I'm no saint. The only way this city gets fixed and those with magic can live free is with the Dragon Kings' help."

His eyes turned hard. "Doona finish that thought."

"I've told you before, and I'll say it again—leave me. It doesn't matter what happens to me. What matters is you stopping the Divine and returning to your people."

He bent until he was even with her face. "I'm only going to

say this once more. I'm no' leaving you. I doona care if it starts a war."

No one had ever put her first in anything. It was a new, glorious feeling, but she didn't allow herself time to enjoy it. "I'm not worth that."

"You're worth that a thousand times over."

Her eyes burned with tears, and her throat clogged with emotion. What might her life had been like if she'd had someone believe in her so unreservedly all along?

Shaw lifted his hand, his thumb catching one of her tears. "It's a moot point because I willna allow this to start a war."

"You might not have a choice. You don't know what the Divine wants."

He blew out a breath as he straightened and walked back to the table to look over the drawings. "In my vast experience, those like the Divine want to use, coerce, or force those like me for one reason—power. We're the dominant ones on my realm. We're about to find out where we stand on this one."

"Can the Divine trap you with anything?"

Shaw turned his head to her and shrugged. "He's obviously using someone with magic. There could be others. I willna know until I stand before him."

"Alone," she said, her stomach clenching with dread.

"Alone."

"What about Merrill?"

Shaw placed his hands on the table and leaned on them. "He's here. He's being followed. Some are obvious, but others are no'. You doona need to worry about Merrill. He already has his plans."

"To get away?"

"To get out and bring reinforcements if needed. To get to me if necessary. I'm sharing everything I learn about the citadel with him."

She walked to a chair and curled a leg under her before sitting. "That makes me feel a little better."

"Cullen is nearby, and other Kings could be here within moments. You doona need to worry."

Nia studied his face as he looked over the plans once more. "You're worried."

His gaze lifted to hers. "I'm being prepared. We know next to nothing about the Divine. No one who has seen him will speak of him. No one can say anything about him because they only hear whispers and rumors. We have nothing to go on. That means I have to think of everything."

"As good as you are, you can't think of every possibility."

"I have to try. Too many lives are at stake."

Nia parted her lips to speak, but the tolling of the bells at the temple interrupted her.

Shaw straightened as he glanced toward a window. "What is that for?"

"It signals they've discovered a child with magic." The fury that stole through Shaw made her shiver. Not out of fear for herself, but for anyone stupid enough to get in his way. "You can't intervene."

"Why the bloody hell no'?" he bit out.

She gave him a flat look. "You know why. They're watching us. And Merrill. The city might not know that children were rescued, but the priests, soldiers, and the Divine do. They'll be on heightened alert."

"No' to mention, it could be a ploy to see if Merrill or I react."

"Exactly. We have to keep to the plan."

Shaw fisted his hands, a muscle in his jaw jumping. "I doona like it."

"Neither do I. But what choice do we have?"

He turned his back to the window. "There's one thing I've no' told you."

"What?"

"Every dragon is born with magic."

"You told me that."

He shook his head. "Aye, we have magic, but each of us is born with a special ability to go along with it. For Merrill, he can breathe a beam of searing light. Con can heal anyone of anything except death."

"What can you do?"

"I can create illusions."

"What does that mean?"

He twisted his lips. "It means that I can use my power to make others see something else entirely than what's real."

She smiled for the first time that day. "Why didn't you tell me sooner? Now I'm not worried about you going to see the Divine."

"I wouldna go that far, lass. There are all kinds of magic out there. I never go into battle and underestimate my opponent. Your leader wants me to come to him. That tells me he thinks he has an advantage. He might. He might no'. I willna know until I get there."

And just like that, the churning in her stomach returned. Nia didn't know if she would survive the anxiety coursing through her. "How long do you think we have?"

"No' long."

"I was told to bring you to the citadel when I was sure you had fallen in love with me. We get to set the day."

He smiled sadly. "We have a day. Two, tops. Then, they'll send for us."

"That isn't how things are supposed to happen."

"Something has changed. And I think it shifted everything."

Nia rubbed her temple as she began pacing. "Part of me wants to just get this over with. I can't handle the waiting."

"Then let's go."

She jerked to a stop and looked at him. "I was joking."

"I wasna. If we go, we get to set the tone. I've no doubt they've begun planning, but we'll put them on the defensive. I've been thinking it all day, but I wasna sure you were ready."

She wasn't. Not by a long shot, but what Shaw said made sense. If going now gave them a slight advantage, why not take it? "Okay."

"Really?" Shaw asked, his brows raised in question.

Nia nodded.

"Do you need to send a message to the citadel?"

Her mind raced as she shrugged. "Probably, but wouldn't that let them know what we have planned?"

"Yes," he said with a grin.

She had no idea what was going on in his head, but she didn't question it. Instead, she went to the door and called for Sadie. When the servant arrived, she gave her the message. Sadie hurried away to have it delivered to the citadel.

Nia closed the door and faced Shaw. "Now what?"

"We get ready while you continue practicing what I showed you earlier."

Did he really expect her to remember those self-defense moves, as he called them? Now? Nia could barely recall how to walk. This would test everything she had ever learned. She had never doubted herself before, but she had never had so much to lose, either.

At least, she wasn't going alone.

Her eyes moved to Shaw. The past few days had been a lovely dream, but she was waking from it and being thrown into a nightmare. Whether she came out of it alive or not was yet to be seen. She didn't like her chances, but she had one with Shaw.

Her legs were wobbly as she walked to her wardrobe. The last time she had been this terrified was when she'd stolen the bread for herself and her siblings. That day had ended in her slavery. One way or another, this one would end in her freedom.

Whether by death or not was up to Fate.

CHAPTER THIRTY-ONE

Merrill watched the dice game as he leaned against the wall with a mug of ale in hand, but his attention was on the soldiers quietly taking up positions along the street. He wasn't the only one to notice, either. The revelry in the bar was gone, leaving a hushed stillness tense with apprehension.

He had looked for Tomar all day yesterday and last night, but he couldn't find the soldier. Or the man didn't want to be found. Either told Merrill all he needed.

How excited he'd been to come to Zora, how thrilled to see the dragons once more. Merrill had been awestruck at the beauty. Not to mention watching the dragons. Zora was proof that it didn't matter what beings lived on a realm, evil always found a way. Of course, there was a cosmic balance of good and evil, light and dark, but that didn't mean he couldn't get angry about it.

Just when the Kings had found peace on Earth, a new adversary arrived on Zora. Was it a coincidence that it was also the time that Varek had been brought here? Doubtful. Merrill wanted answers. Hell, every King did, but he wasn't sure any of them would get them anytime soon.

His and Shaw's mission in Stonemore was supposed to be simple. Unfortunately, nothing was ever simple. At least, not when it came to the Dragon Kings.

Merrill finished his ale and softly set the empty tankard on a nearby table. The unease that had plagued him for over a day now intensified. Brandr and Eurwen didn't want a war, but Merrill suspected there was no getting around it. The mere fact that the Kings were on the human's land was enough to push many to want to attack.

The mortals were scared. Afraid of those with magic teaming up with the Kings. And the humans should be frightened. They should be cowering in a corner, begging to be spared. But they wouldn't. They never did. Because they didn't see what they did as wrong. The humans feared what they didn't understand. Their narrow-minded, intolerant ways were destroying the very foundations meant to propel a community. Add that to the power and greed innate in most humans, and it was a catastrophe waiting to happen.

Merrill didn't know or understand why the Dragon Kings had to be a part of it again.

He was tired of war, weary of fighting enemies that wanted to destroy them or something else. He longed for the days before the mortals had come to Earth, when it was just the clans and the Kings. There was no use in looking to the past, though. It was over and finished. The universe had moved on.

Everyone had.

No matter how many times Merrill told himself that, he

couldn't dislodge the despair that took hold. He was careful never to show the other Kings. No one had been there to see his rage when Varek had gone missing. By the time Merrill told the others, he had composed himself so no one knew a thing.

All he wanted to do was return to his mountain on Dreagan and sleep away the next several millennia, but that wasn't an option. The dragons needed protection. They had failed once. Merrill wouldn't do it again. He didn't care what it took this time. They were Kings on Earth with no dragons. What was the point of their existence?

The dragons no longer needed Kings on Zora. No one needed the Kings.

He looked out the pub window at the soldiers. Brandr and Eurwen didn't want a war. But it would be so easy to go out there and strike down every soldier and priest. Merrill closed his eyes as the urge rushed through him, intoxicating and loud. He could fly to the citadel and show the Divine just who the bastard was dealing with. If he wanted to speak to a Dragon King, then he could talk to Merrill.

In minutes, he could quell the tension growing in the city.

In seconds, he could end the Divine's reign.

There would be no war because he would ensure there was no one to rise against. The humans with magic could live peacefully with those who accepted them. No more children would be murdered simply because they had been born with magic. Then, the Kings could hunt down the invisible enemy intent on killing them.

"Merrill!"

He jolted at the sound of Shaw's voice in his head. *"Aye?"*

"I've been calling your name for some time. What's going on?" Shaw asked angrily.

Merrill opened his eyes and took a deep breath. The rage began to ebb as he looked around the pub at the human faces lined with worry. *"More soldiers."*

"That's why you didna answer me?"

"What's going on? Do you need my help?" The best way not to answer something was to ask another question.

Shaw went silent, letting Merrill know he knew what Merrill had done. *"We're going to the citadel in less than an hour."*

"They're expecting something from one or both of us if the soldiers are any indication. I suppose you heard the bells?"

"We did. What did your contact in the army tell you?"

"Nothing. I can no' find him."

"That's worrying."

Merrill grunted in agreement.

"Others with magic could be working with the Divine, so be careful," Shaw said.

"Always."

"Merrill, I need to know that you're okay."

For a heartbeat, he considered revealing his thoughts to Shaw but then decided against it. *"I'm good."*

"I've alerted Cullen. He's passing on everything to Con and the twins."

"Shaw, they'll try to kill Nia."

Shaw paused. *"They'll try."*

"Are you sure you should let her go?"

"She has to do this. But I'm no' leaving without her."

"Understood."

"If I can no' get to her—"

"*I'll find her,*" Merrill finished.

"*They're going to separate us. I had thought to find her, but I know the best thing is for her to leave the citadel and get to the lower levels and you.*"

"*I agree.*"

"*Take her to the canyon. I'll meet you there.*"

Merrill sighed. "*You'd better come quickly, because if you doona, Cullen and I will return.*"

"*I doona plan on hanging around.*"

Shaw severed the link. Merrill pushed away from the wall and walked to the window for a better view. The Divine had an iron grip on this city.

It was time to break it.

Cullen emerged from the hidden door in the canyon while Tamlyn and Sian moved the children—and themselves—to a secure area of the underground city. He climbed the canyon quickly and easily thanks to his strength and speed. When he reached the top, he stared at the forest separating him from Stonemore.

He heard a sound behind him and turned to find Nari. The wildcat made low, growling sounds as she paced back and forth, her gaze locked on the forest.

"You sense what's coming, too," he said to the cat.

Nari glanced his way with her green eyes before walking to stand near him.

"This isna really your fight. No' that I wouldna appreciate the help, but I'd rather you stay here and guard the city."

The wildcat sat and flicked her long, black tail.

Cullen chuckled. "I doona like sitting out of a battle, either. I'm hoping this doesna turn into one," he said as he looked at the city. "But it seems the Divine wants something, and he's tired of waiting."

When he glanced down, Nari was gone. Cullen looked for her and found the cat already down the canyon and trotting to lay near the door. She camouflaged herself well behind the roots so no one could see her. He gave her a nod when she settled and looked his way. Cullen didn't know how or why the wildcat had befriended him, but he liked it.

His smile faded as he focused on Stonemore. He was ready to shift and fly to the city to aid his friends. Since he would like a word with the Divine himself, Cullen really hoped Shaw or Merrill called for him.

Eurwen stood outside on the cliff at Cairnkeep and exchanged concerned looks with her mate, Vaughn, and her parents. "We didn't want a war."

"Where's Brandr?" Con asked, his black eyes searching for his son.

Vaughn shrugged. "He's been patrolling. He knows what's going on."

"He should be here," Con stated.

Rhi touched his arm, her face grim. "Our son knows what's at stake. You can communicate without him having to be here."

"What if the Divine tries to attack Shaw and Merrill?" Eurwen asked.

Vaughn crossed his arms over his chest. "That would be stupid."

"There's magic being used there," Rhi reminded them.

Con shook his head of blond hair as his nostrils flared, a sign that he was furious. "I'd feel better if Brandr were here."

"We have the Kings. And the four of us are here," Vaughn reminded them. "Let's no' forget that Cullen is close to Stonemore."

Rhi shoved a lock of black hair from her face. "Two Kings are in Stonemore. That should be enough to make any human tremble with fear. Though I find it ironic that the one King who hates to talk is the one going before this leader."

"It should've been Merrill. He's the calmer of the two. But what's done is done," Vaughn said.

Eurwen looked around at the dragons. She didn't want a war. Everything she and Brandr had done was to prevent that from happening. How had they come to this?

"It hasn't happened yet," Rhi said as she came to stand beside Eurwen. "There's no use worrying about it until it happens."

Eurwen looked from her mother to her mate. "It's an eventuality. I just have to accept that."

"It willna be a long war. That, I can promise," Vaughn replied.

Con nodded before storming away. "We need to ready everyone."

Eurwen called Brandr's name in her mind once more. *"Enough, brother. You answer me soon, or I'm coming to find you."*

Brandr paused in his trek. He looked over his shoulder and gazed in Eurwen's direction. He knew that tone in her voice. She would make good on her threat. They might need him if the Divine decided to attack the Dragon Kings. It was his duty to stand next to his sister. She had Vaughn now, though. Con, Rhi, and the other Kings would also rush to aid Merrill and Shaw if it came to it.

"Brandr!"

"I'm here," he answered.

"You're needed at Cairnkeep. When are you coming back?"

He hesitated a little too long.

Eurwen sighed loudly. *"Do I need to be worried?"*

"No."

"That means yes. Tell me what's going on. Please."

Brandr squeezed his eyes closed for a moment. He didn't want to tell her, but he'd known it was only a matter of time before she demanded a reply. *"I'm getting answers."*

"Bloody hell," she gasped. *"You're with the humans."*

"We both know we should've done this a long time ago. I'm correcting that mistake."

"You shouldn't be alone."

"That's exactly what I should be."

She was silent for a heartbeat. *"And if you run into our new enemy? Or what if you encounter others with magic who attack?"*

"Then I'll deal with it. I have to do this, sis."

"I know," she said softly. *"Stay in touch, or I will come looking for you."*

He couldn't help but smile. *"I will."*

Brandr severed the link. Eurwen was used to him

disappearing for long periods of time. She would halt anyone's questions about his absence. For now. The last thing she wanted was war, so Eurwen would make sure that no matter what happened at Stonemore, the killing stopped.

Brandr wondered if it would've been better if only Eurwen ruled. It wasn't the first time he'd had that thought. He slowly faced forward. He hadn't answered anyone who'd communicated with him, but at least he knew what was going on. There was no doubt in his mind that the dragons would triumph.

Unless the unknown adversary made an appearance.

His hand curled into a fist. The attack on him had been the first, and it wasn't a good experience. Con and the Kings had been in battle after battle since they'd first become Kings. Eurwen and Brandr had lived in relative peace since arriving on Zora. But all of that was about to change.

"Unless I stop it."

He lifted his chin and kept walking.

CHAPTER THIRTY-TWO

Shaw kept hold of Nia's hand as they rode in the cart to the citadel. She didn't speak. While outwardly composed, he had come to know her well enough to see that she was holding herself together by the force of her will alone.

"Remember everything I told you," he whispered over the clomping of the horse's hooves on the stone.

She met his gaze and nodded.

Her breathing was rapid, as was the pulse at the base of her throat. Her hand shook slightly in his. For the last couple of hours, as they'd readied for the meeting, he had gone over and over some self-defense moves with her. He prayed it would be enough. Hopefully, no one would think her enough of a threat to put her in a room with multiple guards. Once she got free, she was to leave the citadel immediately and find Merrill. They would all meet up at the canyon.

It was a sound plan. One that would only work if everything went as it should. But that never happened.

"Doona wait for me," he told her for the hundredth time.

She swallowed and blinked nervously. "What if I can't find Merrill?"

"Get out of the city and make your way through the forest. Cullen will be waiting." When she dropped her gaze, he squeezed her hand. "You can do this, lass. Look how far you've come. You can do anything."

Her lips trembled as she tried to smile. "So much can go wrong."

"No matter what happens to me, you're going to get away. You promised."

"It doesn't feel right to leave you at the citadel."

He winked at her. "I'm no' the one you should worry about."

This time, she did smile. It was fleeting, but it was there. "What if I never see you again?"

"You will."

She leaned to the side to look ahead. "There's something I need to tell you."

"You doona need to say anything."

Nia put her finger to his lips to silence. "For someone who doesn't talk, you've not shut up."

He chuckled but didn't say anything.

"Thank you."

Shaw frowned.

Her hands framed his face. "Thank you for showing me the truth, for opening my eyes to the reality I'd chosen not to see. But most of all, thank you for believing in me. No one ever has."

He took one of her hands and placed a kiss on her palm. Shaw searched her eyes. His chest tightened with an emotion he couldn't describe. The closer they came to the citadel, the more he didn't want her there. So many things could go wrong with Nia ending up dead. That simply couldn't happen.

Words clogged his brain, but they were all jumbled. He didn't know how to say them. It seemed the right moment, but he couldn't get them past his lips. His throat was frozen, unable to move. The cart came to a halt then. Shaw glanced out and saw soldiers approaching. His gaze swung back to Nia.

Just before the soldiers reached them, she leaned forward and placed her mouth on his. She searched his gaze and parted her lips to speak when the cart door opened. He gave her hand another squeeze before she stepped to the ground. Shaw followed and straightened to find himself standing at the impressive entrance to the citadel.

The structure itself was several stories high, extending nearly to the very top of the mountain, with each level smaller and smaller to the very top. The tall columns and large entrances gave it a spacious feel. Shaw spotted a few balconies and imagined there were quite a few more for the incredible view. Armed soldiers were stationed every ten feet, wearing different armor than those in the city—no doubt to set them apart so everyone knew when they were dealing with someone from the citadel.

Shaw held out his arm to Nia. She glanced at him as she tucked her hand into the crook of his elbow. He felt her tremble slightly, but she kept her head high and her back straight. He walked them up the steps to the large wooden door. Shaw glanced behind him to see the gate they had ridden through with a battlement and several soldiers standing at attention. He had missed that because he had been focused on Nia. It would be an obstacle she would have to get through, but he knew she could do it.

Her fingers tightened on his arm, drawing his attention. He looked ahead to see two soldiers stationed at the door, watching them. When they approached, one of the guards opened the door. As Shaw passed, he noted the dual swords each wore.

Inside the citadel was more splendor. The sandstone floors had an intricate design of geometric shapes and swirls that he found appealing. A tapestry easily forty feet wide and twenty feet tall hung on the wall ahead of them, depicting the mountain and Stonemore with roses climbing and weaving along the border.

"Ah, you've arrived," Amsden said as he approached from the left.

Shaw bowed his head. "I'm honored the Divine would allow my visit on such short notice."

"The Divine never refuses Nia." Amsden's smile was a little too cocky, too confident. "Follow me."

If they attacked, the steward was the first one Shaw would kill. "I have to admit, I'm shocked I'm here. I'm no one." Shaw wanted to push to see how much information—and lies— he could get.

Amsden glanced over his shoulder as he kept walking. "I informed the Divine of your travels. We're very curious about where you've visited."

"Do you no' send explorers out?"

The steward laughed. "We do, but not to the distance we believe you've traveled. We want to know as many details as you can give us."

So, they wanted information on dragon land, Earth, or both. Surely, the humans knew they couldn't win in a battle with the Kings. And if they couldn't win here, then they surely wouldn't get to Earth. Shaw couldn't imagine what their endgame was. Power, surely, but to what end?

Amsden walked them through long corridors with high ceilings and magnificent arches. The attention to detail on the floors, columns, and ceilings was beautiful. If this meeting was happening for any other reason, Shaw might have taken his time to look everything over. But all he wanted to do was get in front of the Divine and find out what he wanted.

The steward stopped before a set of doors. He turned to face them with his hands behind his back and a smirk on his face. "Nia, my dear, I'm afraid your presence has been requested elsewhere. I'm sure it won't take long, and then you'll be brought back to us."

Even though Shaw had predicted this, it still made his chest tight. He held Nia fast when she would've pulled away. Every fiber of his being screamed not to let her go from his side. All the words he'd been unable to say earlier spun in his head in a frenzy. He didn't know what was happening. Or why.

"Nay," he stated.

Amsden raised a brown brow. "Excuse me?"

Shaw was as surprised as the steward by his outburst. He quickly gathered himself. "I'm quite...taken...with her. I'd like her to remain by my side. I'm sure you understand."

Amsden held his gaze for a long time before drawing in a long breath. "She is quite the catch."

"Exactly. I can no' believe no one has claimed her before now, but I'm no' willing to let her go."

"I'm afraid she cannot get out of the request. I assure you, she won't be long," Amsden replied coolly.

Shaw wanted to punch him. The violence that he wanted to enact on the man surprised even him.

"You wouldn't want to pass up this opportunity," Nia said, a smile on her face as she looked at him. "I'll return as quickly as I can."

Shaw met her gaze and saw the tightness of her mouth. She was subtly telling him to go without her. He knew it was what he had to do, but that didn't mean he had to like it.

She winked and blew him a kiss. "I'll see you soon."

Then she pulled her hand from his arm and walked to a waiting soldier he hadn't seen arrive. Shaw fought not to yank her back, to take her into his arms and fly far from the horrible city. The sinking feeling inside him grew the farther she walked from him, as if he somehow knew that he would never see her again. That thought made him want to throw back his head and roar. He was the dominant one here. He was the one who could —and *should*—call the shots.

Nia paused and turned to look at him over her shoulder. Then, the smile she gave him was genuine. She was ready for whatever came. It was time that he remembered why he was here.

Shaw drew in a shaky breath and pulled himself together. The violence demanded to be released, but he held himself in check. For now. Then he faced Amsden. The steward had watched all of that with interest. Thankfully, it would help confirm the act of him being in love with Nia. Love.

Fuck.

No. It couldn't be. Fate wouldn't do that to him. He'd done everything to keep himself from being attached. He was just worried about her. Nia was risking everything. Aye, that was it.

He was concerned. So, what if he'd come to care for her a little? Their forced proximity and fake relationship would lend itself to some feelings, but he knew better than to fall in love.

"You really do have feelings for her," Amsden said.

Shaw smiled as he recalled his role. "How could I no'? Look at her. She's beautiful with a body I can no' get enough of."

"She is stunning." Amsden's gaze landed on Nia's retreating back, the longing there for anyone to see.

Which made Shaw want to rip the steward's head off and use it as a ball to kick around. "I'm happy she's been so selective. Otherwise, she might have been someone else's."

The steward jerked his gaze to Shaw's. He cleared his throat at having been caught staring. "Does that mean you plan to remain in Stonemore?"

"Depends on many factors," Shaw said with a smile.

Amsden shifted as if suddenly nervous. "Right, then."

Shaw inwardly smiled as the steward turned around and opened the door. Shaw took one last look at Nia to try and see where they were taking her, but she was already gone. He clenched his jaw and walked through the doorway into another corridor.

"What do you think of our city?" Amsden asked.

"It has its pros and cons."

"We've built an empire that few on the realm can compete with."

The pride in his voice grated on Shaw's nerves. "How do you know if you've no' sent out more explorers? The fact that you want me here proves you can no' be sure whether that is fact or no'."

"You're very perceptive," Amsden said with a chuckle as he

glanced over his shoulder at Shaw. "If any cities or villages were left, I'd suggest you ask them who the greater city is. But only we remain."

Shaw lengthened his strides to come even with the steward. "Is that because the other cities died out or because you attacked them?"

"I would suggest you curb your words in front of the Divine. They won't be tolerated."

He'd hit a nerve. Shaw bit back a smile. "I doona like being threatened."

"That wasn't a threat. It was a fact."

Shaw glanced at the steward to see a bead of sweat falling from his receding hairline. Amsden didn't like being alone with him. Good. Shaw wanted the wanker frightened. Everyone in the citadel should be quaking in their boots. They were at his and Merrill's mercy, but they acted as if the roles were reversed.

If they harmed a single hair on Nia's head, they would find out exactly how violent a Dragon King could be.

Amsden turned right and went up a flight of stairs. He moved quickly as if to get ahead of Shaw. Amused, Shaw caught up with him.

"You almost seem as if you're running from me," Shaw said.

The steward laughed, though the sound came out nervously. "Why would I do that?"

"I'm wondering the same thing."

Amsden flashed him a forced smile and continued down another hallway with a deep blue runner along the length, leading to another set of doors. Two soldiers stood guard. Shaw flexed his fingers. Was he finally going to come face-to-face with the Divine? He couldn't sense any magic around him, but that meant nothing.

They had traveled far from windows and natural light. Torches were spaced to shed their beams, the orange light dancing upon the floor in a wild, riotous display.

"You get to discover what few know," Amsden suddenly said as he slowed.

Shaw quirked a brow. "What's that?"

"Parts of the citadel are carved within the mountain."

"What parts?"

"All kinds."

Shaw narrowed his eyes on the steward, causing Amsden to look away anxiously.

Amsden pointed to the doors as he came to a stop. "Go through there. The Divine is waiting."

"You willna be joining us?"

"It's a private conversation."

Shaw could well imagine what *private* meant. Well, if they wanted to trap him, they could give it a shot. If he destroyed half the citadel and city while breaking free, it was no one's fault but theirs.

He turned to see Amsden hurrying away. "If any harm comes to Nia, I'll be looking for you."

The steward quickened his steps.

CHAPTER THIRTY-THREE

Daelya's heart thudded erratically in her chest as the door opened. She wanted to run, to be anywhere but there. Her gaze locked on the tall man with long, black hair as he came into view. Resolve and wariness hardened his handsome face as his eyes scanned the room. Her breath locked in her chest.

Then his gaze landed on her. She couldn't help but take a step back. He was a Dragon King, after all. She felt the strength of his magic, the sheer dominance of the being himself. And those who mastered her thought they could control him? It was almost laughable. She knew what the outcome would be, which was why she hadn't told her master everything.

Besides, they deserved what was coming.

Daelya wanted to say so much to Shaw, to warn him. He quirked a brow as he strode through the nearly empty room toward her. She had to force herself to stand her ground near the doors to the balcony. Her blood rushed in her ears as her brain screamed at her to run.

Shaw's eyes scanned her as he stopped before her. "Who might you be?"

Behind her was a door where the others waited. The one to her left was one she prayed they never opened. If she said nothing to Shaw, she would likely be killed in the resulting battle. If she dared to speak, the Divine would kill her instantly. Either way, she would finally be free.

"Daelya," she answered.

"Are you to take me to the Divine?"

Shaw drew close enough that she could see that his eyes were green. Daelya had never been brave enough to get a glimpse of the dragons. This would be her only chance. Her one attempt to balance the scales once more. "Run," she said in the barest whisper.

His brows drew together as he stiffened.

She pleaded with her eyes for him to leave, but he simply smiled. That was when she realized that he suspected something. Of course, a Dragon King would come prepared. But would it be enough? It had to be.

For everyone's sake.

Shaw looked out the doors to the balcony beyond. Then he swiveled his head to the other side and looked at the wall there. The sun was sinking, darkening the room. The shadows grew, causing her to want to rush to the light, but he didn't seem fazed by them in the least.

"Is the Divine coming?" Shaw asked her.

Daelya's lips parted, ready to tell him everything, when the door behind her burst open and warriors flooded the room. To her shock, Shaw grinned, his eyes burning with reckoning as they surrounded him. Someone grabbed Daelya's hair and tossed her to the side. Her body slammed against the wall, but a rush of footfalls drowned out her cry of pain. She curled into a ball, trying to protect herself from being trampled.

Nia's thoughts ran wild with what could be happening with Shaw as she paced the small, richly appointed chamber. Had he met with the Divine? What did the Divine want? And when would she see Shaw again?

She sat on the curved settee, hoping that would calm her nerves. She couldn't shake the feeling she was being watched, but she couldn't figure out by whom or how. Her skin prickled with unease, so she knew it wasn't her imagination. Someone was there. She had to remain calm. She wouldn't give them anything.

Especially about Shaw.

The door opened, and Amsden stalked in as if he ruled the citadel. The way he raked his eyes over her made her want to gag. He had always repulsed her. Everyone at the citadel felt that way, but his position gave him them power to do what he pleased with whomever he wanted, whenever he wanted.

Amsden leaned his skinny frame against the wall and crossed his arms over his chest. Anger rolled off him in waves as he glared at her. "How did you do it?"

"Do what?" she asked coyly.

His nostrils flared. "Don't play with me. How did you get Shaw to fall in love with you?"

She smiled serenely so he didn't see how scared she was. "I was taught the art of sex and seduction. Done correctly, I can have anyone eating out of my hand."

"Once again, you've proven how resourceful you are."

Nia's stomach clenched. The compliment was anything but. "I do what the Divine asks of me."

"So, you do," the steward said with a sneer.

Now she wished she were standing. He might be against the wall, but he was so much taller. Right now, she didn't like anything that put her at a disadvantage. "Is the Divine displeased with me?"

"On the contrary."

The derision in his voice only made her more nervous. Her stomach churned as her blood turned to ice. "I don't understand your anger."

"Do you really think you'll get your freedom?"

"It's what the Divine offered if I delivered a Dragon King. Shaw is here."

Amsden barked a laugh as he dropped his arms and pushed away from the wall. He stalked to her and put his finger against her forehead before shoving her against the back of the settee, his face contorting with fury and satisfaction.

He loomed over her for a moment. Of all the people to bully her, it had to be him. Normally, Nia would play the part everyone expected of her, but being with Shaw had shown her another way. She straightened and watched Amsden warily. What she wouldn't do for a weapon. Or a Dragon King.

"With all the things you know, do you honestly think you'll get to walk out of Stonemore?" He bent and put his mouth near her ear. "How naïve of you."

Her flesh crawled with fear. Nia tried to move away and get to her feet, but Amsden grabbed her and shoved her onto the cushions. Before she knew it, he had her on her back. Everything

Shaw had taught her went straight out of her head. She tried to push Amsden away. Despite his lanky frame, he was stronger than he looked.

The sound of ripping material yanked her from her shock. Shaw's voice filled her head. *Focus. Strike the eyes, nose, throat, and groin. Any one of those will incapacitate your attacker.*

Amsden had her hands over her head and held them there with a secure hold. She attempted to wiggle loose. He shifted to grab her hips. It was all the time she needed to jerk up her knee, connecting with his groin. He let out an outraged cry and fell to the side, clutching himself. Now free, Nia rolled from the settee to her feet.

She only got one step before a hand clamped around her ankle and yanked it back. She pitched forward, landing heavily on the floor and banging her forehead against it. Pain radiated outward like a blast. Dots swam in her vision.

Nia fought against the darkness pulling her under. She refused to become unconscious and let Amsden have her body. With her eyes open and blinking, she clawed at the floor while he continued tugging her back. Finally, she rolled over and attempted to kick him with her free leg. He anticipated that and laughed as he shoved her foot away.

"I watched that night the priest took you," Amsden said. "I saw all of it. How he couldn't control himself. And how you didn't fight. It's always been fun to watch."

Fury consumed her. She tried to kick him again and again. He couldn't dodge them all. The few she landed made her smile, but him managing to crawl over her once more wiped away the satisfaction. Then he backhanded her.

The pain took her breath. Lights flashed behind her eyes. The darkness tried to take her once more, and she struggled against it. It took more effort this go-round, costing her more time. When she came to, Amsden knelt between her legs with his trousers open and his dick in his hand.

Panic shot through her until she realized that he was limp. A laugh bubbled out of her. "What's wrong? You can't get hard when someone's fighting you?"

"Shut your fucking mouth. It's your job to get me hard. Do it!" he commanded.

She glared at him. "No."

"Do. It."

"Never."

"By the time I'm finished with you, no one will want you," Amsden threatened.

Something snapped inside Nia. She sat up and quickly jabbed the stiffened fingers of her hand like a blade to his throat. His eyes bugged as he gasped and choked. She shoved him away and scrambled to her feet as she hurried from the room, closing the door behind her.

She glanced around to see if anyone was near. When she didn't see anyone, she looked down at herself. Her sleeve was torn, and she knew her hair was a mess. She rushed to the servants' quarters. Nia's foot slipped on one of the stairs, and she tumbled down the last few of them.

The world went black. She had no idea how long she was out before she opened her eyes. Her head swam with dizziness. She had to use the wall to get to her feet. Everything hurt, and she wasn't sure how she would get out of the citadel to find Merrill looking as she did. It wouldn't be long before someone found Amsden, or he found others and ordered everyone to look for her. Nia swiped at the useless tears and straightened from the wall, only to come face-to-face with several servants.

"Stop staring and help," Corrine said as she descended the stairs to come even with Nia.

Nia looked at the courtesan in confusion.

Corrine smiled. "Come on. Let's get you changed and your hair fixed."

"They'll punish you for helping me."

"Not if they don't find out."

Nia glanced at the servants.

"We've all had to deal with Amsden's attention. You're the first who fought back."

Nia glanced back up the stairs, her thoughts on Shaw. Her entire body hurt, but there was no way she could leave the citadel in her current state. Going with Corrine might lead to her death, but what choice did she have?

Corrine's arm was gentle as it wrapped around her and guided her. It wasn't long before they were in the courtesan's room. The beautiful, black-skinned courtesan was gentle as she helped Nia remove her torn clothing and put on new ones. Corrine tossed Nia's ruined garments into the fire before sitting Nia down to redo her hair.

"There," Corrine said with a smile, meeting Nia's gaze in the mirror.

Nia turned to face her and grabbed her arm. "I owe you."

A calculating grin curved Corrine's lips. "Yes, you do. Now, go so I can call in my marker later."

The atmosphere of the city had changed. Merrill walked from the bar onto the street. Mothers hurried their children into buildings. Men kept their gazes on the ground, seemingly too afraid to meet anyone's eye.

And the soldiers watched all of it with gleeful enjoyment.

The resentment inside Merrill festered. The best thing for everyone would be for him to find his mountain on Dreagan and sleep. Too bad for everyone in Stonemore that couldn't happen. Merrill looked at the sky. It appeared as if someone had drawn a horizontal line. Above it was a deep blue. Below it, everything was vibrant orange and coral. It didn't last long as the mountains swallowed the last bit of sun, devouring it and sending them into darkness.

Merrill had never minded shadows or the night. They hid so very much. Monsters lived in the dark. If Stonemore wanted to see a monster, he would show them one.

His head swiveled so he regarded the citadel. Shaw and Nia were there. He should be with Shaw, not waiting for something to happen so he could join the battle. Because there would be combat. No ruler lined the streets with soldiers without preparing for a fight.

Merrill suddenly realized that he was alone on the street with the soldiers. The door of the pub behind him slammed shut with finality. He smiled as he dropped his gaze to the soldiers. Their fear and apprehension filled the air.

"This is almost too easy," he murmured.

CHAPTER THIRTY-FOUR

There was no room to shift. Shaw could do it, but he'd possibly send the citadel crashing down around everyone, including Nia. He couldn't take that chance. So, he battled the men and women who swarmed him.

They wore formfitting, sleeveless tunics showing armbands. He'd seen the likes of which with one other—Jeyra. As Shaw used his body to defend himself, he realized that these people were from Orgate. The very city that had trapped two dragons and tortured them for years. They hadn't taken kindly to Jeyra's betrayal, or news of her choosing a Dragon King over them.

Shaw kept calling to Merrill and Cullen, but no one answered. And his sword wouldn't appear either. He'd felt an oppressive presence when he came into the room, but it'd never entered his mind that something would hinder his magic.

He knew his power, an innate ability like shifting, wouldn't be affected. But there were at least two dozen warriors. Despite his skill and speed, some of their weapons managed to connect, drawing blood. It infuriated him. He could end them in a split second if he wanted. Didn't they realize who they fought? Shaw used his power of illusion to appear in several places in the room.

The warriors didn't know who to fight. They each went after one of him, and Shaw spun around and slammed his elbow into the face of a redhaired warrior near him. Blood spurted from the warrior's nose as bone cracked. Shaw then dropped to one knee and grabbed another warrior's leg, yanking. The man landed hard on his back. Shaw rolled atop him and grabbed the man's hand that held the sword. After wrestling it from him, Shaw was back on his feet.

He lost count of the number of warriors he killed. Though he did catch sight of the woman who had been with him when he first entered. Daelya hunkered in a corner, her eyes glued to him—the real him, not one of his illusions. She must be the one who'd told the Divine who he was. But Daelya had warned him. Why? That would be something he'd find out later. Right now, he had to stop this fight.

Just as he started to turn, Shaw saw a finely dressed, blond-haired woman and a bearded man in the same attire of the warriors watching him. They both stood outside of the battle, seemingly unconcerned for their safety. That sent warning bells off in his head.

A blade sliced across his back. Shaw felt every inch of it. He arched in pain and spun around. That's when he caught sight of the balcony. He grabbed hold of the warrior he was fighting and shoved him through the open doors, over fallen bodies and out into the open. Shaw peeled back his lips and sank his blade into the man's chest before turning around, ready to shift and put an end to all of this.

The explosion came from inside the room. The shockwave sent him tumbling backward, debris cutting and biting into his flesh as it flew into him. He slammed into something hard, and then there was nothing but air. Shaw heard screaming. On instinct, he reached out his hand and grasped hold of something. He blinked until his eyes came into focus and found himself dangling from the mountain face below the balcony.

Shaw was about to pull himself up when he felt something. It was unlike anything he had felt before. He wasn't even sure what *it* was. A person? An animal? Something else? But it was there. Though it made no sense, he felt as if it were trying to communicate with him. Shaw wanted to release his hold and fly to find Nia, but something compelled him to stay.

And he feared that *something* was the same thing he felt.

Besides, there were things he needed to learn. Who was the woman who'd told him to run? Who was the couple watching the battle? How the hell had the Orgate warriors come to Stonemore and the citadel? Not to mention, he still wanted to find the Divine.

Shaw used his strength to flip up and over the balcony to land on his feet. His illusions were gone. A few Orgate warriors rolled on the floor, wounded, but none looked as though they would get up and attack. Which was too bad because he was in the mood for a fight now.

He stepped over bodies, searching for Daelya. He found her inside near the corner where he'd last spotted her lying on her side. Shaw hurried to her and pulled away the bodies that had ended up on top of her. He checked her pulse. It was faint but steady. He scanned the room to find the couple. He found the woman lying unconscious, but the man was gone.

Shaw started to the blonde when he noticed the door in front of him. It was the same one that had garnered his attention when he first walked into the room. His feet moved of their own accord toward it. Even when he knew he should turn away and find Nia, he remained. His hand rested on the handle, ready to open it.

"Don't."

He snapped his head to the side to find Daelya. A thick stream of blood ran from a head wound, then down her cheek and onto her clothes. "What's inside?"

"The reason you were brought here."

Shaw frowned. "The Divine, then?"

Daelya shook her head. "Something much worse."

Questions formed at the same time his hand turned the handle of its own accord. Daelya's eyes widened, her mouth opening on a scream. Shaw couldn't stop himself as the door cracked open. He turned his head to look inside when Daelya shoved him aside. Shaw sprawled on his back, watching helplessly as she was sucked into the room, the door slamming shut behind her.

A war cry split the air behind him. Shaw tore his eyes from the door to find a warrior with a long, light brown beard laced with gray coming at him with a double-edged war axe. Shaw called to his sword. This time, it appeared. The pommel filled his hand instantly. He brought the weapon up in time to stop the attack.

"You'll pay for what you've done!" the warrior bellowed.

Shaw shoved him away and jumped to his feet. "Pay for what?"

"Taking what was ours." The warrior sneered, hate and fury blazing in his gray eyes.

He realized this was the same man who had been standing with the woman. "You'll have to be more specific."

"Your kind made one of ours betray us."

"Your anger is blinding you. *You* betrayed Jeyra."

That only enraged the warrior more. They circled each other, waiting for the perfect chance to strike. "I've come for my revenge."

"Against a Dragon King? The odds are no' in your favor."

The man smirked. "We held one before."

"Good luck getting a second." Shaw lunged as he swung his blade down, the tip of his sword slicing the warrior's neck.

The man blinked in shock as his lips moved, but no words came. He grasped his wound as blood flowed between his fingers before he dropped to his knees. He was dead before his body hit the floor.

Shaw felt the pull toward the door again, but he kept his gaze away from it. He walked out onto the balcony and heard the battle below. *"Merrill? Do you have Nia?"*

But Merrill didn't answer him. Shaw looked at the dead around him. He had more questions now and no one to answer them. Then he thought of the blonde. He started toward her when he heard screams from within the citadel.

"Nia," he said as he rushed from the room.

It felt so good to let the anger out. Merrill struck down soldier after soldier. He never attacked, but if they came at him, he ended it. It was how it had always been. He might never start a fight, but he always finished them.

When he lifted his head, he was breathing heavily. He looked down at his hands. They were coated in blood. So was the rest of him. He blinked it out of his eyes as his gaze moved over the lifeless bodies lying around him in a circle, some stacked on top of others. With the sounds of battle gone, the city was eerily quiet.

Merrill's eyes moved down the street to where he found a group of soldiers clumped together, watching him as if he were some crazed demon that needed to be put down. Shite, maybe he was. A look behind him showed more soldiers. But none of them appeared to have any inclination to come at him. He wouldn't either with the pile of dead around him.

The explosion had set everyone off. A portion of the citadel had blown away while men screamed as they tumbled down from the lofty height. Merrill didn't see any of those men shift, so he knew none of them were Shaw. That didn't mean Shaw wasn't in trouble, though. He had taken a step to go and find out about his friend when the first soldier had struck him. The blade had sliced into his upper arm. That was all it took for Merrill's attention to shift to the men around him.

He made his way over the pile of dead and headed toward the soldier who'd waited at the end. When he reached the group, the soldiers parted, moving away from him quickly. Even the priest soldiers kept their distance while eying him suspiciously. Merrill didn't care. Not about the humans or the war Brandr and Eurwen were trying to avert. It didn't matter what the Kings or dragons wanted. The humans always dictated what happened.

They were always in control, somehow, even though they didn't
have magic.

And, frankly, Merrill was sick of it.

Someone had to remind the mortals who had the power.
Who could wipe them out. He hadn't planned on it being him,
but now that it was, he wasn't sorry. About any of it. If anyone
else stood in his way, he'd react the same. He was done pushing
aside his emotions, ignoring the ache deep within him. There
was no running from the misery within any longer.

It had rested in him, eating away at everything he was.
Leaving him a shell of what he'd once been.

He continued from the fourth to the fifth level. The gate was
barred—as if that would stop him. He shifted and took to the
sky. Screams sounded as humans caught sight of his true form.
Merrill ignored them and flew straight to the citadel. He
returned to human form on the broken balcony, his eyes taking
in the clothing of the dead.

"Orgate," he murmured.

This meeting had been a trap. Wrath burned hotly as Merrill
strode inside the room. There were three doors other than the
one to the balcony. Two of them, one on either end of the room,
were open. It was the one directly opposite him that was closed.
He frowned, sensing something within.

Merrill stared at the door. He wanted to go to it and see what
was inside. It was important. He could feel it. Just as he felt
something attempting to communicate with him. Was there
some creature within? Someone with magic being held? If so, he
would free them.

He took a step when a moan reached him. His head whipped
to the side. Merrill's gaze landed on a woman dressed in fine

clothes, her blond hair askew. He made his way to her, pausing
to stare at her. He couldn't decide whether to leave her or help.
Finally, he bent and pulled the bodies off her. Her lashes fluttered
open as he squatted beside her. She blinked several times and
rolled onto her back. It allowed him to see that the right side of
her face was scarred from long-healed burns that went down her
neck before disappearing beneath her top.

"Are you hurt?" he asked.

Her blue eyes widened a fraction. She licked her lips and
shook her head before wincing.

Merrill held her gaze, watching for her to do anything that
would give him reason to kill her. "What happened?"

"Ambush," she croaked before swallowing.

"Who are you?"

"Villette."

"Do you work for the Divine?"

She stared at him for a second and then shook her head.

Merrill got to his feet and held out his hand. "Good.
Otherwise, I would've had to kill you."

She hesitantly slipped her hand into his, and he pulled her to
her feet.

"We need to go before the Divine's goons come, and I have
to kill more." Merrill waited for her to respond, but she simply
met his gaze. "Are you addled?"

"No."

He released her hand and walked to the door. "You have your
freedom now. Go."

"Can't you hear that? The soldiers here are looking for
anyone to hurt. No one can go out there now."

Merrill followed her gaze outside to see chaos everywhere.

Soldiers and residents alike. Nia. He'd promised Shaw that he would get to her, but how could he now? Merrill called Shaw through their link, but he didn't get an answer.

"I know another way," Villette said.

Merrill eyed her. "I doona need your help. I flew up here, and I can fly out."

"But I can't."

"Then I'll fly you out," he replied coolly. She eyed him suspiciously, which caused Merrill to curse inwardly. How could he have forgotten that humans were afraid of him? He and Shaw had been sent to help the humans with magic, and while Merrill might be dealing with his own demons, that didn't mean he had to take it out on an innocent.

Suddenly, he felt something pull at him. His head swung back to the closed door. What was inside?

The woman suddenly took his hand and tugged him. "Come with me. I know another way through the mountain."

CHAPTER THIRTY-FIVE

Soldiers blocked every way Nia went. Fear clawed at her, burning a hole through her chest and sinking into her bones. She wasn't getting out of Stonemore. She probably wouldn't get out of the citadel alive. Worse, she dreaded that something had happened to Shaw in the explosion. She kept glancing at the night sky in hopes of spotting sapphire scales, but there was no dragon. She kept reminding herself that he couldn't be killed by anything but another King, but she couldn't stop the worry.

Nia flattened herself against the fence. She could hear the soldiers both inside and outside the citadel patrolling. They cut down anyone they viewed as a threat. She glanced toward the citadel. Had they found Amsden? Was he looking for her now? She didn't want to wait around to find out. She had to get out of the city, but first, she had to get past the soldiers at the gate.

"Ma'am?"

Her head jerked toward the sound. Relief surged through

Nia when she saw Sadie. She grasped the servant's hand and pulled her against the wall. "What are you doing here?"

"Soldiers brought us. Told us this was the safest place."

Nia shook her head. "I don't think any place is safe. We need to leave the city."

"Why?"

"Look around."

Sadie shook her head. "The Divine will protect us."

Nia realized she couldn't force Sadie. She smiled and nodded. "Good luck."

"Wait," Sadie said as she grabbed her hand. "Where are you going?"

"Far away."

Her brows drew together. "The Divine owns you."

Nia pulled her arm free. "We had a deal. I delivered a Dragon King. I've won my freedom." She turned and started walking away without waiting for Sadie to reply.

"Stop her!" Sadie screamed to the soldiers. "She's a slave, trying to run away."

The soldiers descended upon Nia like a swarm. They grabbed her arms, and no amount of fighting and kicking got her free.

"She's responsible for all of this," Sadie told the soldiers, stirring their already fever-pitched anger to new heights. "She brought the Dragon King here."

Fury darkened the soldiers' faces.

Nia glared at Sadie. "On the Divine's orders. Let me go."

But the soldiers' bloodlust had been agitated. Everything she said fell on deaf ears. She struggled against their hold as they roughly dragged her up the steps to the entrance of the citadel. Their fingers bit into her flesh and yanked on her hair and clothes. Sadie continued egging them on. Nia could no longer hear what her servant said, but it didn't matter. The soldiers did, and they believed her.

As they dragged Nia toward one of the balconies, she caught sight of Amsden with a group of soldiers. His smug look made Nia want to kick him in the groin again. Amsden soon fell out of sight as they took her outside once more. Terror made her stomach drop to her feet when she spied the balcony.

Shaw ran through the citadel, shouting for Nia. He heard the screams from below as well as the shouts of the soldiers within the fortress. All hell had broken loose in Stonemore. He prayed that Nia had gotten free and was with Merrill even now, but each time he tried to speak to Merrill, his friend didn't answer.

Whether it was because something blocked their communication or Merrill was in trouble, Shaw didn't know.

"Nia!" he bellowed.

His heart pounded an erratic beat against his ribs. He couldn't shake the feeling that she was in trouble. It was the look Amsden had shot her that troubled Shaw the most. The steward was a problem, and Shaw would take care of that issue once and for all.

Shaw slid to a stop when he spotted Amsden. The steward motioned six soldiers around him toward something. Shaw inwardly smiled at finding Amsden alone. He started toward him. Amsden did a double-take when he spotted him. Satisfaction filled Shaw when the steward's face paled.

As he approached, Shaw saw the four slashes down Amsden's

face that were no doubt from fingernails. Anger roiled violently inside him. Shaw didn't need to ask who had made Amsden bleed. He knew it had been Nia.

Images of all the things Shaw wanted to do the steward flashed in his mind. He wanted to make Amsden scream in pain and beg for death. Shaw fisted his hands as the rage built. He stalked to Amsden.

"Wh-what are you doing here?" the steward asked as he stumbled backward.

Shaw smelled the fear on him. "Did you really think I would succumb to a trap? Even one with Orgate warriors? That just proves you know *nothing* about Dragon Kings."

"I-I wasn't part of it."

Shaw scowled at him. His next response would determine how he died. "Where's Nia?"

Despite the fact that he shook uncontrollably with fear, delight filled Amsden's smile as he pointed in the direction the soldiers had gone.

Unease shot down Shaw's spine as he turned his head. He caught a glimpse of the soldiers lifting something. His heart clutched when he spotted brunette hair—Nia's hair. And then they threw her over the balcony.

Shaw bellowed as he started running. He shifted before reaching the balcony, knocking every soldier off the side. Shaw somehow had the wherewithal to use his power so the residents didn't see him shift into his true form. Instead, they saw a bird. Shaw tucked his wings and dove toward Nia as the soldiers shrieked while they plummeted to their deaths.

A scream locked in Nia's chest as she tumbled through the air. Everything was a blur as she plunged to the ground, the wind whooshing in her ears. She couldn't stop thinking about Shaw. His name was on her lips as she closed her eyes and prepared to die.

Suddenly, she stopped falling. She opened her eyes to find herself looking at sapphire scales. Nia lifted her head and gazed up at the chest and neck of a dragon. Tears blurred her eyes. Shaw had saved her. He had saved her. She sobbed as she rested her cheek on the inside of his hand, grateful to be alive.

Something whistled past them. Then more whistles. *Arrows,* Nia thought. Shaw pressed the hand that held her against his chest and flew faster. She wanted to look down upon the world and see it from his vantage point, but she didn't have the energy for anything but being held securely by him.

Nia had no idea how long they flew before Shaw landed. He gently laid his hand upon the ground and opened it. She climbed out and faced him. The moonlight fell upon him, making his glossy sapphire scales appear nearly black. He towered over her. She gasped at his size and took several steps back to get a better look at him.

He watched her carefully with mirror-like, platinum-colored eyes. She stumbled as she walked to the side to see more of him. His scales were large and shiny but became finer and less thick on his neck. He had four limbs with long, black talons that looked as if they could cut a mountain in two. Shaw's dragon head was blocky with a mane of bony spikes that sprouted from the back of his head, and two long, misshapen horns that extended from his forehead.

Something drew his attention. His head snapped back

toward Stonemore, and he growled. She felt the rumble of it and spotted the rows of razor-sharp teeth when his lip lifted for an instant. His tail twitched before it curled around him at the same time he folded his huge wings against his body. Then, he looked back at her.

She had wanted to see him, but she hadn't been prepared for all of it. She had seen drawings of dragons and had heard others speak of them. The few glimpses she'd caught of Cullen had made her think she would be prepared to come face-to-face with Shaw in his true form, but nothing could do that.

Was he terrifying? Absolutely.

Would she run if she didn't know him? Without a doubt.

Did she feel threatened by him? Not for an instant.

He had saved her life. He had believed in her when no one else had, and he had shown her how to protect herself. She might have gotten free of Amsden but getting out of the citadel had been another problem altogether.

Nia walked to him and wrapped her arms around the arm that had caught her. Hers didn't go halfway around his, but she didn't care. She wanted him to know that she didn't fear him. Nia smiled as she realized his scales were warm. She hadn't internalized that when he'd held her in his palm.

She reluctantly released him. The instant she did, Shaw shifted into his human form. He was naked for a heartbeat before clothes covered him. He said nothing as he dragged her into his arms. The tears came then. She held tight as she put her head into the crook of his neck and cried.

"You're safe now," he whispered over and over.

It took a while for the tears to subside. Even when she finished, they remained locked in their embrace. She didn't know where she was, and she didn't care. She was free of Stonemore and the Divine, released to do whatever she wanted. And the only thing she wanted was Shaw.

All her life, she had closed herself off to keep her heart safe. Nothing could have prepared her for Shaw and the feelings he invoked. He'd shown her the life she could have, and the love she could know. That glimpse was all it had taken to break down every barrier she had. And it had happened slowly, without her even knowing that Shaw had taken up residence in her heart.

Was it love? She didn't know what the emotion was, but she suspected it was love. Her life had been about survival. Shaw had opened other doors and stood by her as she tested each one. He didn't want to control her or own her. It was the first time she realized there was another way.

What did she do with all this information now? Their relationship had been an act, something to bring him to the Divine. There had been no promises, no exchange of words about what might come next.

And that was why she couldn't let go of him now.

She was scared that once she did, he would disappear from her life. She had known the fierce lovemaking, the gentleness, and the determination of a Dragon King. No one in the universe could compare to that. Not now.

Not ever.

Somewhere along the way, she had become Shaw's. It didn't matter if he wanted her or not. She had basked in his smiles and teasing. Had known the heat of his body and pleasure unlike anything she'd experienced before. There wasn't a single spot on her that he hadn't kissed, licked, or caressed. The pleasure, the peace, the freedom. He had given her so much.

She leaned back to look into his fern green eyes. Torment contorted his face. She smiled to let him know that she was okay. "Thank you."

"If I hadna gotten there in time…"

"Shh," she said as she shook her head. She cupped his face. "You did get to me. That's all that matters. Don't think of anything else."

His eyes blazed with some emotion that made her heart catch. "I can no' stop thinking about it. Nia, I–"

"Shaw!"

Nia wanted to scream at whoever had interrupted them. She dropped her arms to her sides, the moment broken.

CHAPTER THIRTY-SIX

Shaw was a wreck. His emotions were all over the place. He wanted to return to Stonemore and find Amsden and incinerate him in dragon fire, but at the same time, Shaw didn't want to be apart from Nia.

When he saw her go over the balcony, he'd never known such fear, never felt such panic. He couldn't get to her fast enough. Every time he closed his eyes, he saw how close the ground had been before he finally reached her. He had barely gotten to her in time. A few more seconds and…

Now, she was the one comforting him.

He was scared and confused about his feelings, but he had to tell her. He had to get them out. Once said, he would never get them back, but that didn't stop him. Fortunately, Cullen interrupted them.

Shaw pulled his gaze from Nia's and looked over her head to find Cullen at the top of the canyon, the wildcat, Nari, at his side. Shaw drew in a steadying breath. It had to be Nia's near-

death that had him about to confess…something. He needed
time to think, to consider before he did anything rash.

"It's Cullen," he told Nia. "We're at the canyon I told you
about. You'll be safe here."

She gripped his arms, her fingers digging into his muscles.
"Me? What about you?"

"There are some who need to be dealt with." Shaw motioned
Cullen to them.

Nia shook her head, an argument on her lips.

"What the fuck happened?" Cullen demanded as he drew
near.

Shaw forced himself to release Nia and ran a hand down his
face. "Too much. I called for Con to come with Brandr and
Eurwen."

Cullen's face was grim as he nodded. "And Merrill?"

"I doona know. I've been calling for him since I was inside
the citadel." Shaw looked at Nia. "Did you see Merrill?"

"No," she said with a shake of her head.

For the first time, Shaw smelled the tinge of blood from her.
He bent closer and saw the traces of blood at her hairline. "What
happened? Who hurt you?"

"It doesn't matter."

"The fuck it doesna," he bellowed.

Cullen put a hand on him. "Easy, brother."

Shaw shoved him away. "Doona dare tell me what to do. You
were no' there. You didna see them toss her off the balcony to her
death."

Cullen's head snapped to Nia as his brows drew together. Nia
wrapped her arms around her middle and stared at the ground.

Shaw briefly closed his eyes and tried to rein in his fury. Then he looked at Nia. "Please, tell me what happened."

"Amsden happened." She lifted her chin and met his gaze. "He tried to...you know."

Yeah, Shaw knew. And he would fucking kill the bastard.

Nia smiled when she said, "I used what I learned from you. I kicked him in the groin and punched him in the throat. It felt amazing."

"Good for you," Cullen said with a nod.

Shaw was glad that Cullen had spoken because no words were getting past his wrath. Nia would never give him details, but he didn't need them. Shaw knew exactly what kinds of *things* the steward would've done to her.

"It was Sadie," Nia said.

Shaw was jerked from his thoughts. His gaze focused on Nia's face. "What?"

"She found me when I was trying to leave the citadel. Another courtesan gave me a change of clothes and cleaned the blood from me so I wouldn't be stopped. I thought I could get out and find Merrill, but Sadie shouted for the soldiers. She told them I brought you to the citadel. The soldiers refused to hear that the Divine had ordered me to do it."

Shaw reached for her hand and felt a small measure of peace when she wrapped her fingers around him. "They wanted blood. Nothing anyone said would've stopped them."

"Did you see the Divine?" Nia asked.

Shaw felt Cullen's gaze on him, as well. He licked his lips, ready to answer when Vaughn announced his arrival in his head. Shaw squeezed Nia's hand. "Come with me, please. I'm going to deliver the story, and I know the others will want to hear from you, too."

"I'll get Tamlyn," Cullen said as he ran back to the canyon and jumped to the bottom.

Nia gave a curious glance to the wildcat. "Is that a pet?"

"I'm no' sure what Nari is, but she helped Cullen, and she's been here ever since." Shaw began to walk toward the border, but Nia tugged on his hand to stop him when she spotted the dragons coming their way. "They willna harm you."

She swallowed nervously. "No human is supposed to cross the border."

"You're with me," he said with a smile. "That makes all the difference."

Nia's look told him she wasn't entirely sure that was true, but she didn't resist when he began moving again. As they walked, Shaw looked toward the forest. His enhanced hearing could still detect sounds of fighting from Stonemore. He tried once more to contact Merrill. When his friend didn't respond, worry soured him.

Shaw looked forward again before crossing the border. Nia paused, still holding his hand. She looked down to see a golden aura surrounding the arm that protruded from the barrier.

"It's a magical barricade that alerts when someone has crossed it," he told her.

Nia took a deep breath and squeezed her eyes closed as she walked through it. Once on the other side, she opened her eyes and looked behind her. "I didn't feel anything."

"You're no' supposed to."

Her attention shifted to the dragons who approached.

"The gold dragon? Is that...Con?" Nia asked in a whisper.

Shaw nodded. "With his mate Rhi riding him."

"Peach with gold wings. Is that Eurwen?"

"Aye. The teal dragon is Vaughn, her mate."

Nia blew out a breath. "I never thought to see one dragon. Now, I've met three and am about to meet three more."

The ground trembled as Vaughn, Eurwen, and Con landed. The three shifted into human form, careful to call clothes as they did. Shaw pulled Nia with him as they all began walking toward the group that met them halfway, along with Cullen and Tamlyn.

"Where's Merrill?" Con demanded.

Shaw shrugged. "I didna see him. I've been calling for him since I was inside the citadel."

"You actually got in?" Vaughn asked.

Shaw looked into Vaughn's blue eyes and nodded. "It was a trap."

"Why does it always have to be a trap?" Rhi asked in frustration.

Shaw looked at each of them. "There was a woman there, Daelya. I saw recognition in her eyes. She told me to run."

"Did you know her?" Eurwen asked.

"Never seen her before, but she knew me. Perhaps she was the one able to detect magic. I didna get a chance to inquire."

Con's voice was calm as he asked, "What kind of trap?"

"About two dozen warriors from Orgate were waiting to attack," Shaw explained. "I tried to reach out to Cullen, Merrill, anyone."

Cullen frowned. "I didna hear anything."

"None of us did," Vaughn added.

Shaw ran a hand over his jaw. "I couldna call my sword at

first, either. It wasna that I had my magic taken, but it was dulled. That's the best way I can explain it."

"But you did get your sword eventually?" Eurwen asked.

Shaw nodded.

"Obviously, you bested the warriors." Con was pleased with that.

Shaw grunted, wishing he had more of them to fight. "They're angry Jeyra turned from them to us. At least those warriors were. None are alive to report back to Orgate."

"That may or may not be a good thing," Eurwen said as she exchanged a look with Vaughn.

Shaw agreed. "I went to shift to finish off what warriors remained when there was an explosion. I have no idea where it came from, but it was in the room with me. I caught hold of the balcony and pulled myself to find everyone dead or unconscious. Until the leader of the warriors appeared, and we had a discussion that ended with his death." Shaw paused, thinking of the door and the unease that had gripped him then—and now.

Rhi's silver eyes held concern. "What else? You're holding something back."

"There's something I doona understand." Shaw glanced at Nia to find her watching him silently. "I felt a pull, like something was calling me to a door. I didna hear voices, but that's what it was. I went to the entrance. Daelya regained consciousness at that time and told me not to open it. I tried to listen to her, but my hand turned the knob anyway. She shoved me away, and then she was gone."

"Gone?" Tamlyn asked, shock widening her eyes.

Shaw nodded as the memory played in his head. "Something behind that door sucked her in and slammed it closed."

"The Divine maybe?" Eurwen offered.

Vaughn raised a brow as he met Shaw's gaze. "Did you see the Divine?"

"Besides the warriors and Daelya, there was only another woman there. She looked important, but she was unconscious when I left to search for Nia."

Every eye turned to her then. She held his hand with a death grip, but otherwise looked calm. Shaw squeezed her hand. He remained quiet as Nia told her story. She glossed over Amsden's attack, just as she had with him, but he couldn't blame her for that.

"I can't believe they tried to kill you," Rhi stated angrily.

Shaw moved closer to Nia. He didn't care what it looked like to everyone else. He only knew he needed to be beside her. "I got to her in time."

"What's the plan?" Cullen said. "The fact that Merrill hasna checked in is worrying."

Con crossed his arms over his chest and looked toward Stonemore. "Merrill is smart. He's probably laying low and waiting to get out after Shaw's dramatic exit."

"That shouldn't stop him from answering," Rhi pointed out.

"Two dragons over Stonemore in as many weeks," Eurwen said with a shake of her head. "We're trying to avoid a war, but it looks like we're headed straight into it."

Shaw lifted one shoulder in a shrug. "That depends on the humans."

"No," Rhi said with a shake of her black-haired head. "There's the Divine, whatever was behind that door, Orgate, the crone, and the invisible enemy we're still trying to find. We came to fight whatever attacked the dragons, and we've stirred up something else entirely."

A muscle in Cullen's jaw jumped. "Then the mortals shouldna have murdered defenseless children."

"Cullen's right," Eurwen said. "Brandr and I turned a blind eye to things on the other side of the border for too long. I don't want a war, neither does he, but that doesn't mean there won't be one."

Shaw frowned as he realized Brandr wasn't there. "Where is your brother?"

Eurwen swallowed. "Away."

"Away, where?" Shaw pressed.

"That's something I'd like to know, as well," Con stated tightly.

"Brandr, and now Merrill no' answering." Vaughn sighed loudly. "I doona like this at all."

Eurwen shot Vaughn a dark look. "I've spoken to Brandr."

"Then where is he?" Con asked, crossing his arms over his chest.

Rhi's brows furrowed as she looked at her daughter. "Eurwen, where is Brandr?"

Eurwen released a long sigh. "He's on the other side of the border."

"I figured," Con said softly and dropped his arms to his sides.

Eurwen nodded. "He said he had to do it. That he needed to make up for what we failed to do. I should be with him."

"He's better off alone," Rhi said. "I might not like that he is, but he'll move more freely by himself."

Vaughn shook his head. "He should've let us know before he did that."

"We would've stopped him," Eurwen said. "What's done is done. He promised to keep in touch."

Shaw had had enough of talking. "It's been a rough day. Nia needs to rest."

"She can stay with us," Tamlyn offered.

Con dropped his arms. "That's a good idea. Shaw, come with us. We'll start planning our next step."

Shaw didn't move. "I'm staying."

Con searched his gaze for a long, silent minute. Then the King of Kings bowed his head and turned away.

CHAPTER THIRTY-SEVEN

It was a dream. What else could explain Nia standing before multiple Dragon Kings, a Dragon Queen, and the King of Dragon Kings, not to mention a Fae?

A Fae. A real Fae. Nia had been awestruck by Rhi's beauty. Her inky hair and silver eyes were a beautiful combination. And she looked just like anyone else, just as Shaw said she would. Except more beautiful. Con was stoic, but there was no denying his passion for defending those he cared about. Con and Rhi made a striking couple as both were gorgeous. And Eurwen. Their daughter had a combination of both parents that made her just as stunning.

Nia's gaze moved to Vaughn. While Shaw and Cullen had a wild, untamed look about them, Vaughn was the complete opposite. He was composed, unruffled. Though his love for Eurwen, and hers for him, was undeniable in the way they kept looking at each other, emotion shining in their eyes.

The same was true for Cullen and Tamlyn. Nia couldn't wait

to talk to the Banshee more. Tamlyn was a dark beauty with a quiet conviction that made Nia like her instantly. Since Tamlyn was also an outsider to the Dragon King world, Nia hoped they could be friends. Because she really needed one right now.

Shaw had surprised her by stating that he was staying at the canyon. The look that passed between him and Con was silent, but it held a wealth of meaning. If only she knew what had been shared between them.

Rhi walked to her and took her hands. The Fae shared a dazzling smile. "Thank you for helping us. If you ever need anything, all you have to do is call my name. I'll hear you."

"You can do that?" Nia asked, shocked.

Rhi's smile broadened. "I've learned that Fae are a myth here, but we're very real. We have different kinds of magic than the dragons. We might not be able to communicate telepathically, but a Fae can hear their name called over great distances. We can then find who called for us and go to them."

That would've been helpful to know when Nia was battling Amsden. She had gotten out of that situation herself. Barely. But she had done it. "Thank you."

"No one from Stonemore will harm you now," Eurwen said.

Shaw grunted. "Nay, they fucking willna."

Rhi shot him a dark look before squeezing Nia's hands and releasing them. "Rest. We'll return soon."

Nia returned Eurwen's small wave. Vaughn bowed his head to her, and then the four of them headed out the same way they had arrived.

"Hi," Tamlyn said, drawing her attention.

She turned to the Banshee and looked into Tamlyn's hazel eyes. "Hello."

"You look like you're about to pass out."

Nia hurt everywhere. Her head pounded, and she didn't know if it was from her fall, when Amsden attacked her, or because the very beings she had spent her entire life fearing were talking to her like old friends.

Shaw's arm suddenly came around her. "Let's get you inside," he said softly.

She didn't realize until he pulled her against him how much effort she had used just to stay on her feet. Shaw walked her slowly to the edge of the canyon. She looked down the hillside covered in vines, trees, and other shrubs and jerked back, dizzy. Any other day, she might be up for such a trek, but she wasn't sure she could make it now. She had never been afraid of heights before, but being thrown from the balcony had changed that.

Shaw lifted her into his arms without a word. She met his gaze, and he winked at her as she wrapped her arms around him. She touched his face, delighted that he was with her. She didn't feel like she had to be strong in front of him.

"Close your eyes," he told her.

She quirked a brow. "Why?"

"I'm going to jump us to the bottom."

Nia didn't question him as she let her lids fall shut. An instant later, she felt a rush of cool air, and then the soft impact as Shaw landed. The way his arms held her securely made her never want to let go. She made herself look away from his handsome face to the canyon around her.

She had no idea where they were going. It looked like a dead-end until she saw Tamlyn and Cullen walk toward the rock face and vanish behind some large roots protruding from the canyon wall. That's when she saw the hidden door.

Shaw gently set her on her feet and took her hand. They walked through the doorway into an alcove. There was so much to take in that Nia could barely register it all. Giant faces, a perfectly cut staircase of stones that led them deeper underground as torches lit the way. The sound of dripping drew her attention. That's when she saw the network of tree roots high above them where water trickled down into a large pool. It was obvious that a civilization had once been here by the architecture alone.

"Is that a bruise?" Tamlyn asked with a frown.

Nia immediately reached up to hide the part of her face that had been backhanded. Shaw peered around from the other side, his face a mask of fury. "It's fine," she said.

"Sian can tend to your wounds." Tamlyn waited.

Nia knew she could refuse, but she wouldn't mind a few minutes alone to gather her thoughts. She pulled her hand from Shaw's and turned to the Banshee. Tamlyn smiled as she motioned for Nia to follow. She forced herself not to look back at him. Instead, Nia focused her attention on the corridor Tamlyn led her down. It wasn't long before she found herself in a kitchen.

The builders had made the ceilings high to give the illusion of space. Nia had to admit that it became difficult for her to remember that she was underground. The only thing missing was sunlight, but there was enough light to help.

"Sian is a wonder with her skills as an Alchemist," Tamlyn said. She paused beside a long bench next to a table. "Sit while I get you some food."

"I don't think I can."

"When was the last time you ate?"

Nia thought about her day and shrugged. "I was too nervous to put anything in my stomach."

"Between what you endured and the shock, you need something," Tamlyn said as she moved about the kitchen.

Nia closed her eyes as her head throbbed harder. Her thoughts took her back to the soldiers yelling at her, hatred in their eyes. She had been one of them, but they had turned on her. They'd thrown her to her death simply because Sadie had spoken lies. Sadie. Nia had known better than to trust anyone, but Sadie had become like a friend. Look what that had gotten her.

"Here you go."

Nia jumped at the sound of Tamlyn's voice. She looked down to find a plate full of different meats, bread, and cheese.

Tamlyn put a soft hand on her shoulder. "It's going to be hard, but rest easy. You're safe here. Cullen and Shaw will make sure of that. Try to eat. I'll be right back with Sian."

Thankfully, Tamlyn didn't wait for an answer. Nia wasn't sure she could've given one. She gazed at the food with distaste, but she also knew the Banshee was right, she needed to eat. She would need her strength. Being in a weakened state didn't do her any good.

Nia reached for the bread first. She bit into it, feeling the softness of it and letting the yeasty, slightly sweet aroma fill her nostrils. The taste exploded in her mouth, making her eyes fall shut, and her stomach demand more. She ate the entire slice and reached for another, adding some cheese and meat to it.

By the time Tamlyn returned with a petite woman with long, wavy brown hair and pale green eyes wearing a short apron over her long tan gown, Nia had devoured three slices of bread.

Sian removed her thick leather gloves and smiled. "It's nice to have visitors. Tamlyn told me all about you, Nia. I'm Sian."

Nia smiled in greeting as she swallowed her food. "Hello."

Sian's smile vanished as a frown replaced it. "You've got some bruising I see." She moved closer. "Is that blood?"

"My head hit the floor pretty hard," Nia said.

Sian flashed her a grin. "Don't worry. I have everything needed to get you cleaned up and feeling better."

She rushed away, leaving Nia with Tamlyn. "You were right. I was hungry."

Tamlyn shrugged as she sat on the opposite side of the table. "Sometimes, our bodies don't let us feel things in a stressful situation."

"Stressful. It was certainly that," Nia murmured.

Sian returned, carrying glass bottles of different sizes and colors. She set them down and ladled water from a large barrel in the corner. After she returned with it, Sian gathered one of the torches and set it on the table for more light. Nia watched the flames, noting they looked different from the fire she was used to seeing.

"It's Sian's creation," Tamlyn said. "It burns for days instead of hours. That allows us to keep everything lit here so we aren't in darkness."

"That's amazing."

Sian grinned, pride in her face. "Thank you. Now, hold still. This might sting."

Nia flinched when Sian touched the broken skin with a piece of cloth soaked in something from a tall, slender vial. She held still as Sian moved aside her hair to better get to the lesion. After the initial stinging, the throbbing of the abrasion began to lessen. Surprised, Nia shot a look at Sian.

"She has a gift," Tamlyn replied with a chuckle.

Sian shrugged before spreading some salve on the cut with gentle fingers. "It's what I love."

"Are you with a Dragon King?" Nia asked.

Sian paused for a moment, her expression falling in sorrow. "I'm with someone else. She's gone at the moment."

Nia glanced at Tamlyn to see her lips pinched, worry filling her eyes as she looked from Sian to Nia. Tamlyn shrugged as if to say, "*It is what it is.*" Unaware of the exchange, Sian moved to the bruise forming on Nia's cheek.

"You were very brave," Sian said. "Do you have family in Stonemore that we need to help?"

Nia realized she had no one. Not a single soul as a friend. She couldn't even claim Shaw, because everything between them had been a ruse. "No."

"It took a lot for you to turn away from your life and help us," Tamlyn replied. "None of us will ever forget it."

Nia laughed, though she didn't feel any mirth. Her gaze dropped to the table as sadness and misery rose. "Shaw opened my eyes to the truth. It wasn't anything to leave behind. I have nothing. No one. My father left, my mother disappeared, and my sister and brother died. I was left utterly alone, only to be brought to the citadel as a slave. I thought life might be better because I was clothed, housed, and fed. Little did I know I would be attacked and then moved to train as a courtesan." She lifted her gaze to Tamlyn. "I did what everyone should do against oppressors."

Sian slowly lowered her hand. "My sister and I were slaves. I got away, but she's still there." Sian sniffed and set a bottle before her. "Drink all of this."

Then she was gone.

Tamlyn reached across the table and squeezed Nia's arm. Her gaze moved over Nia's shoulder, and she knew they weren't alone. Tamlyn didn't say anything as she rose and walked away. Nia stared at her plate. It felt like an eternity before she heard footsteps approaching. She recognized Shaw's pants as he stopped beside her. He straddled the bench to face her and waited.

Nia was scared to look into his eyes, afraid to see something there she didn't understand. Or worse, not see anything at all. She had never been in such a situation. People talked about love all the time, but she had rarely seen it and had never experienced it. How could she say the glorious, amazing, terrifying things she felt now were love?

And what if she did? Shaw was from a different world. There was no reason for him to stay on Zora, much less with her.

"Lass," he urged in his deep, soothing voice.

She took a breath and looked at him. His fern green eyes searched hers. Concern sparked when he gently touched the injured side of her face. "We didna have much time to talk. No' about, well…" He paused as if trying to find the words. "We both admitted the attraction between us."

"Yes," she said.

"The way I feel with you, how my body responds, is unlike anything I've ever felt. I-I—"

She put a hand on his arm and made her lips curve into a smile she didn't feel. "I don't need you to say anything. I know what we were. I won't cling to you and beg you to stay." Nia stood and turned to leave, unable to say more before she burst into tears. But Shaw's hand stopped her.

Her heart thudded as a tiny shred of hope sprouted.

Suddenly, he was in front of her. She didn't know how he'd moved so fast or so quietly. He touched her chin to force her head up so her gaze would meet his. His throat bobbed as he swallowed.

"I'm no' good with words. I never have been. Actions were what I showed everyone, because words could be twisted and used to manipulate and lie." His brows drew together for a heartbeat. "But I've realized that words are important, and there are those who need to hear them. Please, be patient as I try to get them out."

Nia nodded, struck by the honesty in his voice.

He drew in a breath and licked his lips. "I viewed my job as King as the most important thing in my life. I found comfort in my brothers and my brethren. Then my brothers were gone. We Kings had always been close, but when we were all that was left, our bonds grew even tighter. We became a family. I thought it would always be like that, but some Kings began to find their mates. While I was happy for them, I saw love as a weakness. We had duties to protect our realm, and by dividing that with someone else, it could cause an issue. It's why I never let myself get close to anyone."

Here it came. Nia braced herself. This was when Shaw would tell her that he might want her body, but that was all it would ever be for him. It hurt more than she wanted to admit. A hole was opening where her heart had been, and the pain was so vast, it might swallow her whole.

"Never in my wildest dreams did I think I'd come across someone who filled my thoughts every hour of every day."

Her breath caught. Could he... Did he mean...her?

"I need to feel you in my arms every night, and I need to find you in the morning when I reach for you. I crave you in ways I didna know was possible. It doesna matter how many times I take your body, it's never enough. Yet, I'm more content than ever."

She stared at him, unsure of what to say. Or if she should even respond.

He pressed his lips together in frustration. "Do you understand what I'm saying?"

Nia parted her lips and tried to answer, but she gave up and shrugged.

"Bloody hell," he murmured. "I didna know how hard it would be to tell you that I love you. I should've spoken more instead of staying quiet. What idiot thinks it's better no' to speak?"

Her heart missed a beat. "What did you say?"

"That I need to speak more."

She shook her head as tears gathered. "Before that. Say it again. Please."

Fern green eyes searched hers in confusion. Then Shaw suddenly smiled. "I love you."

The rush of relief was so great, Nia had to close her eyes. Tears fell down her cheeks. She looked at Shaw. "I love *you*."

His arms came around her. He held her tightly and kept saying over and over, "I love you."

They stayed like that for several minutes.

Finally, he released her, only to cup her head in his hands.

His eyes were wet as he gazed at her. "A dragon always knows his mate. I've found mine in you. There's much about my world you doona know, but I'll show you all of it. Just say you'll be mine. Say you'll spend eternity with me. I'll show and tell you every day how much you mean to me."

Just like that, her happiness could be snatched away. "I'm not immortal."

Shaw laughed. "I might have forgotten to mention that when mated to a Dragon King, you can only die when he does."

Her mouth went slack with shock.

"Is that an aye?" he asked with a grin.

She threw her arms around his neck and kissed him. "I can't imagine life without you. Yes. My answer is yes!"

EPILOGUE

"Are you sure I'm supposed to be here?"

Shaw grinned at Nia's question. After three days at Iron Hall, Shaw and Cullen had gotten word about the mating ceremony. When a King was mated at Dreagan, the ceremony was held beneath Dreagan Mountain where only the Kings and their mates could attend. That rule didn't apply on Zora. Both Shaw and Cullen had taken advantage of that fact. They wanted their women to see what it was like to bind themselves to a Dragon King.

"Aye, *m'eudail.*"

The way she smiled every time he called her his darling made him want to rip her clothes off and have his way with her. The most painful—and freeing—thing he'd ever done was open his heart to her and tell her everything. Words would never come easily for him, but at least with Nia, he could say them.

He couldn't believe he had ever believed that falling in love was a weakness. It was the opposite. He felt stronger, more whole. After her shock at discovering that she would live for as long as he did, they had spent their time tearing each other's clothes off and discussing the future. There was much they wanted to do, but both realized all of it would be on hold until things got sorted on Zora.

Shaw looked at Nia, who watched everything with wide-eyed enthusiasm. All the Kings were in attendance, even those from Earth. Including Melisse. After all, no one missed a mating ceremony. The mates were also there. Shaw had introduced Nia to many of them, but others waited to say hello—though it would have to wait until after the ceremony.

Everyone was in their finest attire. The Kings in kilts, and the women in gorgeous dresses. Dragons flew around, watching, while others perched on nearby mountains to observe. Shaw drew in a breath and smiled. He'd never thought to see such a day again. Zora might not be their world, but they could visit. And that was enough.

Hector came up between Shaw and Cullen. With a low voice, he asked, "Still no sign of Merrill?"

Shaw clenched his jaw. There was no way Merrill would refuse to answer any of them. The only explanation was that he couldn't. Did someone have him like they had captured Varek? Was he in some deep, dark hole, unable to communicate?

He'd held out hope that Merrill would make it back. Truth be told, Shaw had been so wrapped up in his love for Nia that he had forgotten his friend. That was unforgivable. "I'm going to find him."

"We all are," Cullen whispered.

Hector blew out a breath. "Two missing Kings isna good."

Their conversation was halted when Varek walked up. Worry

gripped Shaw. Merrill should be up there with his best friend. Shaw prayed nothing had happened to Merrill. There would be a meeting soon to discuss the next steps, but for now, there was a mating ceremony.

Nia squeezed his arm and gave him a reassuring smile. He winked at her. She gave him strength. One day, they would be standing up there exchanging vows. For now, it was enough that she had agreed to be his.

Varek wore a wide grin, his happiness palpable, his attention focused on something behind everyone. A moment later, Con appeared with Jeyra on his arm. Her long red hair had been pulled back loosely on the sides and flowed down her back. Then he noted Jeyra wore an armband on both arms that sported a large, green amethyst on each. Con always gave a mate a gift, and these were from him.

Even Shaw had to admit her hair contrasted nicely with the lichen-colored dress she wore. Jeyra was a warrior for her people and had spent her life in pants. But she glowed in the strapless tulle gown with a glittered and pleated skirt in a voluminous A-line silhouette that ended in a dramatic, sweeping train.

The way Varek reached for Jeyra when she stopped beside him made everyone chuckle. Con wasted no time in starting the vows. As Shaw listened, all he could think about was one day saying those words to Nia and having her repeat them to him. She squeezed his hand, and they exchanged a look. She smiled, letting him know that she was thinking about their ceremony, too.

"Soon," he whispered. "I'm yours, *m'eudail*. Eternally."

"My eternal dragon." She blew him a soft kiss.

His heart swelled. He'd been terrified of love, but now that he had it, he couldn't imagine how he had lived without it. Their future was as uncertain as it had ever been, but Shaw wasn't worried. Not so long as he had Nia.

Jeyra jerked slightly when the dragon eye tattoo appeared on her left upper arm above the armband, a sign that she was mated to a King.

Shaw leaned close to Nia's ear and said, "I can no' wait until you're sporting that tat."

"Me, either," she replied huskily.

Cheers went up in celebration of another King mated. The dragons joined in and roared, the sound deafening. Varek let out a loud whoop and dragged Jeyra to him for a long kiss. Everyone smiled and laughed at the joyous occasion, but it was tinged with worry and apprehension. Shaw wished they could spend the evening celebrating as they always did, but that wouldn't happen this time.

"I doona like this," Ulrik said as he walked up. "I doona like leaving when two of our own are missing."

Shaw met his gold gaze and nodded. "Aye, but someone needs to watch Dreagan and Earth."

"I'm going to return Eilish to Earth and then come back here," Ulrik stated.

Cullen laughed. "Good luck with that, brother. Your mate willna let that happen."

Hector wore a big smile. "Nay, she willna, but I'd like to see the argument."

Ulrik glared at both of them. "We should all be here."

"We should, but that isna what's happening," Shaw said. "We're going to find both of them."

Ulrik placed a hand on his shoulder as he sighed. "I know. Good luck to all of you."

They watched him walk back through the Fae doorway to Earth with the mated Kings and their women. That seemed to signal the end of the evening. The rest of them gathered around. Since Jeyra called Zora home, she and Varek had chosen to stay and fight.

"There could be several reasons for Merrill no' answering," Con addressed everyone. "We're going to find out why. Both he and Brandr are Dragon Kings. They're highly skilled and powerful. But as we're learning, there are those on Zora with magic we've never encountered."

Ranulf shrugged. "That's never stopped us before. It willna now."

Con looked around the circle, stopping at Rhi, who stood to his right. "Our enemies are growing. We're here as guests, and we're trying no' to begin a war. Eurwen and Brandr are the rulers of this realm. Remember that."

"No," Eurwen said, her silver eyes blazing. "You're no longer here as guests. You are Dragon Kings. Every dragon that's here now is descended from bloodlines going back to Earth. Each of you willingly came to help when asked. My father is right, we have unknown adversaries. My brother and I are partly to blame for that. We went out of our way to ignore anything having to do with the humans. That was our mistake, one that needs to be rectified. We need to know what magic is out there, and who is dangerous. All of you have risked everything time and again to protect Dreagan and Earth. Brandr and I are asking you to do it again here."

Kentigern bowed his head to her. "That's the thing. You doona need to ask. We're more than willing."

Shaw joined the rest as they nodded in agreement.

Eurwen drew in a shaky breath. "Then let's get started."

Brandr squatted down in the tall grass atop a hill and looked at the village in the valley below. He'd been walking for days. Nothing looked out of the ordinary in the town, but he wasn't taking anything for granted.

He had spent much of his time alone. He'd encountered others twice during his travels. The first had steered clear of him. The second had shared an evening fire and asked many questions. Brandr had answered them all as well as asking his own. That was how he'd learned of this village. He plucked a piece of grass and twirled it between his fingers.

If he wanted to learn, he had to venture into the heart of where humans lived. If he could suffer it on Earth, he could handle it on his realm. The answers he sought were out there—so were his enemies—and he wouldn't shy away from either.

Villette kept her pace quick. Merrill followed closely behind in the narrow tunnel that led through the mountain. She lifted the torch high to light their way. He hadn't said anything since she'd pulled him into the tunnel. He kept trying to communicate with the other Kings, which put a strain on her already taxed power.

It took everything she had to keep the beast at bay on an

average day. She had believed she was strong enough to spread herself and hinder Shaw, but that had backfired. The beast tried to communicate with Shaw—then Merrill. That ignited her drive to achieve her goal. She was back in control now. She didn't want to divert her magic again, but she had no choice. She had a Dragon King, and she wasn't going to let him go. Which meant, he couldn't talk to his brethren.

Everything she had worked so hard for could've been destroyed today. It made her sick to think how close it had come to just that. Had she not woken when she did.... Villette didn't want to think about that. About what would've happened had the beast gotten free.

Her thoughts returned to Merrill. He likely wouldn't give up easily in his quest to talk to his friends. She would have to distract him eventually. For now, she was able to keep the messages from getting out or in to him. But she needed to rest and regain her strength.

Merrill was handsome with a blend of chestnut brown and blond hair and dark blue eyes. He had something violent and brutish about him. Something she had noticed when he landed in the room, but not something he'd had when he walked through Stonemore's gates. Was it because Shaw was gone? Or something else? She'd soon find out when she started digging.

"Who are you?" he demanded.

She looked at him over her shoulder, the scarred side in shadow. "I told you. But you didn't share your name." She had to make him think that she didn't know him.

"Villette," he replied. "How did a woman of obvious means such as yourself come to be in that room?"

Her steps slowed. She stopped and faced him. "I told you, I don't work for the Divine."

"You didna answer my question. You know this route well. Which means, you know the citadel."

The torchlight danced in his blue eyes. "I know this path well because I've used it for many years."

"Why were you in that room?" he pressed.

"To observe." No need to lie.

His eyes narrowed. "Observe what?"

"Dragon Kings, of course."

Merrill took a step closer. "Your kind knows nothing about us."

His intense stare was meant to make her uncomfortable. If only he knew who he was dealing with. "I want to learn."

"You may regret saying that," he said before brushing past her.

Villette released a victorious smile. The plan was working perfectly.

Dreagan

Henry stood in the Dragonwood and looked in the direction of the Fae doorway to Zora. He wished he could see it for himself, not that it would make his decision any easier. Or maybe it would. He didn't know any longer.

For so many years, he'd known who he was, what his purpose was. At least, he had thought he did. Then he'd discovered the Dragon Kings and learned that he and his sister, Esther, were

part of a group of powerful Druids from the Isle of Eigg that
policed Druids. He was the JusticeBringer. Esther the
TruthSeeker.

Everything about them had been lies. Their real birthdates,
their names, everything.

"Henry?"

He squeezed his eyes closed at the sound of his sister's voice.

"Nikolai said he saw you. Why didn't you come to the
manor? It's been months since you've returned my calls or texts.
I've been worried."

Henry opened his eyes and released a breath. "I needed some
time alone."

"From me?"

"From everyone."

She paused for a moment. "But you're back. Right?"

"Do you feel it?" he asked without turning around.

"Feel what?"

He'd hoped that she would have felt the call just as he did,
but it looked as if that wasn't the case. Just as he had known
where to find the Druids being killed for their magic, he was the
only one who felt the draw to Zora. He didn't want to go. He
knew if he crossed through the Fae doorway, he would die on the
other realm.

"Henry?" Esther said as she came up beside him and touched
his arm. "You're scaring me."

Finally, he looked at her. He stared into her dark brown eyes
and smiled. "I'm glad you found Nikolai."

"I know that tone." Her face tightened, and she latched onto
his arm. "What are you planning?"

"Nothing."

She shook her head of long, brunette hair. "Don't lie to me. Not me."

He turned to face her. "Something on Zora is calling to me."

Esther glanced to where the doorway had been marked for everyone not a Fae to see. "No."

"I don't want to go."

"Then don't."

"I don't have a choice," he said softly.

Her nostrils flared. "The hell, you don't." Her brow furrowed as she stared up at him with fear in her eyes. "Please, don't go. There are no Druids there."

"You don't know that."

"I have a bad feeling, Henry. I'm begging you. Don't go."

He looked at the doorway. "I'm not sure I have a choice."

Thank you for reading DRAGON ETERNAL! I hope you loved Shaw and Nia's story as much as I loved writing it. Next up in the Dark World is the much anticipated Reaper book, DARK ALPHA'S COMMAND (Balladyn's book!).

BUY DARK ALPHA'S COMMAND now at
https://donnagrant.com/books/dark-alphas-command/

To find out when new books release
SIGN UP FOR MY NEWSLETTER today at
http://www.tinyurl.com/DonnaGrantNews

Join my Facebook group, Donna Grant Groupies, for exclusive giveaways and sneak peeks of future books. If you loved the Dragon King series, you'll be thrilled to know Kendrick gets his HEA in the next book, DRAGON LOVER...

Can she learn to love the man—as well as the dragon within?

Buy DRAGON LOVER today at
https://donnagrant.com/books/dragon-lover/

Keep reading for an excerpt from DARK ALPHA'S COMMAND and a sneak peek at DRAGON LOVER...

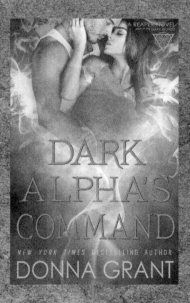

From *New York Times* bestselling author Donna Grant® comes another action-packed installment in her thrilling Reaper series, featuring a brotherhood of elite assassins who wage war on the Fae at Death's behest—and the women who dare to love them.

There is no escaping a Reaper. I am an elite assassin, part of a brotherhood that only answers to Death. And when Death says your time is up, I'm coming for you...

I've been a part of so many different worlds I'm not sure who I am or where I fit in anymore. Honestly, with everything I've been through, being called across realms and encountering the beautiful Druid who instantly captures my attention—and my heart—shouldn't have surprised me. But it did. Not as much as discovering how it feels to brush against her magic, however. Now, we must navigate these new waters and fight against our latest threat, hoping that our combined power and that of our allies is enough to defeat our foe. Because the Fae Others want to end the Reapers, the Dragon Kings, and take over the realm, and their leader is one of the most formidable enemies we've ever faced. The battle won't be easy, but with this strong, resilient mortal by my side and some help from our friends, it's a fight I'm more than willing to enter—as long as it means she's by my side. Forever.

Death's Realm

Balladyn's eyes snapped open, his heart racing as he gasped for breath. The yawning, opaque terror occurred abruptly, like a hard punch to the gut. Only one thought went through his head: *find it.*

Without hesitation, he teleported to the Fae doorway. Just before he stepped through, he remembered his vow to Death. Balladyn clenched his jaw at the physical pain that gripped him when he halted. He needed to find Erith and tell her what was happening. But the thought of wasting that time when he could be searching for whatever called to him made him want to bellow with annoyance.

He was being pulled in two.

"Balladyn."

Erith's calm voice reached him. He turned his head to the goddess and stared into her lavender eyes.

She looked him over before lifting her chin, a small frown puckering her forehead. "What is it?"

"I...don't...know," he managed to get out. The alarm and distress were so boundless he could barely speak. He braced his hands on either side of the doorway. It was the only way to stop himself from just walking through—and hopefully ending the torment that had him in its merciless grip.

Erith nodded to someone on Balladyn's other side. He didn't bother to look. It was most likely her consort, Cael. Balladyn dropped his chin to his chest. He had to go. He *needed* to leave.

Right that instant. If he didn't...

"You want to leave."

It wasn't a question. "I have to," he ground out. His body shook as he fought to remain where he was. Every second was excruciating. If he left, the agony would end. He didn't know how he knew that, only that the knowledge was there.

"Tell me what's happening."

He squeezed his eyes shut. The words stuck in his throat as the pain intensified. The compulsion to find whatever called to him across the realms was too great to resist. He parted his lips, wanting to tell Erith what he felt, but he couldn't. Balladyn pushed away from the doorway and started to walk through it.

"Wait," Death commanded in a sharp tone.

Her order froze him immediately. The ensuing deluge of despair made him throw back his head and bellow. He had to get...*fek*. He had no idea where he needed to go, only that he had to go. Immediately.

"Follow him. Don't let him out of your sight," he heard Erith say. Then, "Go, Balladyn."

The instant she released him, he was through the doorway. He let whatever pulled him determine his course. He was mildly startled to find himself not just on Earth but in Belfast. He paused long enough to orient himself in the narrow, old-town street. The night was cold and rainy. Lights strung over the road and suspended from each building lit the area and reflected in the puddles on the ground as locals and tourists rushed to get out of the rain.

Balladyn didn't look behind him to see who followed. All that mattered was locating who or what had reached through time and space to him. His head snapped to the right when he felt the sharp tug again. He strode down the street until he came to a narrow alley. He heard nothing over the steady beat of the rain. When he turned to go down the lane, he felt a hand on his shoulder.

"This could be a trap," Eoghan cautioned.

Balladyn looked into the molten, silver eyes of the Reaper who led their team. "I have to."

Eoghan released him and nodded, letting Balladyn know without words that his team was there and would watch his back.

Balladyn blinked the rain from his eyes and started walking. With every step, something urged him to hurry. He was running by the time he reached the end where it opened to a small area. He slid to a stop and let his gaze scan the space. It was dark and quiet. Nothing stirred. Then he smelled it—blood.

The sound of a slight cough reached him. His head swung to the side, and he made out the shape of someone on the ground.

Balladyn rushed over. The instant he knelt and saw the red hair, his breath caught. He found himself staring into the beautiful face of Rhona, the head of the Skye Druids.

"What the hell?" Bradach asked in a shocked whisper.

Balladyn glanced down at Rhona's body and found her hands clutching her abdomen, blood running quickly through her fingers. Her heartbeat was faint, her breathing shallow. She wouldn't live much longer. Certainly not long enough for him to get her anywhere that someone could help her.

Another bellow rose within him. He didn't know what Rhona was doing in Ireland or what had happened to her, but he couldn't let her die. Not like this.

"Rhona? Open your eyes," he begged. "Look at me."

But she didn't move. Suddenly, he remembered reading about some ancient magic in one of the books in his library. Without hesitation, the words he had read filled his mind. The magic sprang forth and wrapped around Rhona.

"What the hell did you just do?" Ruarc demanded.

Balladyn lifted Rhona in his arms. "I have a library of books. I made use of some ancient knowledge in one. This won't last long. She's lost too much blood. We have to get her to safety."

"She could be a trap for us. I hate to say it, but the Six could've learned of our connection to Skye through Sorcha and me," Cathal said.

Rordan grunted. "Not only is Rhona Sorcha's cousin, but she's also the leader of the Druids."

"We'll find our answers later," Eoghan said. "Cathal, fill Erith in on everything and return with Sorcha. Dubhan and Bradach, you two take a look around. See if you can spot any of the Fae

Others, the Six, or their soldiers. The rest of us are going to Skye."

Balladyn didn't wait for Eoghan to finish speaking before teleporting inside Rhona's cottage. It was dark inside, but he saw well enough to make his way down the hall to her bedroom. He gently laid her on the bed. When he stepped back and saw the blood on his arms, his heart clutched painfully.

"What now?" Rordan asked.

Balladyn turned his head to Eoghan. "We need Druids."

"Can we trust them?" Ruarc questioned.

Eoghan blew out a breath as he flipped on the light in the room. "We don't have a choice. Rhona needs their healing."

No sooner had he spoken the words than Cathal arrived with Sorcha. Tears welled in her eyes the minute the Druid spotted Rhona on the bed. "I'll get the others," Sorcha said and turned to her mate.

The urgency driving Balladyn had stopped when he found Rhona. He didn't know if she had called to him or if it had been something else. As far as he knew, no one could penetrate time and space to reach a Fae other than Death. Not even someone as powerful as Rhi could do that. So how had the message reached him?

"The Druids aren't going to be happy to see all of us," Eoghan pointed out. "We need to remain veiled."

Ruarc grimaced. "Should we even stay?"

"I'm not leaving her," Balladyn stated.

Eoghan quickly said, "None of us is. We need to know what happened."

They could only get answers through Rhona, and only if the Druid lived. Balladyn kept his gaze on her hands. There was more blood than he'd initially realized. It soaked her wet clothes. The magic he used had paused it, but he had no idea how long that would last. The Druids needed to get there. Soon.

They heard approaching cars. Balladyn regretfully moved away from the bed and veiled himself. He never took his eyes off Rhona as he backed himself against the wall just as the Druids rushed into the room with Sorcha.

Disbelief registered on all their faces, but they held their tongues and took their places around the bed. They held their hands over Rhona's body just as the blood started to pour through her fingers once more. The Druids began to chant. Balladyn's chest squeezed with an iron-vise grip as he silently urged them to go faster. He would've offered his magic if he thought it would have done any good.

Rhona's flame-red hair lay wet and limp against the dark blue sheets, and the moisture from her soaked clothes seeped into the bed linens. Her skin remained pale, the kind of sunken pastiness that preceded death. He fisted his hands, feeling another bellow rising. Balladyn had no idea what was wrong with him. It had been a long time since he had lost control of his emotions as he had earlier with Death.

The Druid leader might not be a huge fan of the Fae, but she had recently helped the Reapers. What could she have gotten herself mixed up in that'd left her dying alone on a street in Ireland? The more he thought about it, the more he had to know the answer. One way or another, he would find out everything.

Tense minutes passed in unbearable slowness before Balladyn saw color begin to return to Rhona's face. He didn't breathe easy until the Druids slowed their chanting and then finally stopped. He eyed the group of five, noting the sweat on their faces, their ragged breaths, and the exhaustion in their expressions. Saving Rhona had taken a lot of healing magic.

"What the bloody hell is going on?"

Balladyn slid his gaze to the man who had spoken, his Scot's brogue thick. His dark blond hair was cut short. He was of average height with a stocky body and a fuzzy beard that looked like an animal living on his face. He directed his close-set brown eyes at Sorcha.

"You know as much as I do, Evan," she replied.

He snorted. "Somehow, I doubt that."

Cathal, who had remained by his mate's side since he had gone with her to gather the Druids, glared at Evan. "She's not lying."

"Enough," said an older woman, her gaze directed at Evan. "Kerry, Lyra, and I will get Rhona cleaned up. When we're finished and rested, we can talk."

Sorcha nodded. "I'll help you."

Balladyn looked at Eoghan and shook his head, letting Eoghan know that he wasn't leaving Rhona for a second.

Eoghan flattened his lips but issued a brief nod before motioning for the other veiled Reapers to leave the room. They teleported out quickly after. Balladyn watched Cathal lean down and whisper something to Sorcha before Cathal's gaze briefly met his. Cathal then turned on his heel and walked out.

"Thank you, Violet," Sorcha said as she walked to the woman.

Violet didn't smile. She had her gray hair trimmed in a short bob that ended right below her ears. Locking her blue eyes on Rhona, she twisted her hands nervously. Despite the lines on her face, Balladyn could still see hints of the beauty she had once been.

"That magic was…" Lyra couldn't finish. She shook her head of black curls currently pulled away from her face by a scarf. Deep brown eyes lifted to look between Sorcha and Violet. Her dark skin still wore a sheen of sweat. "I didn't think we would be able to heal the wounds."

"There were so many of them," Kerry whispered and gently touched Rhona's cheek. She shifted her full-figured body, her short, thin brown hair hanging limp around her full face.

Anger churned within Balladyn. *Who* had done this to Rhona? And why?

"We healed her," Sorcha said.

Though they didn't say it, Balladyn saw that they believed they had come very close to losing Rhona. His hesitation in leaving Death's realm when he'd first felt the pull had nearly resulted in her death. If he had waited even another few seconds, she would likely be dead. That thought made him want to destroy something.

Violet shook herself. "Come. Let's get Rhona changed and cleaned. She doesn't need to see any of this when she wakes."

While the four of them removed Rhona's clothes and wiped away the blood, he let his mind wander back to the alley where he had found her. Balladyn went over everything in his mind's eye, trying to see if he had missed someone or something. When he looked at the bed again, Rhona was dressed in a black shirt and lying beneath fresh sheets. Kerry was the first to leave the room. Violet and Lyra both touched Sorcha's shoulder before they, too, filed out.

The half-Fae, half-Druid stared at the bed as she said, "Thank you for finding her, Balladyn."

He lowered his veil and bowed his head to her.

Tears fell down her face when she turned to him. "How did you know where she was?"

"I have no answer. I've never felt anything like it before."

She nodded slowly. "The Druids will want to know."

"Eoghan or Cathal can tell them everything. They and a few others were with me. I'm not leaving Rhona's side."

Sorcha tucked an auburn curl behind her ear and smiled before she left.

Balladyn swung his gaze back to Rhona. How had he known that she was hurt? Was she the one who had called to him? Skye Druids were the most powerful of all Druids on the realm, but he hadn't known she had that ability.

If it had been her.

But who else could it have been?

BUY DARK ALPHA'S COMMAND now at
https://donnagrant.com/books/dark-alphas-command/

NEXT IN THE DRAGON KINGS SERIES...

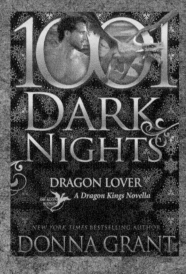

New York Times and *USA Today* bestselling author Donna Grant returns with the next exciting story in the *Dragon King* series.

Can she learn to love the man —as well as the dragon within?

Sensual. Clever. Daring. There's only one thing Kendrick yearns for—peace that has eluded the Dragon Kings. Zora may have been made in the image of Earth, but it's a far cry from home. For too long the Kings have been on the defensive, betrayed time and again. When Kendrick has an opportunity to stop a foe, he takes it. Except he isn't the only one tracking it. Soon, he finds himself face-to-face with an exquisite swordswoman who holds him enthralled.

As an Asavori Ranger, Esha has dedicated her life to protecting her people. She trains relentlessly to become one of their best warriors, forsaking everything else. When a treacherous new enemy invades their lands, she vows to destroy it. Esha's rash decision has her path crossing that of a mysterious, handsome man. He's trouble the Rangers don't need, but she can't walk away from him—and that could be the downfall for both of them.

Buy DRAGON LOVER today at
https://donnagrant.com/books/dragon-lover/

ABOUT THE AUTHOR

New York Times and *USA Today* bestselling author Donna Grant has been praised for her "totally addictive" and "unique and sensual" stories. She's written more than one hundred novels spanning multiple genres of romance including the bestselling Dark King series that features a thrilling combination of Dragon Kings, Druids, Fae, and immortal Highlanders who are dark, dangerous, and irresistible. She lives in Texas with her dog and a cat.

www.DonnaGrant.com
www.MotherofDragonsBooks.com

facebook.com/AuthorDonnaGrant
instagram.com/dgauthor
bookbub.com/authors/donna-grant
amazon.com/Donna-Grant/e/B00279DJGE
pinterest.com/donnagrant1

Made in the USA
Las Vegas, NV
17 June 2022

50384809R00195